LEGENDS & LATTES

A NOVEL OF HIGH FANTASY AND LOW STAKES

TRAVIS BALDREE

TOR

A TOM DOHERTY ASSOCIATES BOOK
NEW YORK

LEGENDS & LATTES

Copyright © 2022 by Travis Baldree

Cover art by Carson Lowmiller
Cover design by Peter Lutjen

A Tor Book
Published by Tom Doherty Associates
120 Broadway
New York, NY 10271

www.tor-forge.com

Tor® is a registered trademark of Macmillan Publishing Group, LLC.

The Library of Congress Cataloging-in-Publication Data
is available upon request.

ISBN 978-1-250-88608-8 (paperback)
ISBN 978-1-250-88609-5 (ebook)

Our books may be purchased in bulk for promotional, educational, or business use. Please contact your local bookseller or the Macmillan Corporate and Premium Sales Department at 1-800-221-7945, extension 5442, or by email at MacmillanSpecialMarkets@macmillan.com.

First Edition: 2022

LEGENDS & LATTES

For anyone who wondered where the other road led . . .

LEGENDS & LATTES

Viv buried her greatsword in the scalvert's skull with a meaty crunch. Blackblood thrummed in her hands, and her muscular arms strained as she tore it back and out in a spray of gore. The Scalvert Queen gave a long, vibrating moan . . . and then thundered to the stone in a heap.

With a sigh, Viv slumped to her knees. The persistent twinge in her lower back flared up, and she dug in the knuckles of one huge hand to chase it away. Wiping sweat and blood from her face, she stared down at the dead queen. Cheers and shouts echoed from behind her.

She leaned closer. Yes, there it was, right above the nasal cavity. The beast's head was twice as wide as she was—all improbable teeth and uncountable eyes, with a huge, underslung jaw—and in the middle, the fleshy seam she'd read about.

Jamming her fingers into the fold, she pried it open. A sickly golden light spilled out. Viv slid her whole hand into the pocket of flesh, curled her fist around a faceted, organic lump, and yanked. It came free with a fibrous ripping sound.

Fennus moved to stand behind her—she could smell his perfume. "Is that it, then?" he asked, only a little interested.

"Yep." Viv groaned as she hoisted herself to her feet, using Blackblood as a crutch. Without bothering to clean the stone, she stuffed it into a pouch on her bandolier, then propped the greatsword on her shoulder.

"And that's truly all you want?" Fennus squinted up at her. His long, beautiful face was amused.

He gestured at the walls of the cavern, where the Scalvert Queen had entombed untold wealth within sheets of hardened saliva. Wagons, chests, and the bones of horses and men hung suspended amidst gold, silver, and gemstones—the shiny castaways of centuries.

"Yep," she said again. "We're square."

The rest of the party approached. Roon, Taivus, and little Gallina brought with them the exhausted but exultant chatter of the victorious. Roon combed muck from his beard, Gallina sheathed her daggers, and Taivus glided behind them both, tall and watchful. They were a good crew.

Viv turned away and strode toward the cavern's entrance, where dim light still filtered through.

"Where are you goin'?" hollered Roon, in his rough, affable voice.

"Out."

"But . . . aren't you gonna—?" began Gallina.

Someone shushed her, most likely Fennus.

Viv felt a prick of shame. She liked Gallina the most, and probably should have taken the time to explain.

But she was done. Why drag things out? She didn't really *want* to talk about it, and if she said anything more, she might change her mind.

After twenty-two years of adventuring, Viv had reached her limit of blood and mud and bullshit. An orc's life was strength and violence and a sudden, sharp end—but she'd be damned if she'd let hers finish that way.

It was time for something new.

1

Viv stood in the morning chill, looking down into the broad valley below. The city of Thune bristled up from a bed of fog that hazed the banks of the river bisecting it. Here and there, a copper-clad steeple flashed in the sun.

She had broken camp in the predawn dark, and her long legs had eaten up the final few miles. Blackblood weighed heavy on her back, the Scalvert's Stone tucked in one of her inner jacket pockets. She could feel it like a hard, withered apple, and reflexively touched it through the cloth from time to time to reassure herself it was still there.

A leather satchel hung over one shoulder, stuffed mostly with notes and plans, a few chunks of hardtack, a purse of platinum chits and assorted precious stones, and one small, curious device.

She followed the road down and into the valley as the fog burned away, and a lonely farmer's cart tottered by, stuffed with alfalfa.

Viv felt a rising sense of nervous elation, something she hadn't felt in *years*, like a battle-cry she could barely hold in. She'd never prepared as much for any one moment. She'd read and questioned, researched and wrestled, and Thune had been the city she'd chosen. When she'd crossed every other location off her list, she'd been absolutely positive. Suddenly, that conviction seemed foolish and impulsive, yet her excitement remained undimmed.

No outer wall surrounded Thune. It had sprawled far beyond its original, fortified boundaries, but she sensed herself approaching the edge of *something*. It had been ages since she'd stayed in one place more than a handful of nights, the duration of a job. Now, she was going to put down roots in a city she'd visited maybe three times in her entire life.

She stopped and looked around warily, as though the road wasn't entirely vacant, the farmer long gone into the mist. Withdrawing a scrap of parchment from her satchel, she read the words she'd copied.

> *Well-nigh to thaumic line,*
> *the Scalvert's Stone a-fire*
> *draws the ring of fortune,*
> *aspect of heart's desire.*

Viv tucked it carefully away again, exchanging it for the device she'd purchased a week before from a thaumist scholar in Arvenne—a witching rod.

The small, wooden spindle was wrapped in copper thread, which covered the runes inscribed along its length. A wishbone of ash was fitted over the top and into a groove so it spun freely. She held it in her fist, feeling the copper thread absorb the warmth of her palm. The spindle gave a barely perceptible tug.

At least, she was fairly certain it was a tug. During the thaumist's demonstration, there had been a stronger pull. Viv pushed down the sudden thought that it had all been a parlor trick. As a rule, folks with a fixed address avoided swindling an orc twice their height who could snap a wrist if they shook hands too firmly.

She took a deep breath and strode into Thune with the witching rod before her.

—+—

Thune's wakeful noises rose as she moved farther into the city. At the outskirts, the buildings had been mostly wooden, with some river stone foundations interspersed. The deeper she ventured, the more stone prevailed, as though the city had calcified as it aged. Muddy dirt gave way to a smattering of stone lanes, then cobbles near the city's core. Temples and taverns huddled around squares featuring statues of people who probably used to be important.

Any doubts about the witching rod had evaporated. It definitely pulled now, like a living thing—brief twitches growing into insistent tugs. Her research hadn't been in vain. Ley lines were clearly threaded beneath the city, powerful avenues of thaumic energy. Scholars debated whether they grew where people settled or gathered folk near like warmth in winter. What mattered to Viv was that they were *here*.

Finding a potent ley line was only the start, of course.

The little wishbone of ash-wood twitched left and right, tugging one way for a time before reversing and pulling like a fish on a hook in another direction. After a while, she didn't have to look at it. The feel of it was enough, and Viv paid more attention to the buildings she passed.

The device ushered her down the major thoroughfares, through the squiggling alleys that stitched them together, past blacksmiths and hostels and markets and inns. There were few people her height on the streets, and she never found herself crowded. Blackblood tended to have that effect.

She passed through all the layers of smell that made up a city—baking bread and waking horses and wet stone and hot metal and floral perfume and old shit. The same smells you found in any city, but underneath them, the morning scent of the river. Sometimes, between the buildings, she could see the blades of the waterwheel at the flour mill.

Viv let the rod lead her where it wanted. A few times the tug was so strong she stopped and inspected the buildings nearby— but disappointed, she'd continue onward. The rod would resist for a while, until it seemed to give up, finding a new direction in which to surge.

At last, when it yanked *hard*, she came to a semi-dazed stop and found what she needed.

Not on the High Street—that would've been too much to hope for—but it was only one removed. Kerosene streetlamps dotted the length, extinguished now, and like as not, you wouldn't be knifed there after dark. The buildings on Redstone showed their age, but the roofs seemed in good repair. All except one in particular, and here, the witching rod drew her closer.

It was small for what it was. A battered sign hung from the single remaining iron eyehook—PARKIN'S LIVERY—the paint of the embossed letters long since flaked away. There were two large, iron-bound wooden doors, but they were ajar, and the crossbeam was leaning against the wall nearby. Another smaller, orc-sized door was amusingly padlocked to the left of it.

Viv ducked her head in for a look. Light filtered from a hole in the roof above, and a handful of clay shingles lay shattered across the broad alleyway leading between six horse stalls. A ladder of dubious sturdiness led to a loft, and to the left, a small office with a back room. The sour smell of moldering hay came from the trough at the back. Dust swirled in beams of light, as though it never settled.

It was as perfect as she could hope for.

She tucked the witching rod away.

When she reemerged into the growing traffic of the street, she spied a knobbly old woman sweeping the stoop across the way. Viv was pretty sure she'd been sweeping since her arrival, the threshold no doubt sparkling at this point, but she continued to attack it with determination, shooting Viv a surreptitious look every other second.

Viv strode across the street. The old woman had the good grace to appear surprised, mustering something approaching a smile as she did.

"Do you know who owns this place?" asked Viv, pointing back at the livery.

The woman was less than half her height and had to crane to make eye contact. Her eyes disappeared as she compressed her face into a considering tangle of wrinkles.

"The livery?"

"Yep."

"Wellll." She dragged the word out thoughtfully, but Viv could tell there was nothing wrong with her memory. "That's old Ansom, if I recollect properly. Never had much of a head for business, that man, not for trade nor husband's work, neither, to hear his old lady tell it."

Viv didn't miss the woman's suggestive pump of the eyebrows. "Not Parkin?"

"Nope. 'Twas too cheap to change the sign when he bought it."

Viv's smile was amused, her lower fangs prominent. "Any idea where I can find him?"

"Couldn't say for certain. But I imagine attendin' to the only work he never failed at." She tipped her free hand, bringing an imaginary tankard to her lips. "If you really want to find him, I'd try the places on Rawbone Alley. Head about six over." She gestured to the south.

"At this time of morning?"

"Oh, *this* business he's serious about."

"Thanks, miss," said Viv.

"Oh, *miss*, is it!" cackled the woman. "You c'n call me Laney. You plannin' to be my new neighbor . . . ?" She made a give-it-over motion.

"Viv."

"Viv," said Laney, nodding.

"I guess we'll see. Depends on whether he's as bad a business-man as you say."

The old woman was still laughing as Viv left for Rawbone Alley.

——◆——

No matter what Laney said, Viv didn't really expect to find the much-maligned Ansom at this time of day. She figured she'd ask after him in any swill-joint with an open door and, once she knew his haunts, track him down after the day wore on.

Turned out, she only needed three stops before she found him in residence. The tavernkeep looked her up and down after she asked, raising his eyebrows pointedly at Blackblood's hilt over her shoulder.

"No trouble from me, just business," she said evenly. She tried to look less imposing.

Apparently satisfied that she wasn't spoiling for a fight, he cocked a thumb at the corner and went back to swabbing the grime of the bar-top into new and more interesting locations.

As Viv approached the table, she got the overwhelming impression that she was entering the den of some elderly woodland beast. A badger perhaps. Not a dangerous sense, but the feeling of a place where he spent so much time that it had absorbed his smell and become essentially his.

He even looked like a badger, a big, greasy black beard striped with white tangled across his chest. As wide as he was tall, he occupied so much space between the wall and table that when he inhaled deeply, the thing rocked up on its legs.

"You Ansom?" asked Viv.

Ansom allowed that he was.

"Mind if I sit?" she asked and then sat anyway, leaning Blackblood against the back of the chair. Truth be told, she wasn't really accustomed to asking permission.

Ansom stared at her over puffy lower lids. Not hostile, but wary. A tankard sat before him, nearly empty. Viv caught the tavernkeep's attention and gestured at it, and Ansom brightened considerably.

"Much obliged," he muttered.

"I hear you own the old livery on Redstone. That true?" asked Viv.

Ansom allowed that he did.

"I'm looking to buy," she said. "And have a feeling you might be looking to sell."

Ansom seemed surprised, but only briefly. His gaze sharpened, and while he might not have had a head for business, Viv was pretty sure he had one for haggling.

"Maybe," he rumbled. "But that's some prime real estate.

Prime! I've had offers before, but most of 'em don't see past the place to really appreciate the value of the *location*. That is to say, they underbid."

At this point, the tavernkeep swapped his tankard for a fresh one, and Ansom visibly warmed to his subject.

"Oh, yes, so many embarrassing offers. I have to warn you, I know what that lot is worth, and I can't see myself selling to anyone but a serious businessman. Er . . . business*woman*," he amended.

Viv flashed her toothy and amused grin, thinking of Laney. "Well, Ansom, there's all kinds of business." Very conscious of Blackblood leaning behind her, she thought of how easy her business—her old business—would've made this negotiation. "But I can say for sure that when I do business of any kind, I'm always serious."

She reached for her satchel, removed the purse of platinum chits, and hefted it. Withdrawing just one, she held it between thumb and forefinger, inspecting it and letting it catch the light. Platinum was a currency hardly ever seen in a place like this, and she'd need to exchange it for lower denominations soon, but she'd wanted some on hand for just this sort of moment.

Ansom's eyes widened. "Oh, uh. Serious. Yes! Serious, indeed!" He took a long pull of his beer to cover his surprise.

Sly dog, thought Viv, trying not to smirk.

"As one serious businessperson to another, I don't want to waste your time." Viv leaned on an elbow and slid eight platinum chits across the table. "That's probably eighty gold sovereigns. I think that covers the value of the lot. I'm sure we can agree that the building is a loss, and I think the odds of another . . . *businesswoman* tracking you down to pay cash on the barrelhead is vanishing."

She held his gaze.

He still had the tankard to his mouth, but wasn't swallowing.

Viv began to withdraw the chits, and he hurriedly reached out, pulling up short before touching her much larger hand. She raised her eyebrows.

"I can see you've got a keen eye for value." Ansom blinked rapidly.

"I do. If you want to take a moment this morning to bring the deed and sign it over, I'll wait here. But I won't wait longer than noon."

Turned out the old badger was a lot nimbler than he looked.

———+———

As Viv made her mark on the deed and pocketed the keys, Ansom scooped the platinum into his purse, looking relieved the deal was complete. "So . . . I didn't figure you to be interested in livery-work," he ventured.

It was common knowledge that horses didn't like orcs much.

"I'm not. I'm opening a coffee shop."

Ansom looked nonplussed. "But why would you buy a horse stable for that?"

Viv didn't answer for a moment, but then she stared hard at him. "Things don't have to stay as what they started out as." She folded the deed and tucked it into her satchel.

As she left, Ansom hollered after her. "Oh, and hey! What in the eight hells is *coffee?*"

———+———

Viv had three more stops to make before returning to the livery.

The Exchange at the trade depot put some copper, silver, and gold in her purse, and then she was off to the Athenaeum at the small thaumic university on the north bank of the river. She'd wanted to know the location anyway, in case she needed to do any reading.

More importantly, the Territorial Post ran between the scattered Athenaeums and libraries in most major cities, and it was dependable. Those copper-clad steeples she'd seen made it easy to locate.

Seated at one of the big tables between the shelves, she wrote two letters, using a few sheets of her parchment. The smell of paper and dust and time put her in mind of all the recent reading she'd done in places just like this.

A lifetime of training her muscles and her reflexes and her hardness of mind, traded for reading and planning and amassing details. She smiled ruefully as she wrote.

The gnome at the post counter couldn't stop goggling at her as she stamped the wax seal. The woman had to take the addresses twice, she was so flustered at seeing an orc in the building.

"I'm looking for a locksmith. Know of anyone reputable?"

The gnome's mouth hung open a moment longer, but she recovered herself and flipped through a directory behind the counter. "Markev and Sons," she replied. "Eight two seven Mason's Lane."

She gave some sketchy directions.

Viv thanked her, and then left.

Markev and Sons was there, as advertised. A silver and three coppers lighter, she left with an enormous and quite heavy strongbox under one muscular arm.

—+—

Back at Parkin's Livery, as the sun set, Viv unlocked the office door, rebarred the stable doors, and hauled the strongbox behind an L-shaped counter in the office. She stowed the deed and her funds inside, locked it, and strung the key around her neck.

After some testing with her feet and fingertips, she found a loose flagstone in the main pathway between the stalls and, flexing mightily, levered it up and out. She scooped earth from beneath and then carefully placed the Scalvert's Stone in the hollow. Covering it with the dirt, she replaced the flagstone and took a stiff and shedding stable-broom to the area to ensure it looked undisturbed.

She stared down at it for a few moments, all her hopes centered on this small stone, buried like a secret heart in Parkin's Livery.

No, not a livery anymore.

This place was Viv's.

She looked around. *Her* place. Not a temporary stop or a spot to sling her bedroll for one night. Hers.

The brisk evening air swirled through the hole in the roof, so for tonight, at least, it would probably feel like any other night under the stars. Viv glanced up at the loft and the ladder leading to it. She tested one of the lower rungs with a foot, and it shattered like balsa. She snorted, unstrapped Blackblood, and with both hands, tossed it into the loft, startling a bunch of pigeons that escaped through the roof. Gazing after it for a moment, she then unfurled her bedroll in one of the stalls. There'd certainly be no campfire, and there were no lanterns to speak of, but that was all right.

In the dimming light she surveyed the interior, amidst horse apples of antiquity and the dust of neglect. She didn't know much about buildings, but it was clear that this one needed an unbelievable amount of work.

But at the end of it? Something she built up, rather than cut down.

It was ridiculous, of course. A coffee shop? In a city where nobody even knew what coffee was? Until six months ago, *she'd* never heard of it, never smelled or tasted it. On the face of it, the whole endeavor was ludicrous.

She smiled in the dark.

When at last she lay back on her bedroll, she started to list her tasks for the following day, but didn't make it past the third.

She slept like the dead.

2

Viv woke in the predawn indigo to the growing murmur of the city outside. The pigeons cooed in the loft where they'd returned to their nests. She rose and checked on the flagstone above the Scalvert's Stone. Undisturbed, of course. Gathering a few things, she slipped into the street, chewing the last of her hardtack and inhaling the moist morning scent of shadows giving way to sun. She felt limber and coiled, like she was up on her toes, ready to break into a sprint.

Across the street, Laney had swapped her broom for a bowl of peas and sat on a three-legged stool shelling them. They traded amiable nods, and then Viv locked up and left in the direction of the river.

She found herself humming as she walked.

In the receding morning fog, Viv made her way to the shipyards clinging to the bank of the river. The place was alive with the clatter of hammer and saw, shouts muffled by the mist. What she wanted was fixed in her mind, but she didn't expect to find it right away. She could be patient, though. In her experience, you had to be. After long hours spent reconnoitering or staking out a beast's lair, Viv had made peace with the passage of time.

She bought some apples from a rattkin urchin hawking them from a burlap sack, found a stack of crates out of the way, and settled in to observe.

The boats here weren't large—mostly keelboats and little fishing boats best suited to the river. A dozen or so were up on the long quay, attended by small knots of shipwrights, being scraped or tarred or repaired. She watched them as they worked, keeping an eye out for what she wanted. The crews ebbed and swelled as the morning progressed.

Viv was on her last apple when she found what she'd been looking for.

Most of the crews worked in twos and threes, big men with big voices, scrambling over the hulls and hollering to one another as they did.

A few hours on, though, a man of smaller stature appeared, hauling a wooden box of tools half as large as himself. His ears were long, body wiry, skin leathery and olive, with a flat cap pulled low over his brow.

You didn't see hobs often in cities. Humans disparagingly called them "pucks" and shunned them, so they liked to keep to themselves.

Viv could relate, but she was more difficult to intimidate.

He labored alone at a small dinghy, while shipwrights and dockworkers alike avoided him. She watched his diligent, fastidious work. Viv was no woodworker, but she could appreciate craft. His tools were meticulously organized, sharp and well cared for. There was a deliberate economy to his every motion as he used drawing knife and plane and other things she didn't recognize to shape a new gunwale.

She polished off her apple and watched him at his work, trying not to be too conspicuous about it. Lurking was a well-used part of her skill set, after all.

It was noon when he tidily replaced his tools and unwrapped a lunch from his toolbox, and Viv approached.

He squinted up at her from under his cap, but said nothing as she loomed over him.

"It's nice work," said Viv.

"Hm."

"At least, I expect it is. I don't know much about boats," she admitted.

"I expect that dulls the compliment a touch, then," he replied, his voice dry and deeper than she'd expected.

She laughed, then looked up and down the quay. "Not many here that do the work alone."

"Nope."

"You get a lot of work?"

He shrugged. "Enough."

"Enough so you wouldn't like to have a lot more?"

He removed his cap then, and his look was more speculative. "For someone who don't know much about boats, seems odd you're expectin' to need much ship-wrightin'."

Viv dropped to her haunches, tired of towering over him.

"Well, you're right. I don't. But wood's wood, and craft's craft. I watched you work. Live long enough, you realize some folks can be handed a problem and some tools, and they'll sort it out. And I never think twice about hiring that sort of fellow." Although, she reflected, the tools and fellows had been historically a lot larger and a lot bloodier.

"Hm," he said again.

"I'm Viv." She held out a hand.

"Calamity." His own callused paw was swallowed by hers. Her eyes widened.

"Hob name," he said. "You can call me Cal."

"Whichever you like best. I don't need your name to suit me."

"Cal's fine. The other's too much a mouthful."

He folded the linen back over his lunch, and she now felt that she had his full attention.

"So, this . . . work. That a here-and-now sort of prospect or—?" He flapped his hand at some vaporous future.

"Here-and-now, well-paid, and with the supplies you ask for, not the ones I choose for you." She withdrew her purse, opened it, removed a gold sovereign, and extended it to him.

Cal held out his hands as though to catch a toss, but she deliberately placed it in one palm. He pursed his lips and bounced it in his hand. "So. Why me, exactly?" He made to hand the coin back to her, but she declined.

"Like I said, I watched you work. Sharp tools. You clean as you go. Your mind's on your business." She looked around at the conspicuous absence of men nearby. "And you do it even when some might say it's wiser not to."

"Hm. So you want me for my lack of wisdom, eh? It ain't boats you want built. What exactly have you got in mind?"

"I think I have to show you."

————+————

"*Wrack and ruin,*" Cal swore under his breath. He removed his cap to tuck it into the top of his breeches.

They stood outside Parkin's Livery, the stable doors thrown wide, and Viv experienced a momentary twist of uneasiness.

"Don't know much about roofin'," he said as he peered up at the hole.

"But you can figure it out?"

"Hm," he replied, in what Viv was coming to understand was an affirmative.

He walked slowly around the interior, kicking at the stall panels, stomping on the flagstones. Viv tensed when he walked over the one above the Scalvert's Stone.

He peered back at her. "How many you plannin' to hire?"

"You have someone you like to work with, I'm not opposed. Other than that, I'm a ready pair of hands, and I don't tire easy." She held them up in demonstration. "It's not a livery I'm wanting though."

"No?"

"Ever hear of coffee?"

He shook his head.

"Well, I need a . . . a restaurant, I guess. For drinks. Oh!"

She went to her satchel and withdrew a set of sketches and notes. Suddenly, she was unaccountably nervous. Viv had never cared much for the judgment of others. It was pretty easy to ig-nore when you had three feet and six stone on most of the folks you encountered. Now, though, she worried that this small man would think her a fool.

Cal was waiting for her to continue.

She found herself rambling. "I came across it in Azimuth, the gnomish city out in the East Territory. Was there for a . . . well, it doesn't matter what I was there for. But I smelled it first, and I came across this shop, and they made . . . Well, it's like tea, but not like tea. It smells like . . ." She stopped. "And it doesn't matter what it smells like, I can't describe it, anyway. At any rate, imagine I'm opening a tavern, but with no taps, no kegs, no beer. Just tables, a counter, some room in the back. Here, I did some sketches of the place I saw."

She thrust the papers at him and felt color rising in her cheeks. Ridiculous!

He took the pages and examined them, paying careful attention to each, as though he were committing every line to memory. After several agonizing minutes, he returned them. "Those your sketches? Not bad."

If anything, she flushed hotter.

"And you're plannin' to stay here, too?" He cocked a thumb at the loft. "Seems that's suited."

"I . . . yes."

He put his hands on his hips and stared into the bay where the stalls stood.

She'd half-expected him to turn on his heel and leave, but now she was beginning to think she might've chosen just right.

"So . . ." He walked around the space again. "Seems you could keep the stalls. Cut 'em down some. Tear out the doors, box it in along the walls for benches. Take some long planks, set 'em up on a trestle in between. Then, you got yourself some booths and tables here along the sides. Tear down that wall into the office. The counter might do. Need to check for rot."

He kicked at the splintered wood from the ladder and raised his eyebrows at her. "Gonna need a new ladder. Couple bags of nails. Whitewash. Paint. Clay tile. Some river stone. Bags of lime. Might want a few more windows in the place. And . . . a *lot* of lumber."

"So you'll do it?"

He gave her another one of his long, speculative looks. "What'd you say? I do things when it seems wiser not to? Well, if you're helpin', I guess so. Gimme some of that parchment and a stylus if you've got it. We're goin' to need a list. A *long* list.

Tomorrow, we can see about gettin' the orders filled and how much flatter we can make that purse of yours." For the first time since she'd met him, he offered a thin little smile. "Not gonna ask how much it'll cost?"

"Do you figure you even know, yet?"

"Don't suppose I do."

"Well, then." Viv dragged an old tack crate away from the wall, blew away the dust, and handed him a stylus.

They bent over the parchment together as Cal started writing.

—◆—

Cal left in the late afternoon to complete his work on the dinghy, promising to return in the morning. Viv tucked away the materials list and then stood in the hush of the livery, where the low noise outside seemed hardly to intrude. She looked out the doors and across to Laney's porch, but found it empty.

She suddenly felt very alone, which was odd. Viv had spent plenty of time with no company to speak of—long treks, lonely campgrounds, cold tents, dripping caves.

But in a city, she was almost never alone. One of her crew would've been with her.

Now, in *this* city, filled with people of all races and backgrounds, the solitude was terrible. She knew three people by name. None of them were really more than an acquaintance, although Laney seemed friendly at least, and Cal was strangely calming to be around.

She locked up and headed toward the main thoroughfare— pointedly *away* from Rawbone Alley.

You feel you need company? Well, fine, here we are. New place. New home—for good this time.

Viv found the brightest, loudest establishment she could,

a restaurant and pub that seemed to do good business, with no staggering drunks in the street out front and no puddles of piss to step over. She ducked under the lintel and entered, and there was a momentary drop in the conversational volume, but Thune was pretty cosmopolitan, and orcs weren't unknown, just a little unusual. The noise picked right back up.

She took a deep breath and tried to relax her face into a non-threatening expression, something she'd been practicing. Not hauling a greatsword around and wearing plain clothes hopefully added to the effect.

There was a long, clean bar-top, sparsely populated, and a mirror on the wall behind. Lanterns blazed throughout the dining area. It wasn't cold enough for a fire, but the room was still cheerfully lit.

The tables were mostly occupied. Viv drew up a stool at the bar-top, and she tried not to fidget. She felt awkward—so many people, so close—and for the first time, she wasn't just passing through. It suddenly seemed that any faux pas or stumble here might follow and shame her forever, before she'd even properly settled down, irrational though the thought was.

A moon-faced man approached, red cheeked, his ears just a touch pointed. Probably a little elf in him, though his girth hinted at a very human metabolism. "Evening, ma'am," he said and slid a chalk slate menu in front of her. "Eating or drinking?"

"Eating." She smiled, trying not to bare her lower fangs too much.

His expression didn't change a whit. Rapping a knuckle on the slate, he said, "The pork's good! I'll let you think on it," and breezed away.

When he returned minutes later, she ordered—the pork—and while she waited for her meal, she gazed around, musing.

She hadn't dared to think this far ahead before, except in a very abstract way, but with Cal signed up, she allowed herself to dream on it a little.

The café she'd visited in Azimuth had been the very definition of gnomish architecture—precisely fitted wall tiles, geometric shapes, and pavers arranged in intricate, interlocking patterns. The furniture had, of course, been gnomish in scale as well—she'd had to stand.

She'd known her place would be different, but now, she tried to make that real in her head. She looked at the decorations inside the pub, here an oil painting in an old gilt frame, there a huge ceramic vase on the floor with fresh ferns to sweeten the air. A simple chandelier with three fat candles, clearly changed regularly, with no sloppy wax threads.

Viv began to imagine her own place. *Brighter*, she thought, *with that tall barn ceiling. Some light coming in from high windows.* She could see what Cal had meant about the booths as well, but maybe another long table down the middle with benches, a kind of community seating.

Viv saw it with the big stable doors thrown wide, perhaps a few tables there in the entry to catch the breeze and the sun. The flagstones polished. Clean, whitewashed walls . . .

Her thoughts were interrupted by the arrival of her meal, the rich smell of it reaching her first. She discovered that she was ravenous.

"Before you go," she said, "I wanted to ask . . . is this your place?"

The half-elf blinked and then smiled a little wider than his regular, professional pleasantness. "Sure is! Four years now."

"If you don't mind me asking, how'd you get started?"

He leaned on the bar-top. "Well, it's not a family business, if that's what you're asking. And my first place sure wasn't here on the High Street." He chuckled at that.

"And was business slow, at first? Or did they come all at once?" She waved at the room.

"Oh my, slow. Very slow. Fair to say I lost more money than I could afford to . . . and then I lost some more. But these days, I lose *just* enough to get by. You planning to open a pub around here? Can't say I'd advise it." He winked at her, clearly joking.

"Not exactly, but maybe something like it."

He seemed surprised but recovered swiftly.

"Well, best of luck to you, ma'am." He spoke behind his hand in a stage whisper. "I'll thank you not to take my customers, though, hear?"

"Not much chance of that, I don't think."

"Well, that's all right then. Eat up, now, or it'll get cold."

Viv quietly ate her meal and didn't speak to anyone else. Her mood was meditative as she left the pub. She found a chandler's shop still open, bought a lantern, and returned to the livery. There, she lay awake, staring into its flame. The visions of what might someday be were far from the cold and derelict place where she bedded down.

Tomorrow, though, the real work would begin.

3

True to his word, Cal arrived with the dawn. Viv had placed the tack crate out front and was sitting and watching the shadows take shape in the morning sun, contemplating how excellently a mug of coffee would suit her.

The hob hauled in his box of tools and placed it inside the big doorway.

"Morning," she said.

"Hm," he said, but he nodded genially enough. He removed his copy of the materials list from a pocket and unfolded it. "Lots to do. Some of this we'll have directly, some will take time."

Viv produced her purse. Her platinum and most of her sovereigns were in the lockbox, but she figured there were sufficient funds to cover what was needed. She tossed it to Cal. "I think I can trust you to place the orders, if you're willing."

Cal looked surprised. He sucked his teeth thoughtfully for a moment before saying, "I reckon you'll not get the best prices if I'm the one dickering."

"Think it'll go better if it's me?" Her smile was sardonic.

"Well. Maybe it's a wash. And you want to trust me with all of this? Don't fret I'll stroll away with it?" He bounced the purse in his hand.

She gave him a long look, and her expression didn't lapse.

"No . . ." he said, as he took in the size and the shape of her. "No, I suppose you wouldn't."

Viv sighed. "I've lived a long time knowing I'm a threat walking. I'd rather that wasn't the shape of it for you."

He nodded and tucked the purse away. "I'll need some hours."

Viv stood and stretched, knuckling the ache in her lower back. It was always stiff in the cold. "I need to rent a cart, something to haul the junk with. And someplace to haul it."

"The mill for the cart," said Cal. "Figure you can find it. As for the rest, there's a midden out west and off the main road. Cart track hooks south."

"Thanks."

"I'll be off, then." Cal tipped his cap and ambled back down the street.

He was right. The mill was indeed willing to rent her a cart—less a pair of animals—for a full silver, which was certainly more than it was worth. The miller grinned smugly after she paid, no doubt imagining the trouble an orc would face hitching up a horse, but she gripped the traces in both hands, lifted, and easily got the cart moving by herself.

The miller watched her roll it away, scratching the back of his bald head bemusedly.

Viv worked up a healthy sweat and loosened herself up on the trip back. Along the way, she haggled with a stonemason who had three or four ladders at a job site. He parted with one for ten coppers too many, and she tossed it in the back of the cart.

—⫶—

Laney was back on her porch, broom in hand, attacking what Viv had to imagine was the cleanest stoop in the entire Territory. She gave her a neighborly nod and began the hard work of clearing out the old building.

It quickly became apparent exactly how much junk had accrued in the place—rotten lumber, horseshoe iron, a set of rusted and bent pitchforks, a baled stack of grain sacks, crumbling tack, an assortment of saddle blankets thick with mold, and plenty of awkward, cumbersome, and decrepit miscellany. The office had its own share of debris—moth-eaten ledgers, shattered inkwells, and an inexplicable set of winter underclothes gone gray with dust.

Viv snapped the broken ladder, threw it in the cart, set up the new one, and climbed to the loft. Thankfully, there was only a little old hay, the pigeons' nests, and a few scraps of this and that. Blackblood lay there in the dust, already gathering some itself. She picked it up, hefted it in her hands for a second, and then leaned it carefully against the slanted ceiling.

By noon, the cart was piled high.

Filth covered Viv from head to toe, and the livery's interior looked like a sandstorm had passed through, with little dunes and drifts of dirt having resettled after the disturbance. She thought with amusement that she should hire Laney to broom it out, but when she looked in that direction, the old woman was absent.

There was, however, someone else shadowing her own doorway.

Viv's back prickled with a sense she trusted implicitly. It was the reason she was still moving around and breathing, after all.

"Help you with something?" she asked, dusting off her hands and thinking about Blackblood leaning up in the loft, out of reach.

He was dressed stylishly, with a ruffled shirt, a vest, and a broad-brimmed hat. But on closer inspection, his clothing was worse for wear, sweat-stained and a little frayed. His skin had the gray cast of one of the stone-fey, and his features were sharp.

"Oh, no help required," he replied. "We like to welcome budding entrepreneurs to the city when we can, and I'm powerfully curious about what new business you'll bring to the district." His voice was smooth, almost cultured.

Viv didn't miss the reference to a nebulous *we*.

"Oh, so you're a city official?" Viv smiled, and this time she didn't concern herself with how prominent her lower fangs were. She approached him so that their difference in stature was even more apparent. She was pretty sure she knew exactly what this man was, and until recently, she'd have had him by the throat and off the ground already.

He didn't adjust his posture an iota, smiling back. "Not as such. I just consider it my civic duty to welcome new arrivals and to take an interest in their welfare."

"I'll consider myself welcomed, then."

"I didn't catch your name."

"You didn't. But fair exchange is no robbery. Didn't catch yours, either."

"Indeed. I don't suppose you'd mind giving me a little preview of your new"—he looked around her at the cart and waved a gloved hand—"venture?"

"Trade secret."

"Oh, well, I wouldn't want to pry."

"I'm glad to hear that." Viv walked back, grabbed the traces, and lifted, her biceps bunching as she started hauling. It was significantly heavier than it had been that morning. Her lower back lit up in a bright knot of pain. She didn't slow as she approached the door, staring grimly past her visitor who, at the last second, had to depart the threshold less gracefully than he would have doubtless preferred.

"We'll catch up later!" he called after her, as she rumbled the cart down the cobbles to the west, her face set, breathing hard through her nose.

Above, the clouds began to clot and thicken, threatening rain.

Everyone else on the street made certain they were clear of the coming storm.

⸺✦⸺

When Cal reappeared that afternoon, the sky was even darker. Viv was seated out front on the tack box, the cart returned. Her sleeves were rolled up, and sweat striped the grime on her arms.

As the hob approached, Viv saw a bundle under his arm, and when he stopped, he flapped a corner of it at her. "Tarpaulin. Looks like rain. Best we keep the new lumber dry." He tossed her purse to her, and she tucked it away without bothering to examine it.

Viv hauled out the ladder and gathered a few stones from an alley. They both climbed onto the roof and anchored the tarp with the stones over the hole, just as raindrops began to speckle the tile a dusty orange.

When they were back down and inside, listening to the drops

clatter lightly overhead, Cal said, "Well, maybe no deliveries to-day, unless the rain slacks off." He looked around the barren interior. "A good job of it, eh? Looks a fair bit bigger now."

Viv smiled ruefully as she surveyed the place. The emptiness of it somehow made the work to come more daunting. "Think I'm a fool?"

"Hm." Cal shrugged. "Not in the habit of offerin' my less than positive thoughts to somebody like you."

"Somebody like me?" She sighed. "You mean—?"

"I mean somebody who's payin'." He gave her one of his thin smiles.

"Well, as the one paying, I don't see a reason for you to wait around here while—"

She was interrupted by the arrival of a cart with three small, sturdy crates in the back.

"That's promptness for you," said Cal.

Viv headed out into the rain. "That's not the supplies," she called over her shoulder. She had already caught the smell of it.

Signing for the delivery, Viv paid the driver and declined his help hauling the crates one by one into the livery. Each was tidily assembled, with the sides and base cleverly fitted and only the top nailed in place. Gnomish stencils ran along the panels at neat right angles.

Cal watched curiously as Viv gently set down the last one, then indicated Cal's toolbox, giving him a questioning look.

"Have at it," he said.

Hefting a pry bar, she levered up the lid, and there inside was a set of muslin sacks. The scent was even stronger now, and Viv shivered in anticipation. Untying one, she dug a hand into it, and let the roasted brown beans sift through her fingers. She loved the quiet hiss they made as they fell back into the bag.

"Hm. You're right. Not much like tea."

Emerging from her reverie, Viv glanced up at him. "You can smell it though, can't you? Like roasted nuts and fruit."

Cal squinted at her. "Thought you said you drank it?"

Viv nibbled one experimentally, tasted the warm, bitter, dark flavor as it coated her tongue. She felt she needed to explain. "They grind it into powder and then run hot water through it, but there's more to it than that. When the machine shows up, I'll show you. Gods, the smell of it, Cal. This is just a ghost of it."

She sat back on the flagstones and rolled the bean between her thumb and forefinger. "I told you I came across it in Azimuth, and I remember following the smell to the shop. They called it a *café*. People just sat around drinking it from these little ceramic cups, and I had to try it, and . . . it was like drinking the feeling of being peaceful. Being peaceful in your mind. Well, not if you have too much, then it's something else."

"A lot of folks allow you feel peaceful after a beer."

"It's different. I don't know if I can tell you how it is."

"Well, all right then." His look was not unkind. "In the int'rest of your new business, I guess I'll say I hope folks have the same experience you did."

"So do I." She retied the sack, took his mallet, and started nailing the crate lid back down.

When she looked up again, Cal was emerging from the office area. He stopped in front of her and stared at the floor ruminatively for a moment, and she was content to wait for what he had to say.

"Figure you might need a sort of kitchen back there. Stove. Maybe a water barrel and some copper pipe. Hooks for pots an' pans."

"The water barrel's not a bad idea. I should've thought of

that, since I'll need the water. But a kitchen? What do I need that for?"

"Well," he said, looking apologetic. "If you find nobody wants any of the beans and water, at least you can feed 'em."

———+———

As the day drew down, the rain stopped, and the city smelled, if not clean, then at least refreshed. It wasn't quite dusk, but Viv took her lantern and her notes out to the tack box, which had cemented its role as her porch bench. Before she could settle in to reexamine them, she spied Laney across the way, wrapped in a shawl and blowing on a mug of tea.

Viv set the lantern on the box, tucked away her notes, and stepped over the drying puddles to join the woman on her porch.

"Evening," she said.

"It is." Laney nodded at the livery. "Seems you've been mighty busy, *miss*." She grinned slyly when she said it.

"Oh, yeah. I suppose so."

"Sleepin' in there, are you? Hope you're lockin' up at night, dear. It's close to the High Street, but I wouldn't like to see you runnin' afoul of sommat unsavory after dark."

Viv couldn't mask her surprise. As a rule, folk spared little thought for her physical well-being, herself included. She was touched.

"Don't worry. Locked up tight. But, speaking of anyone unsavory . . ." Viv tried to sort out what she wanted to ask. "Had a visitor today. Big hat . . ." She held her hands out wide from her head. "Fancy shirt. Stone-fey, I think. You know him?"

Laney snorted and slurped her tea. She said nothing for a long moment, then sighed. "One of the Madrigal's, I reckon."

"The Madrigal, huh? Some kind of local kingpin?"

"A bunch of stray dogs," spat Laney. "The Madrigal's got the leash." Her wrinkles bunched tight around her mouth. "But the Madrigal ain't to be ignored. When they ask ya to pay"—she gazed sharply at Viv—"and they *will* ask, you'd best bank your coals and pay."

"I'm not sure I can bring myself to do that," she replied mildly.

Laney patted Viv's considerable forearm. "I know you mayn't have thought to 'til now. But seems to me you ain't here to do what you've always done. Am I wrong?"

The old woman had startled her again.

"Well. That's true," Viv said. "Still, for all that, not sure I can roll over for a little man in a big hat and a silly shirt."

Laney chuckled darkly. "Never mind the man in the hat. The Madrigal's what you want to worry about, and nothin' silly about them."

"I'll be careful," said Viv.

They stood in companionable silence for a few minutes.

Viv glanced sidelong at Laney's mug of tea. "Say, you ever have coffee?" she asked.

Laney blinked at her and looked affronted. "Why, I never have. And the way I was brought up, a lady doesn't talk about her maladies," she said primly.

Viv barked a laugh, to the old woman's great annoyance.

——◆——

Viv moved her bedroll and lantern to the loft under the slope of the roof. The smell of coffee beans filtered up through the cracks in the boards, and she inhaled it deeply, like a warm, earthy memory. The tarpaulin thumped like a distant drum in the occasional gust of wind.

In the lantern's light, Blackblood gleamed where it leaned

against the wall. Viv stared at it for a long time and thought about the man in the hat and the Madrigal. She felt a sudden impulse to sleep next to the blade, as she had in a hundred campsites and bivouacs.

She deliberately turned away, extinguished the lantern, and filled her lungs with the dark smell from below.

On the roof, there was a solid thud, followed by a rhythmic heavy padding and a scratching clatter on the tiles, but she was already beginning to doze, and she lost it in the sound of the tarpaulin.

Then she was asleep.

4

The lumber, tiles, and other supplies came in piecemeal over the next few days. Showers came and went, then the sky cleared entirely. When it did, Viv and Cal repaired the hole in the roof, shucking old tiles down through the gap to shatter on the floor. She was surprised at how many of the timbers they had to take up to mend it fully.

Cal was just as methodical and mindful about the repair work as she'd hoped. It was a hard two days of labor for the both of them, but the roof was fully proof against water again.

Next, Cal examined the interior, sounding the boards with a knuckle and several times digging a fistful of dry-rotten wood out and shaking his head at it. After four days of prying out old timber and nailing in fresh, Viv started to wonder if they might have been better off rebuilding the whole damn thing. She rented the cart from the miller again to haul away the debris.

They built a permanent and sturdier ladder into the loft. Viv was a fast study and a reasonable hand with a hammer and nails. Accurately slinging a slab of metal and striking a target was squarely within the realm of her abilities.

When Cal first clambered into the loft and spied Blackblood

glimmering darkly in the corner, he made no comment on it. "Cozy," he said instead. "Be wantin' a bed and dresser, no doubt." "No need," said Viv. "I'm used to sleeping rough." "Used to ain't the same as ought to." But he pressed no further, and that was that.

In the main stable area, they did as Cal had suggested, cutting down the stall walls and converting each into a sort of booth. The hob boxed in neat U-benches along the interiors. They pre-assembled tabletops, and Viv easily orc-handled them into place across trestles.

Viv cut two high windows into the northern and eastern walls, letting the morning sun crawl down from the loft and into the new dining area.

They sanded the office counter and added a hinged extension to the end for extra workspace. Cal repurposed some old tack shelves and moved them to the back wall of what Viv now thought of as the storefront. He also managed to replace some cracked panes in the mullioned front window next to the smaller door.

"Well, doesn't look much like a stable anymore," observed Viv, watching him fit in the last bit of glass.

"Hm. Mighty pleased it quit smellin' like one, too."

———+———

One afternoon, Viv returned from the cooper with a water barrel on one shoulder and a few buckets in hand. She tucked the barrel in the corner, back of the counter. She drew water from the well a few blocks down, and Cal checked for leaks as she filled it.

They converted the backroom of the office into a pantry with more shelves. Viv consulted her notes and excavated a pit that she insulated with clay for cold storage. Cal added a neat, hinged door.

Viv did the ladder-work of whitewashing the front, while Cal rechinked mortar between the river stones low on the walls.

When she strode back inside, arming sweat from her forehead and hauling the whitewash bucket, she found him inspecting the flagstones, checking the sand between. Her eyes went to the resting place of the Scalvert's Stone, and she had to keep herself from rushing forward to interrupt.

"Anything need doing there?" she asked, trying to sound brisk and natural about it. What if he found the Stone? Would he recognize it? And so what if he did? It was fair to say she trusted Cal.

And yet.

He looked up. "Hm. Maybe a little more sand. This one's loose. Might should take it up and pack some underneath." He stomped on the flag she'd buried the Stone under, and her heart leapt.

"I'll take care of it," she said, and her smile felt entirely false.

Cal didn't seem to notice.

"Hm," he said.

And that was that.

Later that evening—after glances up and down the street to reassure herself that the man with the hat wasn't peering in at her—Viv did take up the flagstone. She removed the Scalvert's Stone and held it in her hand. Warm to the touch, it almost seemed to have a lambent yellow glow, independent of the light of the lantern. Replacing it with care, she scooped fistfuls of dirt to relevel the flagstone and smoothed sand into the crevices again.

That night she dreamed of the Scalvert Queen, but when

she drove her hand into its skull to remove the Stone, its flesh drew tight around her wrist. As she tried to withdraw her fist, she couldn't, and the flesh firmed, and the scalvert's many eyes ignited one by one, like signal fires in the dark. Her efforts to free herself grew increasingly frantic, until she startled awake. The nerves in her right arm were alight, her hand tingling with pins and needles.

After lying awake for some time, she finally slept again, and by morning, she'd forgotten the dream.

—◆—

Days passed in a haze of hot work, aching muscles, slivers, dust, and the smells of sweat and lime and fresh-cut wood.

At the end of two weeks, the place looked downright respectable. Viv found herself out in the street a few times a day, hands on her hips, surveying the shop with a rising, warm sense of accomplishment.

On one of these occasions, she was startled to find Laney suddenly beside her. The woman used her broom as a walking stick, leaning her weight on it. Viv had no idea how she'd arrived so silently.

"Well. Fanciest livery I've ever seen," Laney said, then nodded, and went back to her porch.

Unsure why she hadn't done it sooner, Viv set up the ladder and tore down the old Parkin's Livery sign, tossing it into the rubbish pile with real satisfaction.

—◆—

"Goin' to need a new sign," said Cal, his thumbs hooked into the waist of his breeches, staring up at the vacant iron bracket.

"You know," said Viv. "I took a lot of notes. Figured I'd covered

most details. But I never really thought about a sign. Or a name."
She looked down at Cal. "Just never crossed my mind."

It was quiet for a minute, then Cal cleared his throat, and in
the most hesitant voice she'd ever heard from him, he ventured,
"Viv's Place?"

"Good as any, I suppose," she replied. "I don't have a better
idea."

He didn't look satisfied.

"Hm. Maybe . . . maybe . . . Viv's Coffee?"

"I'll be honest, feels strange having my name on anything.
Like putting your own face on the sign."

A pause.

"Could just say Coffee, I s'pose. Don't 'spect there'll be a lot
of confusion."

Viv squinted hard at him and thought he'd outlast her, but
then his mouth quirked at the corner.

"I figure I'll table it for now," she said. "Who knows? Maybe
I'll name it after you. Calamity Coffee has a nice sound to it."

Cal regarded her, sniffed, and then said solemnly, "Well.
You're not wrong."

———✦———

Later that week, the bulk of the construction was complete.
They built a big trestle table, and benches ran between the
booths. She and Cal stained and oiled them all, swept the floors
clean, and set glass in the new high windows.

Viv hoisted a chandelier and secured it to a bolt-plate Cal
set into the wall. As evening drew on, they lit it with a long
taper, both pleased with the glow it cast, the ring-shadow pulsing below.

At the table, with Viv's notes between them, they discussed

some of the finer points of furnishings and rugs and maybe some reeds to freshen the smell of the place.

They both halted their conversation at once.

In the doorway stood the man in the hat, with company to boot. They were less well-dressed, a motley assortment of men—two humans and a dwarf with a cropped beard and clubbed-back hair. Viv saw at least two short-swords and would have wagered there were at least six knives between them, in one cuff or another.

"Wondered when you'd stop back by," said Viv. She didn't bother to rise.

"I'm flattered to have occupied your thoughts," the man said, stepping across the threshold and surveying the renovations with an appreciative nod. "You've been mightily industrious! The old place never looked better. Seems you won't be in the business of horseflesh though."

Viv shrugged.

His smile from the last visit might never have lapsed in all the intervening days. "Look, I enjoy a witty back-and-forth as much as the next man, but I sense you appreciate directness. I'm merely a representative. My friends call me Lack. You can, too. This street—this entire southern quarter—is under the watchful and beneficent eye of the Madrigal." He sketched a bow, as though the Madrigal himself were here to see it.

"You think I need a watchful eye?" Viv's brows rose.

"We *all* need someone to watch out for us," replied Lack.

"This is the part where you let me know about the monthly involuntary donation for . . . what did you call it? A 'beneficent eye'?"

Lack cocked a finger at her, and his smile widened.

"Well, you've said your piece." Viv casually dismissed him by returning to the study of her notes. Cal hadn't budged an inch during the entire exchange, his face rigid.

Lack's voice developed an annoyed edge. "I'll expect your contribution end of the month. One sovereign, two silvers is the going rate."

"What you expect is your business." Viv's reply was mild.

Out of the corner of her eye, she saw the heavies behind Lack make a move to approach—which would have been a laughable mistake—but he stopped them with a gesture.

There was a heavy silence while Viv waited for a rebuttal.

Then Lack and his crew were gone.

Cal let out a long breath and shot her a worried glance. "Listen. You don't want to run afoul of the Madrigal," he said in a soft voice. When the hob normally spoke, it was always even and solid, like he was laying brick. The change in him made her look at him seriously.

"That's what Laney said." She put one of her hands on the table and opened it wide. "But Cal, I think you have a pretty good idea of what these hands have done. Do you really see me bobbing a curtsy to a bunch of men too stupid to know the odds if they were to tangle with me?"

"Hm. I don't doubt you'd lay those four low, no problem. But listen. There's a lot more'n four of 'em out there, and the Madrigal is the sort to make an example."

"I've heard a lot of stories and a lot of legends in my time, and they're always worse than the real thing. I can take care of myself, here."

"Maybe so. This place, though?" He rapped the table with a knuckle. "It ain't fireproof. So, fine, you can take care of yourself, but I figure there's more you got a stake in. Am I wrong?"

Viv frowned and stared at him, lost for words.

Cal got up, leveled a finger at her, and said, "Wait."

He rummaged in some of the last remaining supplies and retrieved a hammer and nails. Up on his toes at the wall behind the counter, he banged some brackets into the wood—one, two, three.

"At least, do this. Put that sword of yours up there," he said. "If you're gonna show 'em you got teeth, at least fix it so you can bite when you need to. Hm?"

———+———

When Viv retired for the night, Blackblood rested on those brackets, a killing slab.

She wished it was still hidden in the corner.

———+———

Viv hadn't expected Cal, but around noon, he showed up riding in the back of a cart next to a big, black stove and several lengths of stovepipe.

She gave him the side-eye as he leapt down. "What's all this?"

He shrugged. "Hm. I said you needed a kitchen. And b'fore you say anythin', it's already paid for."

She tossed up her hands, both amused and exasperated. The horses shied nervously. "Where'd you get this? I'm not a baker."

He gestured at the upper room. "Gets cold here in winter, and no fireplace to speak of. You want to freeze up there in the loft, layin' on the floor, snow on the roof? Gimme a hand with this."

Viv held her peace as she hefted the stove out of the bed of the wagon, one end at a time. Even for her, the heavy iron thing was difficult to maneuver. She eventually got it down and walked it end-by-end into the storefront by way of the big doors.

Cal carried in the stovepipe, piece by piece, and then paid the impatient driver.

She was surprised to find that she was a little winded. Her back was gnawing at her again, too, as she fell onto one of the benches. "Can't let you pay for it, Cal."

"Hm. Too bad. Already paid me too much. Figured if I was gonna waste it on somethin' foolish, this might as well be it."

"Heat for winter, huh?"

Cal nodded. "And if the bean water doesn't work out . . ."

Viv laughed. "Speaking of that." She gestured at the counter, where a mortar and pestle sat next to a few kettles, a tumble of cloth, and some fired clay cups.

"Takin' up apothecary, too?"

"I'll show you. But let's get this thing out of the middle of the floor, first."

At some direction from Cal, she positioned the stove against the west wall, and after some figuring and fussing and cursing, he got the stovepipe affixed. With a little cutting by brace-drill and saw—and some arch comments from Viv—he fed the pipe out through the flange where it met the wall. A few hours later, they had the end run up past the eaves and topped with a rain cap.

They made do with some scrap for kindling and started a small blaze in the side box. The smoke drew up and out just fine.

"All right," said Viv. "Get some water in one of those kettles and put it on."

Cal raised his eyebrows. "Bean water?"

"You want to test the stove or not?"

He shrugged and went about it, filling the kettle from the water barrel.

Viv dug out a handful of coffee beans from one of the sacks, crushed them in the mortar, and poured the grounds into a tube of linen. She stretched the tube over the mouth of one of the clay cups, and when the kettle whistled, she slowly poured boiling water through, a little at a time.

"Is that a lady's stockin'?" asked Cal.

Viv glanced at him. "It's clean. I don't wear stockings."

"Just askin'," he said mildly.

"Hm," she said. It seemed he was rubbing off on her.

"How exactly were you plannin' to use that kettle with no stove?" he asked pointedly.

"Mmmm, needed it to fill the machine that's coming. Just a happy accident."

Viv completed a last spiraling pour and waited for the swollen grounds to steep. Removing the linen sleeve and swirling the cup, she closed her eyes, brought it to her nose, and inhaled deeply.

She took an experimental taste . . . and smiled, nodding. "That's not half bad."

Cal frowned at her.

"Now," she said defensively, "this isn't as good as it'll be when I can make it right. But." She handed him the cup.

He made a big show of sniffing at it. He raised his eyebrows and nodded a little. Very slowly and very delicately, he sipped at it. Then he held it in his hand and stood there.

After what Viv considered an overly generous few moments, she couldn't help herself. "Well?"

"Hm," said Cal. "I'll allow . . . it's actually not that terrible."

—◆—

Later, they sat at the big table, each with their own cup. Cal pretended to ignore his, but Viv caught him stealing cautious sips now and then, when he thought she wasn't looking. She held her own in both hands contemplatively, absorbing the heat and the scent. It felt like completing a loop, like the satisfying click of a clasp snapping closed.

"So," she said. "You can also make these with milk. You might like it."

"Milk?" Cal made a face.

"Better than it sounds. You'll have to try it once I have the machine. The gnomes called it a *latte*."

"Latte? That mean somethin'?"

"Named after the gnomish barista who invented them, I think—Latte Diameter."

Cal gave her a long-suffering look. "Can't explain what one word means with another word nobody knows. What's a barista?"

"Cal, I didn't *invent* the words."

"Folks gonna need a new education just to buy some bean w—some coffee."

"I don't know. I kind of like it. It's more exotic that way."

"Ladies' stockin's and exotic bean water. Gods help us."

5

The jobs board sat at the east end of the largest square in Thune. It was long and low and, beneath newer scraps of parchment or foolscap, furred with the ragged flakes of a hundred others. As Viv scanned the notices, she endured a weary onrush of memory—beast hunts, bounties, and battles. She might've torn down five score of those sheets herself in one city or another, knuckles bloodied, to claim her due for a job done.

She'd even posted a few in her time—a hireling here, filling out a hunting party there.

This one was nothing like the others.

She spiked her notice on one of the many iron studs and read over what she'd written.

ASSISTANT WANTED: MUST BE WILLING TO LEARN
MANAGEMENT & FOOD SERVICE EXPERIENCE DESIRED
ADVANCEMENT OPPORTUNITIES
PATIENCE A PLUS
WAGES COMMENSURATE
INQUIRE AT THE OLD LIVERY ON REDSTONE
AFTERNOON TO DUSK

It was a long shot, but the Scalvert's Stone hadn't let her down yet.

◄──+──►

She returned to the shop but found herself restless and pacing. She'd sent post for her most important delivery on her first day in the city, and while the coffee had shown up promptly, the other parcel had yet to arrive. With the shop repaired and cleaned and nothing upon which to expend her nervous energy, she felt thwarted.

After weeks of steady work and with Cal absent, her hands itched with the inactivity. At last, in exasperation, she gathered her notes into her satchel and hiked to the pub she'd visited on her first night in Thune.

She sat at a table in the back, ordered a meal, and made increasingly irrelevant lists. When noon arrived, her meal remained half-eaten, and her nervous organizational efforts were in shambles, so she lunged from her seat, paid, and stalked back to the shop to wait.

The idea that an applicant would arrive on the first day was, of course, ludicrous. But the Scalvert's Stone . . . well. She either trusted its power, or she didn't. And if she did . . .

> *the Scalvert's Stone a-fire*
> *draws the ring of fortune*

Viv started a fire, boiled water, ground some beans, and made a cup of coffee, which she drank too quickly. Then she made another. And another. As a result, she was nervier than ever and wished she'd written other instructions on the advertisement. Or that her probably misplaced faith in the power of the Stone wasn't keeping her corralled there. Did she really believe it would deliver results so soon?

Blackblood hung ominously on the wall, and she found herself wanting to take it down to sharpen it and to lose herself in the repetitive, familiar action of it, but she forced her gaze away. She found herself annoyed that Cal had made her hang it up and then angry at herself for blaming him, since that was a stupid thing to think. Viv could have juggled the man one-handed. He'd hardly *made* her do anything.

And then, in late midafternoon, there was a rap on the door, and it opened briskly.

A woman strode in, glancing about in a way that was both cautious and confident. She was tall—not as tall as Viv, of course—with glossy black hair cut severely at chin length. She wore breeches and what looked like a sweater, dark and shapeless, with a collar that covered her throat. Her face was aristocratic, her eyes dark. Viv also noted with surprise the short stubs of horn parting her hair, the hint of dusty magenta in her skin, and her whipcord tail. The woman was clearly a succubus.

Viv's head was already buzzing from her fourth cup of coffee, and she started up from her seat.

The woman slowly looked her up and down, but her expression didn't change. She glanced deliberately at Blackblood on the wall and then back. "Assistant Wanted," she said. It wasn't a question. Her voice was throaty, but she spoke precisely.

"Uh, that's right," replied Viv. And just stood there.

The woman's eyebrows slowly rose, and she closed the door behind her. She held out a hand. "Tandri," she said.

"Viv." She awkwardly returned the handshake, cursing herself for drinking so much coffee. "I'm sorry, I didn't expect anyone to actually show up on the first day," she said, which was absolutely untrue, but seemed a good excuse for how scattered she probably appeared.

"I like to be prompt," said Tandri.

"Good. Good!" Viv tried to get hold of herself. She'd hired help before. Sure, they'd been mercenaries and cutpurses, but the principle was the same. Lay out the job, set forth the terms, get a feeling for whether they'd cut and run at an inconvenient moment, and then make the call. Easy.

"So, I'm looking for an assistant. I guess that's clear from the notice. The job's . . . uh, it's sort of . . . um. You ever hear of coffee?"

The succubus shook her head, her hair moving like a liquid curtain. "I have not."

"Well, that's fine, doesn't matter. Tea though? You know tea. I'm opening this shop soon, kind of like a tea shop—but coffee—and can't run it all by myself. I need somebody willing to learn the work, take customers, help with whatever needs doing. Probably some cleaning, too. And they'd make coffee, you know, as needed, after some instruction . . . from me. Uh. I wrote 'food service experience' in the notice. You have that?"

Tandri's expression didn't falter in the slightest. "I do not."

"Um."

The succubus inclined her head at Viv. "Do you?"

Viv's mouth hung open for a moment, until she eventually managed, "I . . . do not."

"I *am* willing to learn. That was higher up on the notice," said the woman.

"That's true." Viv scratched the back of her head. Gods, this was so awkward.

"Advancement opportunities, it also said," prompted Tandri. "What sorts of opportunities?"

"I did write that, didn't I? Well . . . I mean, if things went well . . . I guess it would depend on what your interests were?"

There was a very awkward pause.

Viv wrestled with what she was about to say. She'd never been skilled at putting things delicately. It had never been particularly important up 'til now. Succubi had a reputation for certain . . . biological imperatives. Were their needs and predilections even a choice? She forged onward. "You're a . . . succubus. Right?"

At the implied addendum to that question, Tandri's expression changed for the first time—a pinching of the lips, a tightening around the eyes. Her tail lashed behind her. "I am. And you're an orc. Running a not-tea shop."

"No judgment from me!" Viv babbled, feeling on the precipice of a great mistake, but stumbling forward, nevertheless. "I only ask, because—"

"No, I have no desire to *vamp* your customers, if that's your question." Tandri's voice was icy.

"That . . . wasn't what I was planning to say," said Viv. "I would never assume that. I've just never worked with one of . . . you . . . and I wasn't sure about your . . . needs." Gods, this was agonizing. Her cheeks were aflame.

Tandri closed her eyes and crossed her arms in front of her. Her cheeks were flushed, as well.

Viv was absolutely sure she was about to turn on her heel and leave.

She sighed. "I apologize. Look, I am *very* bad at this. I don't really know what I'm doing." She hooked a thumb at the greatsword on the wall. "This is what I know, what I've always known. I just want to know something else, now. To *be* something else. Everything I said was stupid. I, of all people, ought to know better than to assume anything based on what you were born as. Before you walk out, do you mind if I start over?"

Tandri took a slow breath, in through her nose, out through her mouth. "There's no need to start over."

"Ah," said Viv, disappointed. "I understand."

"Why waste the time? We've covered most of the particulars," continued the succubus, briskly. "So, *wages commensurate?*"

Viv goggled at her for a moment and then stammered, "Three silver, eight bits a week, to start?"

"Four silver."

"I . . . yes, that's fine."

"Acceptable."

"Then, you want the job?"

"I do." Tandri held out her hand again.

Viv shook it in a daze. "Well, then . . . welcome aboard. I . . . thanks." She'd set out to hire an assistant, but she had the overwhelming sense that she'd just acquired a partner without meaning to. She couldn't help wondering who had interviewed whom.

"It's settled then," said Tandri. "A pleasure to meet you, Viv." Then she turned and left, closing the door gently behind her.

"*Patience a plus,*" Viv murmured.

It was several minutes before she noticed that she hadn't even specified when the work would start. But somehow, she wasn't worried about it.

—◄+►—

Viv went directly to the square and tore down her notice, which hadn't hung for more than seven hours. She folded it and tucked it into a pocket, then returned to the shop, where she wiped away the debris of her furtive bean-grinding.

Afterward, Viv went out and ate a hearty meal, coming home pleasantly warm and full. As she sat toying with the witching rod in the dining area, her gaze returned again and again to the place where the Scalvert's Stone rested.

Later, staring at the ceiling from her bedroll, she thought about her impending delivery and the feeling of potential motion building in her. All that remained was for that last obstruction to be kicked away.

She heard a thud on the roof tiles. Heavy footfalls clattered noisily as something large tracked to the western wall. There was a pregnant pause . . . and then a thump.

Viv quietly stole from her bedroll, descended the ladder, and paced the dark and quiet street, trying to see onto the roof before checking the alley to the west, but she found nothing.

6

Viv's lack of concern was vindicated, and Tandri did indeed turn up the following morning. Viv was wringing out her wet hair into the street, a half-full bucket by her side. She'd reverted to camp-bathing after discovering she disliked visiting the nearest bathhouse.

She coiled up her hair and pinned it, then stood, palming water off her face. "I should have said when we'd start," she said. "Can't open yet. Still waiting on a delivery."

"It seemed there was plenty to do already," Tandri observed. She was just as severe and direct as the previous day, with none of the sensual sway that Viv had noted in other succubi she'd met. Although, admittedly, that was a vanishingly small number. Only the syrupy gloss of Tandri's hair and the sinuous lash of her tail hinted at anything but crisp efficiency.

"Oh?" asked Viv.

"I'll need to know what I'll be doing. No time like the present."

"Right. Well, I can't really show you the particulars until the equipment gets here, but the plan for today was to sort out some dishware and furnishings. I'm not much of a decorator, but I've got a few ideas. I was going to find a potter, then see about tables for the street, some chairs, maybe"—she waved vaguely—"some . . . paintings? I thought this would be the easy part, but it's very fiddly."

"If I can make a suggestion," said Tandri. It didn't sound like a question.

Viv made a be-my-guest gesture.

"Thune Market is today and tomorrow, the same as every week. If you want to be thrifty about it and save a lot of needless wandering, that's what I'd recommend."

"Willing to tour me around?"

"It's your silver," said Tandri, and while her tone was as even as ever, Viv thought she caught the ghost of a smile.

In Viv's experience, most of the nonmartial folk she met stepped carefully in her presence, as though cringing from a blow that would never come. She enjoyed the succubus's frank disposition. Cal had an entirely different species of that bluntness. She wondered again about the Scalvert's Stone, and what it promised to draw to her.

Viv locked up and followed Tandri north of the High Street to a long, curving thoroughfare where many of the tradesfolk clearly had permanent storefronts or workshops. She was surprised to note that it was near where she'd visited the locksmith when she'd first arrived. Most vendors had awnings, tables, and displays set up on the wide street, and there was already a thickening mass of shoppers.

They browsed for a few hours, past noon. Viv kept her eyes out for the items on her list, and Tandri deftly steered her away from some bad buys, noting subtle cracks in pottery or poor joins in ironwork. Without prompting or permission, she took over the process of negotiation, and Viv could see that, despite how thoroughly she cloaked herself in neutral clothing and poise—and Tandri didn't trade on physical allure, at all—the merchants responded to . . . *something*.

In the end, Viv paid for a full set of clay plates, mugs, and cups, and a pair of much larger copper kettles. She also secured a hefty box of pewter spoons and cutlery, a utensil hanger, a rug, two wrought-iron tables with chairs to match, five wall-lanterns, assorted cleaning supplies, and a scattering of pastoral paintings that Viv thought looked blurry, but Tandri maintained were *evocative*. In most cases, the succubus secured delivery as part of the deal, although Viv carried the box of cutlery and the utensil hanger under one arm as they left.

After dropping them off at the shop, Viv insisted on thanking Tandri with a late lunch.

There was a fey-run eatery on the High Street that was only open during the day, and somehow it seemed appropriate to the moment. The day was warm, and the smell of the river was strong. They sat at one of the tables in the street.

Fey cuisine was known for its buttery breads and artful presentation, and while Viv wasn't normally particular about what she ate, she had to admit that she'd acquired a taste for it.

"So," she said, as they waited on their meal. "Have you always lived here, in Thune?"

"No," replied Tandri, poised in her seat. "I've lived lots of places." The succubus then smoothly redirected. "And you're clearly not the cosmopolitan sort. Why Thune?"

Viv thought about the ley lines, the real reason she'd chosen Thune, and figured that was thorny to explain. She settled on a truthful but less complicated response. "Research," she said. Viv glanced ruefully down at herself. "You wouldn't know it to look at me, but I do a lot of reading. Anyway, once I got it in my head to do this, I spent a lot of time in Athenaeums, talked to a lot of people, and this seemed the best place for plenty of reasons."

"Coffee," said Tandri, quirking a small smile. "Not-tea. Long-held dream or just a change of pace?"

Viv explained her encounter with it in Azimuth, a little more eloquently than she'd managed with Cal. Tandri looked thoughtful.

"Seems a far cry from what you might've done before."

"Hm, and what line of work do you assume I was in?" Viv arched a brow.

Tandri looked stricken. "You're right, that was stupid, especially . . ."

Viv snorted. "I'm just baiting you. My hide's thicker than that. And for what it's worth, *your* assumption isn't wrong. You don't get this many scars farming."

Tandri gave her a searching look and then appeared to relax.

Their food arrived, and once the fey server left, Tandri lifted her mug of weak beer. "Well. To misplaced assumptions."

Viv raised her own drink. "I'll toast to that."

As they ate, Viv continued. "I think I'd been looking for a way out for years. Adventuring, fighting, hunting bounties—you're either bleeding yourself slow from a hundred wounds or waiting on one deathblow. But you get numb to the possibility of anything different. This was the first time something else made me feel a way I wanted to *keep* feeling. So, here I am, and with some blood still in me."

Tandri nodded but said nothing.

Viv waited, thinking Tandri might have something to say on her own behalf, but she quietly ate instead.

Maybe another time.

Still, it was a very pleasant meal.

———+———

When they returned to the shop, an enormous, gnomish crate sat in the street out front, and waiting atop it, legs dangling, sat a sturdy dwarf Viv knew well.

"Roon!" she cried. "What in all the hells are you doing here?"

He leapt down and approached, tugging nervously at his braided mustache. "Just makin' a delivery to an old friend," he said.

"Come here, you old stump," she said, opening her arms wide.

His face broke into an expression of relief, and he embraced her. "Have to say, wasn't sure you'd want to see me. The way you left . . ."

She got down on one knee to bring their faces closer to level. "I'm sorry about that. If I'd stopped to explain—tried to lay it all out—I thought I'd talk myself out of it. Wasn't fair to you or the others, but . . ." She shrugged helplessly.

He searched her face, then nodded decisively and clapped her on the shoulders. "Well, you can tell us, now you're clear of it. True?"

"Yeah, I can do that." Then she looked up at the crate. "But . . . the delivery?"

"Ah! Well, my brother Canna runs the carriage post out of Azimuth. Saw your name, was curious, an' let me know. I offered to ride security. Done it before. Have to say, after seein' the crate, I'm fair burnin' to know what you're up to." His eyes flicked behind her.

"Oh! This is Tandri. She's working with me." Viv stood and made introductions. "Tandri, this is Roon. We ran together for, oh, for years, I guess."

"Until veeerrrry recently. Pleased to meet you," said Roon.

"Likewise."

"Well, we can't just stand in the street, like this," said Viv. She unlocked the shop, then unbarred and opened the big doors. "Roon, help me move this thing inside."

Together, they hauled it onto the long table. Tandri followed them bemusedly.

"All right," said Viv. "You're curious. You want to do the honors?"

"Don't mind if I do," Roon replied.

He took the edge of the hatchet he kept on his belt and gently popped up the corners of the lid, and they slid it off.

Inside, nestled amidst wood shavings, was a large, silver box, crowded with ornate pipework, gauges behind thick glass, a set of knobs and dials, and a pair of long-handled contraptions along the front.

"Viv," said Roon, who was standing on the bench to peer down into the crate. "I haven't the faintest damned idea what that is."

"It's a coffee machine," mused Tandri aloud. "Isn't it?"

"That's exactly what it is," said Viv, with great satisfaction.

"Coffee?" said Roon. "Is this what you were on about back in Azimuth?" He shot a glance at Tandri. "Couldn't stop *belaborin'* it."

"Yep." Viv smiled at him.

"Well, what in the hells are you plannin' to do with it?" asked Roon.

"Help me get it out of here, and I'll tell you."

—◆—

They shortly had it up on the counter top and the crate out in the street. Viv drew the big doors closed, again. She wasn't interested in another unexpected visit from Lack, especially not right now. With Roon here, she might find it more difficult to rein in her desire to knock him bloody.

A pamphlet was packed into the crate amongst the shavings. Tandri claimed it and perused it while Viv and Roon chatted at the big table.

After Viv explained her plans and what she'd done with the place, Roon gave the building a longer, more appreciative inspection.

"Whew," he said. "Well, Viv, when you go at somethin', you don't go at it soft. Can't say I understand how you plan to make it work, but you never ran into a fight without knowin' how it was goin' to turn out. Guess I'd trust your gut over mine."

"Not sure about that," said Viv. "But I did my best not to leave too much to chance."

Roon squinted at her when she said it and seemed like he might press for more.

"So, how's Gallina?" asked Viv, hurrying past the uncomfortable potential of that topic.

"Can't say she wasn't stung. But you know her, tough as they come. Maybe still sore, but she'll be fine. You know, if you want me to say somethin' . . . carry a letter maybe. . . ?"

"I should write her, but I think I ought to take a little time to think about it. You all still pass through Varian?"

"'Course. Easiest route to most places."

"I'll send her something there, after I figure out what to say. Tell her . . . well, tell her I'm sorry I left the way I did."

Roon nodded, then drummed his hands on the table. "An' speakin' of leavin', I have to be gettin' on. Day's runnin' down, and a long way to go tomorrow. But before I do . . ." He rummaged in a pouch at his belt and pulled out a small gray stone with three wavy stripes engraved on the side.

"Blink Stone?" asked Viv.

"Yep," said Roon. "I've got the match to it on me. I know you're set up here, don't expect any problems, but you ever get into trouble, things don't go the way they should? You toss this into a fire, I'll get the signal, and I'll find you, now that I know where you are."

"It's going to be fine, Roon."

"Well, sure it is. But also . . . maybe someday you find you need to get back out there." He held up his hands before she could protest. "Not sayin' you will! Not sayin' it's even likely. But, better prepared, true?"

She took the stone from him. "Better prepared. Sure." It was the last thing she wanted, but he was doing her a kindness, and after she'd left them behind without explanation. The least she could do was graciously accept a friendly overture.

"Then I'll be off," he said briskly. He rose and embraced her again. He made a short bow to Tandri, adding, "A pleasure, miss."

Viv saw him out. "It was good to see you, Roon. Truly. Give Gallina and Taivus my apologies. And Fennus . . ."

Roon grinned at her. "A swift kick in the arse?"

"Hm," she said.

"I'll see you. Take care, Viv."

And he departed into the night.

◄─✦─►

"Sorry about that." Viv returned to find Tandri still perusing the gnomish booklet. "Honestly, there's no need for you to be here this late. I lost track of time, should have cut you loose an hour ago."

The succubus looked up from her reading. "After all this? I think I have to know how this works. I'm not sure I can stand to be in suspense overnight when it's sitting right here." She briefly touched the gleaming machine.

It looked so modern and glossy, there on the counter. Gnomish engineering really was a marvel. It wasn't exactly like the one Viv had seen in Azimuth, but close enough, and now that Roon had left, her excitement rose, along with some queasy trepidation.

"You already know how it works?" asked Tandri.

"For the most part," said Viv, who stared at it, her eyes roving over curving pipes and polished glass plates.

"Well." Tandri's expression had given way to something with more humor in it. "Don't leave me on tenterhooks."

"Right! So, fire." Viv located the small door along the front and flipped it open. An oil reservoir and wick were just visible. She found a long, sulfur match, struck it, and lit the wick, closing the door after.

"And water . . ." She filled a kettle from the water barrel, opened another door along the top, and carefully decanted water into the reservoir.

While she retrieved a bag of beans from the storeroom, she heard a rising gentle hiss, and by the time she returned, the gauges along the front had begun to twitch.

There was a clever grinding mechanism at one end, and she poured a measure of beans into yet another compartment. She unlatched one of the long-handled devices from the front of the machine and slotted it in below the grinder. Once the right-hand gauge crept into the blue section on its face, she flipped a lever, and a rumbling whine sounded as the beans were ground and packed tightly into the scoop of the handle.

"Can you pass me one of those mugs?"

Tandri obliged, watching the whole process with interest.

"Now, for the final bit," said Viv, reseating the scoop in its original location, placing the mug beneath, and flicking another lever.

A louder, sharp hissing, a gurgle, and the machine thrummed as water surged through the silver pipework. After several seconds of increasing noise, a steady trickle of brown liquid poured into the mug below.

Viv waited a bit too long to cut the switch, but she could tell immediately that she'd mostly done it correctly. The smell that rose from the mug was rich and warm and nutty . . . and perfect.

She brought it to her nose, closed her eyes, and inhaled deeply.

"Gods. Yes, that's it."

Relief and elation surged through Viv in equal measure.

"I really like it this way, but for a first-timer . . ." Viv held the mug under another spout and pressed a trigger along the top, and hot water burbled into the cup until it was nearly full.

She turned carefully to Tandri and held the mug out. "Here. Go on. Careful though, it's hot."

Tandri gravely took the mug and held it in both hands, tentatively sniffing at it.

She brought the brim to her lips, blew on it for several seconds, and then took a very cautious sip.

A long pause.

"Oh," said Tandri. "Oh my."

Viv grinned. This just might work.

7

When Cal next appeared with his tools, Viv proudly displayed the gnomish coffee machine. The hob was inspecting it with interest, thumbs tucked into his belt, when Tandri appeared.

Viv made the introductions.

"Charmed," said Cal, executing a deep bow.

"It's nice work," said Tandri, gesturing to the interior. "I remember what it used to look like."

The hob puffed up a little bit at that, and Viv was sure she saw him struggling not to smile, but he only nodded and said, inevitably, "Hm."

Deliveries from the previous day's excursion began to arrive and continued piecemeal over the balance of the day.

Cal hung the wall lanterns, while Tandri and Viv uncrated and shelved the dishware, rolled out the rug, and arranged the tables and chairs out under the front windows.

Midafternoon, Cal excused himself to run "a little errand." He returned a while later, struggling with the awkward bulk of a wooden signboard. Breathing heavily, he set it down with the front facing away and drummed his fingers anxiously across its top.

"So," he said. "I should've asked, but . . . seemed you were undecided. And nothin' hangin' yet. And after thinkin' it over, I thought . . . well." Viv could swear his cheeks were flushing red. "Ah, gods." He huffed and spun it around for her to see.

The sign was in the shape of a kite shield, and the surface was routed out to leave two words embossed in diagonal script, with a sword whose profile she recognized dividing them.

"You don't have to use it, 'course. Was just a thought, and I had some idle time, and I figured . . . well, you need a sign. Can't have people thinkin' it's still a livery," he said in a strained voice.

The sign read:

LEGENDS
— & —
LATTES

"Cal." Viv discovered her throat was a little thick. "It's perfect."

"Well," he said. And then thrust it at her with both hands.

Tandri nodded thoughtfully. "Very memorable. What's a latte?"

"Bean water with milk," said Cal in a stage whisper, peering around the edge.

Tandri made a face.

Viv laughed and took the sign, holding it up to admire. "Just for that, I'm going to make you a proper latte, and you're going to drink it. I've got a fresh jug of milk in the cold-box, and I was practicing this morning."

"Hm. First, let's hang that sign."

Viv was tall enough that standing on a chair brought her in

reach of the iron sign-arm, and she looped the eyehooks over the spikes. Cal had clearly measured in advance.

They all stood back and admired it.

"One good turn deserves another. How about that milky bean water?" asked Viv, grinning at Cal.

He made a show of grumbling about it, but watched avidly as Viv demonstrated the entire process, finally frothing the milk under a silver spout that jetted steam. When she poured foam into the mug and placed it before him, he eyed it, then her, and after gingerly blowing on it, he took a sip.

His eyes widened. "Well, shit. Milky bean water. I'll be damned." He took another, longer sip and burned his tongue.

"This, I have to try," said Tandri.

Cal gave it over while he whistled air through his scalded mouth.

After a careful sip and a closed-eye evaluation, Tandri pronounced it excellent. "There are gnomes in Thune. Why are they not serving this?" she asked, in a tone of wonder.

"Who knows? But I'd as soon they didn't start," replied Viv. "At least let me get a foothold first!"

"Cheers to that," said Tandri, taking a longer drink. Her tail snapped a pleased whip-crack motion.

"I'll have that back, thank you," said Cal, waggling his hand for it. "Ain't you supposed to learn to make 'em, anyway?"

"I've read the book that was packed in, but there *is* some kind of art to it," she replied as she handed over the mug.

"Come on around here. I'll show you," said Viv. She was smiling, and for the first time, the building, the city, this *place* . . . felt like hers. A place she'd still be tomorrow, the week after, next season, next year . . .

Home.

—+—

"So, opening tomorrow, you said?" asked Tandri, as they all sat together at one of the outdoor tables, sipping their respective drinks.

"I hope to," said Viv. "Not really sure what to expect, though. If I'm honest, I'm nervous about it. Feels like there's something else I should be doing to prepare, but I don't know what that is, so I figure I should just get in there and get bloodied and sort it out as I go . . . as *we* go."

"Well, ideally, there won't be any blood," said Tandri with a wry smile. "But do you really expect folks to just show up at your door? Are you going to advertise?"

"Advertise?"

"Put the word out. Signs. Hire a crier to let people know you're open."

Viv was taken aback. "I'd never thought about it."

"For someone who has planned this as thoroughly as you have, I'm a little surprised by that," said Tandri.

Viv felt both complimented and chastened at the same time. "I just stumbled across the café in Azimuth. I figured it might be the same here."

"There were customers, though?"

"Sure."

"That's advertising by itself. You saw people buying, repeat business. It let you know it was worth investigating."

"Huh. You seem to know a lot more about this than I do. Well . . . what do you suggest?"

Tandri thought about it before answering. Viv liked that about her.

"No harm in opening. We can find our sea legs. The problem

I see is that even if you tell the city what you're selling, nobody knows what it really is, the same as Cal and I."

Cal nodded.

"So," Tandri continued. "Maybe we need to educate them. Hmmm. Let me think on it. Tomorrow, a dry run, but frankly, I wouldn't expect much. I don't want you to be disappointed."

Viv furrowed her brow. "After both of your reactions, I guess I didn't figure it would be such a hill to climb."

"I don't think you should be concerned yet," said Tandri, briefly touching her hand. "I just think we should keep expectations in check."

Viv was ruminating on that when she was startled by another voice.

"Well, miss, seems you've settled right on in!"

Laney grinned at them, her face like a withered apple.

"Laney!" said Viv. "Uh, I guess I have."

"Can't say I can figger what you're about here, but the place looks a treat." She squinted up at the sign. "Nope. Not. A. Clue." She brightened and placed a dish on the table with a dark round loaf on it. "Seems you're celebratin', though, and today's my bakin' day."

"Oh, uh, thank you," stammered Viv. She introduced Cal and Tandri, and Laney nodded and flapped her hands at them.

"Can I get you a chair and a drink?" Viv held her mug up. "I can show you what I'm doing here."

Laney made a big show of peering into the mug and sniffing deeply, but she flapped her hands again. "Oh, no need. My stomach don't appreciate anythin' new, these days. You all enjoy that and bring the plate by tomorrow." She toddled back across the street.

Viv retrieved cutlery, sawed at what they surmised was a fig cake, and they all took experimental bites. They each sat chewing for an extremely long time, laboriously swallowed, mumbled vaguely appreciative words . . . and after a shared glance, burst into laughter, agreeing that the thing was wholly inedible.

They sat and chatted a little longer, and then Cal finished his drink.

"Hm. Seeing as how you're all set, and I'm paid up . . ." he said, looking down at the table. "Suppose the work's done, far as that goes. Plenty to be gettin' on with down at the docks, of course."

"Well, I hope you'll come by," said Viv. It was hard to keep the disappointment out of her voice. She'd gotten used to having him around. "You stop in, and you'll have coffee whenever you want it. I hope you do."

"Might just do that, the need arises," he said.

Viv thrust her hand at him. "Don't be a stranger, Cal."

He returned the shake, his hand swallowed by hers. "You, neither, Viv. Been good work." Somehow, from him, the words were touching.

"It was good to meet you, Cal," said Tandri.

Then, with a nod and another small bow to both of them, he left.

Viv's heart broke a little to see him go.

———◆———

While Tandri rolled up her sleeves and cleaned the mugs in the wash bucket and set them out to dry, Viv went into the pantry and retrieved a long holly garland she'd bought when she'd gone for jugs of milk that morning.

For a long moment, she stared at Blackblood where it was mounted on the wall and then twined the garland from end to end and stood back, eyeing it critically.

"It looks nice," said Tandri, drying her hands and startling Viv out of her reverie.

"I just thought . . . I don't know what I thought."

"Before, you could have picked it up and swung it at any moment," said Tandri. "It was a weapon." She gave Viv a thoughtful look. "Now, it's a relic. A decoration. Something from before."

Viv nodded. "Suppose you're right."

Tandri gave her a little smile that was almost a smirk. "I usually am. Something you'll eventually come to terms with."

"Well, you'll excuse me if I hope you're wrong about tomorrow."

"If I *am* right, don't take it personally."

Viv snorted. "I'll try not to." But she was still worried.

While Tandri tidied up, Viv went to the dining area and the Scalvert's Stone's resting place. She tapped the flagstone with her foot three times, for luck, and then withdrew a much-thumbed scrap of parchment from her pocket.

> *Well-nigh to thaumic line,*
> *the Scalvert's Stone a-fire*
> *draws the ring of fortune,*
> *aspect of heart's desire.*

"I'll be leaving now," said Tandri, coming into the room and startling her again.

Viv hurriedly stuffed the scrap back into her breeches as the woman gave her a puzzled look. "Uh, great! Sure. I'll see you tomorrow. Suppose I should try to sleep, but I honestly don't think I can."

"I'm sure—"

At a sudden clatter and thump, they both turned toward the front of the shop.

Viv ducked her head out the door.

Laney's plate still sat on the wrought-iron table, but the neglected fig cake, which had been nearly whole, was missing.

Tandri joined her at the door and hummed.

"What in the eight hells?" said Viv.

"Well, whoever made off with it," said Tandri, "I feel very, very sorry for them."

8

Tandri was not wrong.

The following day, Legends & Lattes opened to receive customers for the first time.

Viv propped the big livery doors wide, hung a sign that read
OPEN from a peg on the wall next to the window, and waited
nervously behind the counter.

Not one customer appeared.

Viv could admit that it really wasn't surprising. After all
her thoughtful planning, research, and preparation, she hadn't
taken into account the most important thing. Who showed up
to buy something they didn't know they needed?

Tandri had seen the problem immediately.

Why hadn't she?

Tandri arrived with a leather folio tucked under one arm, but
she made no mention of it and stowed it beneath the counter.
The succubus took up a station behind the machine and made
a pair of drinks.

"A bit of quiet makes a good opportunity to practice." She'd
clearly paid attention to Viv's demonstration. Her first attempt
was a little bitter, and the second came out a touch watery.

Still, they were eminently drinkable, and Viv found the aroma calming.

The air breezing in the door was moist and cool, and enticing curls of steam rose from their mugs. Everything was in place, closer to plan than she could have hoped.

Except there was nothing whatsoever to do.

Viv spent the first hours pacing like a penned predator.

Cal made a brief appearance, drinking a coffee while loudly commending its flavor, as though there was anyone to overhear him, until he eventually excused himself with a pained smile.

They did, however, receive one unexpected visitor.

Midmorning, Laney tottered across the street.

"Mornin', dears," she said brightly. "Reckon I should see what all the fuss is about." Although *fuss* was clearly thin on the ground. "Let me have one of those. How much?" She waved a hand at the coffee machine.

Viv thought about the slate menu at the pub she'd visited and cursed herself for failing to think of something similar.

"Uh, half-copper for coffee. That's . . . that's plain. A copper for a latte, that's, uh . . . for one with milk. I thought, with your stomach . . . ?" Viv rubbed her own.

Laney fussed in a pocket of her voluminous dress and slid a copper onto the counter. Tandri dutifully deposited it in the cashbox and set to work.

The old woman chuckled and twittered over the machine as it hissed and ground and gurgled, and she received her milk-frothed mug with a nod.

"Very nice. Very nice," she said. "Thank ya both, dears. Oh! And while I'm here, I'd love to have that plate back, mmm?"

Viv handed it over with thanks.

"Thank ya kindly!" she exclaimed. "Well, got to be gettin' back to m' chores. Don't be strangers, now."

Then she waddled back across the street, plate in hand, leaving the cooling latte on the counter top without taking so much as a sip.

Viv sighed heavily.

Tandri drank the latte.

"So," said Tandri, clutching the leather folio in front of her. Up 'til now, Viv would have said the succubus *couldn't* look nervous. "I mentioned some ideas last night, and back in my room, I did a little thinking."

"Oh?"

Tandri opened the folio on the counter and slid out a sheaf of pages, covered in sketches and text. She shuffled them anxiously. "Yes. Well, I hope you're not *too* discouraged. If we—if *you*—can let people know what they're missing, I think things could be fine." Her gaze met Viv's. "Because it *is* good. This idea."

"I'd hoped so," Viv murmured, surprised. Tandri had been very sure of herself last night, but now she was talking fast, as though afraid Viv would cut her short. She glanced down at Tandri's notes.

"Anyway, these are just some ideas. I thought if you—we—could find a way to get a core clientele, then there'd be some spread from word of mouth. Plus, having customers in the shop will attract others. So. I propose a sort of event."

She turned a sheet around to face Viv. Tandri's sketch was actually quite attractive, and Viv could see the ghosts of drafting lines behind the design she'd made, a combination of block and script.

GRAND OPENING
LEGENDS & LATTES
TRY THE **EXOTIC** GNOMISH SENSATION
FREE SAMPLES
LIMITED SUPPLY!

"You drew this?" asked Viv, impressed.

Tandri tucked a lock of hair behind her ear, and her tail lashed behind her. "I did. Anyway. We commission some posters from the inkmonger. We post them at the jobs board and get signboards for the street. Like this."

She produced another sketch, similar, with a big, scripted arrow pointing in the presumed direction of the shop.

"This is amazing, Tandri," Viv said, and she thought the succubus colored a little. "I'm . . . I don't know what to say. I'm . . . overwhelmed."

"Well, if you're not in business, I don't get paid, either." Tandri flashed a smile.

"Very true."

"The key is making it an opportunity that's limited. We want a lot of people at once, but not too many, or we can't serve them fast enough. So we start with just the street signs. And yes, you'll lose some coin on the free samples, but we're hoping for repeat customers." Viv noticed that Tandri had settled on *we*, and smiled.

"How do you propose we start, then?"

Viv could see Tandri seize the idea fully. "I'll need some

funds, and I'll get these materials together. Tomorrow we start
with the signs. I can paint them this afternoon, put them out
on the street tonight *after* the doors are closed. Then, we see
what's what."

Viv filled her purse from the strongbox and slid it across the
counter to Tandri. "You've got my blessing."

Tandri beamed—a first—then snatched the purse and gathered the folio. As she hurried out the door, she called over her
shoulder, "I'll be back!"

———✦———

Viv's optimism had dwindled rapidly during the morning, trans-
muting into growing despair, but now, her mood lifted. Still,
success remained far from a sure thing. With glances along
the street to make certain no customers were approaching, she
snorted ruefully and shook her head, temporarily closing and
barring the big doors.

She slid aside the table, carefully pried up the flagstone, and
stroked the Scalvert's Stone where it lay nestled in the earth.

"Come on, little lady," she whispered. "Don't make me a fool."

———✦———

When Tandri returned, she labored under the weight of two
waist-high folding signs, her folio awkwardly pinched under one
arm and a cloth bag over one shoulder.

"I clearly didn't think this part through," she panted.

Viv hurried to relieve her of the signs, and Tandri unburdened herself of the rest.

The woman didn't ask if business had improved. It clearly
hadn't. She unpacked the cloth bag, which contained stoppered
inkwells, brushes, and a few curious curved pieces of wood.

Tandri handed over the purse and then set to work.

She sat cross-legged on the floor, rolled up her sleeves, laid her sketches beside her, and began inking. Her hand was steady as she executed clean strokes with her brush, but there was no tension in her mouth. The bits of wood turned out to be stencils that she used to guide some of the longer and more elaborate curves. Tandri glanced occasionally at her sketches for reference, although to Viv's eye she barely needed them.

Less than an hour had passed when she swept a final snaking line across the bottom. She cleaned her brush on a rag and capped the inkwell, then stretched, and kneaded her back as she surveyed her handiwork.

Viv thought it looked quite professional. "Were you a signmaker or something?"

"No. Just always had an . . . artistic bent." Tandri turned to face her. "I'd say we close up now and set them out while it's still daylight."

"You're the expert," said Viv, quirking a smile. "I'll put 'em where you want 'em."

Tandri stepped into the street. "The first in front, here." She pointed to a spot a few feet from the door. Viv carried out both signs, leaned one against the wall, and obliged with its mate, angling it so that the arrow pointed toward the entryway.

"And this one?" asked Viv, lifting the other with one hand.

"I was thinking the intersection where you can see the High Street. This way." She led her along Redstone to the corner. After Viv set the sign down, Tandri checked the sightline in a few directions and fussed with the orientation until she was satisfied.

They returned to the shop just as the lamplighter began setting his taper to the street lanterns.

"So, you think this'll really work?" Viv leaned against the doorframe as Tandri gathered her things.

"Couldn't get worse," said Tandri, emerging with folio in hand.

Viv's eyes narrowed. "I don't know about that," she murmured darkly. Over Tandri's shoulder, she spied someone coming up the street. She'd recognize that hat anywhere.

"What's that?" Tandri turned to follow her gaze as Lack strolled past, alongside a thick man with a lantern on his belt and a badge over his heart.

Lack rested one hand companionably on the Gatewarden's shoulder. He smiled and muttered something, and the badged man barked a good-natured laugh in response.

"Nothing," said Viv.

Lack stopped a few paces away and glanced at Viv in mild surprise, then past her to the shop. The Gatewarden looked puzzled by the interruption.

The stone-fey took a step closer, peering through the window. "Quite the blade, Viv. I do hope you're not showing your teeth." He pointed inside.

The Gatewarden squinted through the glass, as well. "Mmm, indeed," he agreed, patting the hilt of his own short-sword.

"It's sentimental," said Viv, snarling more than she intended.

Tandri looked back and forth between them, gripping her folio tighter. "Should I be worried?" she asked quietly.

Viv wasn't sure how to answer that, for it had dawned on her that there was more to be lost than the shop itself.

Lack nodded, his ruffles bouncing on his chest. "Two weeks," he said. "Just a friendly reminder. Wouldn't want you to forget to set aside a portion."

The Gatewarden didn't so much as blink at that, and any notion of tapping the local authorities for help evaporated.

Viv clenched her fists, then forced them to relax. "Guess we'd better hope things pick up by then," she said. "Can't squeeze blood from a stone."

"Yes, I'm sure you'd know about squeezing blood from things. Or extracting it in . . . other ways. I imagine you can be quite resourceful. Rest assured, we are similarly talented." His gaze flicked to Tandri, and he bowed, not mocking. In fact, his expression was confusingly apologetic.

"Shall we carry on?" prompted the Gatewarden.

Viv and Tandri watched them go.

"What was that all about?" asked Tandri, once they'd disappeared.

"Nothing I can't handle. Don't worry about it."

Tandri's expression was skeptical, but she didn't argue.

"You should get home," said Viv, forcing a smile. "The signs are incredible, and I've already kept you too late."

"You're sure?"

"Positive."

Tandri nodded reluctantly and left, folio tucked under her arm.

As the succubus rounded the corner, Viv stalked over, removed the OPEN sign from its peg, and went inside.

When she closed the door, she tried her best to be gentle about it, but it still rattled on the hinges.

———◆———

As Viv lay on her bedroll, she withdrew the Blink Stone that Roon had given her. She turned it over and over in her hands, thinking about how clear the division between success and failure had once been. That clarity had never been more elusive.

She put away the stone and did not go to sleep for a long time.

9

She'd definitely harbored *some* hope, but when Viv went to hang the OPEN sign on its peg, the sight of three individuals lined up outside the door still startled her—a burly dockworker, a red-cheeked washerwoman, and a rattkin in a big, leather apron dusted with flour.

The dockworker looked her up and down, surprised, then growled, "Free samples?" He hooked a huge thumb at the sign in the street.

"That's right," said Viv, propping the door wide with a river stone. The sky was still dark, and the morning air had a mid-spring bite to it.

All three bustled inside. Viv had the stove lit for heat, and the wall lanterns cast a buttery glow over the interior.

The washerwoman approached the counter and examined a sheet of parchment that Viv had weighted with a few smooth pebbles. She hadn't had time to find a slate, so she'd hand-printed a menu, conscious of the crudeness of her attempt compared to Tandri's stylus work. It was better than nothing, but she'd have her new employee rework it later, if she was willing.

Viv hadn't bothered to add prices to the simple list. She didn't want to scare anyone off. Everything was free for the time being, anyway.

~ MENU ~

COFFEE ~ RICH DRINK BREWED WITH ROASTED GNOMISH BEANS

LATTE ~ COFFEE WITH MILK—CREAMY AND DELICIOUS

"Don't know what none of that is," said the washerwoman, tapping the list with one red forefinger. "Which one is best?"

She'd put a little thought into this. "Do you take cream in your tea?"

"Nah," she replied. "Hot and more of it is how I likes mine. So, it's like tea, is it?"

Viv waggled a hand side to side, then admitted, "No. Not really." She looked at the other two. "How about you?"

"What she's having," said the dockworker, crossing his arms. The rattkin approached, got up on his toes to get a good view of the menu and, after a moment, tapped the latte without uttering a word.

"Done," said Viv. She set to brewing.

As the machine began hissing and grinding and burbling, her first customers gathered around curiously. The rattkin squeaked in surprise when the brew began to gush into a mug, his oil-drop eyes gleaming.

She slid the first mug to the woman, who cautiously picked it up, gave it a deep sniff and a puff of breath to cool it, then took a hefty sip. She screwed up her face for a moment . . . then nodded. "Huh. Not bad, that is," she admitted. "Not tea, that's sure. Not saying I'd pay by the mug, hear, but . . ." She wandered into the dining area and slid onto the bench, hands curled around the mug. Leaning over it, she sighed deeply.

The dockworker received his, smelled it dubiously, and somehow drank it in four long swallows. Viv grimaced and grabbed at her own throat involuntarily. The big man contemplated it, shrugged, returned the mug, and left without a word.

Viv's disappointment was acute, but she still managed to call out, "Uh, thank you!" in her best impression of someone who knew what they were doing.

Tandri slipped in the door and quietly rounded the counter as Viv brewed the rattkin's latte. He waited with hands clasped daintily, his whiskers twitching, snout quivering.

He eagerly received the cup and thrust his nose into the curls of steam rising from the golden cream on the surface. After a delicate sip, he closed his eyes, clearly savoring it, and Viv leaned her elbows on the counter to watch.

The rattkin's eyes opened, and he dipped his head in thanks. He quietly took his mug to a booth, where he sipped his drink and kicked his dangling paws.

"A promising start," said Tandri. "That's all so far?"

"So far."

The washerwoman departed, leaving her mug at the table, and eventually, the rattkin finished as well, delivering his empty cup to the front counter. He bowed politely and scurried out the door, leaving scattered dustings of flour in his wake.

Tandri heated a kettle on the stove, filled the washbasin, and gathered the mugs to soak. "That was a good idea," she said, indicating the menu on the counter. "Really helpful."

Viv gave her a sidelong glance. "You could do better, though."

"Well. *Better* isn't the word I'd use."

"I'm going to pick up a slate and some chalk later. Got the

idea from a pub on the High Street. We can hang it back here, and then you can work the same magic you did with those signs. Is that all right?"

"My pleasure."

Early morning customers—the sort of folks who rise well before dawn to begin the day's labor—arrived in a thin trickle. Viv and Tandri worked in tandem, explaining the menu as best they could and trading off between brewing and cleaning. The shop was pleasant and warm, and the smell of roasted beans permeated the air, drifting out into the street.

More than a few folk clearly followed their noses in the door.

Viv dared to hope.

———+———

The morning surge dried up after a few hours, and business evaporated, even though traffic outside the shop increased.

"And now it's looking like yesterday all over again," muttered Viv.

"Let's not worry yet," said Tandri.

But Viv noticed that the woman was scrubbing mugs she'd already cleaned. Before long, Tandri was aggressively wiping the surface of the machine, polishing it for the fifth time.

The next few hours were frankly agonizing.

At last, around noon, their first post-morning visitor walked through the door.

He was young, tall, and handsome, in an underfed and aristocratic way. His looks were somewhat spoiled by an inadvisable beard—too wispy, too patchy. He glanced around as if searching for someone. A satchel of books weighed down one arm, and he kept looking down at one cupped palm. He wore a split-hemmed cloak, and the pin on its left breast looked a lot like the head of a stag.

He didn't approach the counter, wandering instead into the dining area.

Viv watched him with a wrinkled brow.

"Ackers student," murmured Tandri.

"Ackers?"

"The Thaumic Academy."

"Oh. Visited it my first day here, but didn't know the name. He looks pretty well-to-do. Maybe we'll even get some word of mouth. Students talk to each other, right?"

"They talk, all right," muttered Tandri, with a hint of venom that made Viv look at her askance.

The young man circled the big table and benches twice, then sidled into one of the wall booths, unpacked some books, and began consulting them.

Viv shot Tandri a questioning glance, but the succubus shrugged. They both continued to watch him.

After about twenty minutes, during which Viv grew increasingly perplexed, she approached him and asked, "Anything I can help you with?"

He glanced up, smiled brightly, and replied, "No, thank you!"

"Are you here for the free sample?" she pressed.

"Sample? Oh, no. Nothing for me, thanks!" Then he returned to his study.

Nonplussed, Viv returned to the counter, shaking her head.

He remained there for a full three hours, during which time he busily perused his reading materials, scrawled intermittently on a parchment, consulted his cupped hand again and again, and murmured to himself. Then he packed his things, rose, and approached the counter.

"Thanks ever so much," he said, and with a genial nod, he left.

———+———

After too much listless pacing, Viv abruptly decided that some sort of action was required. She left Tandri with the shop and headed into the city, to the trade district up north. It wasn't a market day, but she still managed to locate a big panel of slate at a sign-maker's and some stubs of chalk. She even found multiple colors. She figured Tandri should have a palette to work with.

It felt good to be *doing* something, at least. The morning rush had raised her expectations for the rest of the day, but on the walk back, she counseled herself against unreasonable hope. Certain hours were just better suited to the business. A restaurant was busiest at mealtimes, and a café was busiest . . . well, she supposed she was discovering when exactly that was.

———+———

"Oh, yes, this will work perfectly," Tandri purred as she took the chalk and slate from Viv. She dug her wooden stencils out of the storage room, set up at the big table, and got to work.

While she drew, Viv stood in the doorway, looking up and down the street. Laney was out on her porch, sweeping as she always seemed to be, and waggled a cheery wave at her.

Was morning *really* the only time she could expect to do business? It certainly hadn't seemed that way in Azimuth—the cafés there had been lively throughout the balance of the day. Perhaps prospects would improve if the idea caught on. She supposed tomorrow would give her an inkling.

When she reentered the shop, she found Tandri examining the finished menu, which leaned against the wall. Again, Tandri's script was far superior to Viv's artistic endeavors, and she'd used the colors to excellent effect. Her text appeared beveled, almost leaping off the slate. She'd also taken some creative liberties with the wording.

⌒ＬEGENDS & ＬATTES ⌒
~ MENU ~
Coffee ~ exotic aroma & rich, full-bodied roast—½ bit
Latte ~ a sophisticated and creamy variation—1 bit

❀

FINER TASTES FOR THE
~ WORKING GENT & LADY ~

She'd even added an artistic rendering of a pair of beans and a mug with an artful curl of steam.

"I like it. You're a hell of an artist." Viv nodded. "Here, I've got a mallet in the back."

Tandri held the sign level while Viv banged a few nails into the wall below the base as a sort of shelf.

"The slate was a good idea," said Tandri. "We can change or add to it easily."

"Change it?"

"If you decide to expand the menu. You never know."

Viv looked around the place and sighed. "I'd hoped we'd have more after noon. Maybe around dinner? Doesn't feel like it's going to happen, though. I don't know if expanding the menu is going to be a real concern anytime soon."

Tandri pursed her lips and tapped them with a forefinger. "Let's wait and see what tomorrow morning brings."

"Free samples still, you think?"

"Yes, let's see about repeat customers, first." Her expression waxed briefly wicked. "Hook them and see if they stay on the line."

"Never was any good at fishing."

"You're in a river town, now. You'll learn."

Viv hoped she was right.

There *were* repeat customers, although Viv supposed "customer" might be too strong a word while the drinks were free. When they opened, the washerwoman and the rattkin were back. The woman had a friend in tow, and there were four others behind them.

The rattkin scurried inside first, wafting a cloud of flour, and pointed wordlessly at the latte on the menu. Tandri brewed for the first rush of customers, while Viv watched the street, nodding to herself as a few stragglers joined the short line.

Business stayed reasonably steady, too, with only a few gaps where one or the other of them wasn't pulling a fresh shot.

"Seems like the fishing is good," murmured Tandri as she passed by with emptied mugs in hand.

"You're the angler," said Viv, smiling. "I guess you'd know." She leaned out to peer into the dining area, where a scattering of sleepy folk murmured in tentative conversation.

She glanced behind her and found that Tandri was up on a

footstool with chalk in hand, adding a new line to the bottom of the slate menu.

Free Samples Today Only!

When she stepped down, she caught Viv's questioning gaze and said, "Let's see if the hook is really set."

—+—

They were still doing slow business as the morning crept toward noon when the Ackers student from the previous day reappeared. He stepped smartly inside, registered surprise at the people sipping their drinks in the dining area and, with only a distracted glance at Viv and Tandri, hurried to a spot in a vacant booth. He unloaded his book satchel again and resumed his scribbling and the cryptic consultation of his palm.

For the next hour, the man did nothing but avail himself of the seating, and Viv grew increasingly irritated. "What is he doing?" she asked Tandri in a loud whisper.

She shrugged. "Coursework? Research? Although why he's doing it *here*, I have no idea."

"Yesterday, I was almost happy to have him, just to fill a seat, but . . . if he's only going to take up room."

"Easy enough to find out," said Tandri, as she rounded the counter.

He gave her a distracted glance as she approached, clenching his hand closed. "Can I help you?" he asked, a bit waspishly.

"You took the words right out of my mouth," said Tandri. "Thanks so much for visiting, and two days in a row. I'm just checking to see if you'd like a sample. I assume that's why you're here?"

Viv had drifted across the room to overhear.

"A sample?" His eyes flicked between her horns and tail, and he seemed puzzled, as though he hadn't been asked the same question the previous day.

"Coffee? A latte? You're aware this is a shop that serves drinks?"

"Oh!" He seemed to recover. "Yes, well, there's no need." He smiled as though conferring a favor. "I'll be just fine without!"

Tandri's polite smile thinned away, but then she deliberately appeared to apply a new one, at a significantly higher wattage. Viv got the distinct impression that Tandri was unveiling the barest edge of something she normally kept cloaked. With a subtle purr, she asked, "Can I ask what you're doing, Mister . . . ?"

"Uh. Er. Hemington," he stammered. "I, um. Well, I would love to, but it's all *very* technical." He attempted to look apologetic.

"I'm very interested in technical matters," said Tandri. "I've sat in on a few classes at Ackers. Try me, maybe?"

"You have?" Hemington blinked. "Ah! Well, er, it's to do with ley lines, you see." He warmed to his subject as Tandri slid into the booth across from him and rested her chin on interlaced fingers. "They crisscross Thune, and Thaumic Thread Theory is preoccupied with the radiant effects on the material realm. That's a fascinating intersection with *my* area of study."

He uncurled his hand, and the imprint of a ring of sigils glimmered a faint blue there. The symbols writhed on his palm, reshaping in little licks of light.

"A ley-compass," said Tandri, pointing at it. Viv started at that.

"Well, yes!" he replied, clearly pleased at her recognition. "But what I'm finding here is truly anomalous. We see scattered minor line nexuses throughout the city and westward toward

Cardus, but I've found a nexus *right here* that is giving some terribly interesting readings. Ley lines pulse, of course."

"Of course," agreed Tandri.

"But this nexus holds *firm*. It's really quite extraordinary. So I'm taking some measurements, assembling some notes. This could be the foundation of a *fascinating* paper, detailing their interactions with ward-glyphs."

Viv had a sick feeling in her stomach and couldn't stop herself from glancing to where the Scalvert's Stone was hidden. She couldn't pretend that it wasn't responsible somehow, and if this student continued with his readings—the mention of a *compass* was unnerving—then where might that lead him?

"That *is* fascinating, Hemington," said Tandri.

"It is? It is, isn't it."

"But, this *is* a place of business," she continued. "Of course, we'd love to have you as a customer, but the seating here is really intended for patrons . . ."

Hemington adopted an expression of annoyed consternation. "I . . . don't really drink hot beverages."

Tandri ignored his protest and smiled at him sweetly. ". . . and fortunately for you, today's samples are free."

"Yes. Well. I, uh. I suppose," he grudgingly allowed. "I . . . will . . . take advantage of that."

"Excellent. I'll bring you a cup." She rose to return to the counter, but then turned back. "Oh, and as a reminder, this is the last day of the promotional period. Only a half bit for our flagship beverage. Thanks ever so much!"

———✦———

As Tandri brewed a cup, Viv whispered, "You were an Ackers graduate?"

"Not a graduate, as such. Just took a few relevant classes."

"Relevant to what?"

"To personal interests," she replied evasively.

Viv didn't press.

Tandri delivered the drink to Hemington, who stared at it doubtfully and made no move to drink it.

After tapping her chin for a moment, Tandri took up the chalk and added another line to the menu.

Purchase Required to Enjoy the Dining Area

—◄+►—

Hemington eventually departed, leaving his untouched drink on the table. At least he had the decency to hover over it for a moment, clearly trying to decide which was least embarrassing—leaving it where it was or bringing the full cup up to the front. As he slunk past the counter, he noted Tandri's fresh addition to the sign. "You know, I *would* buy something. It's just, as I said, I don't much care for *hot* drinks. Perhaps if there was something to *eat*," he said, a note of pleading in his voice.

"Hm," said Viv, in her best impression of Cal. "I'll take it under advisement."

After he left, though, she glanced at the stove the hob had installed, and something niggled at her, a nascent idea.

She let that percolate as she went to retrieve Hemington's mug.

The shop had mostly emptied, although one old dwarf sat tucked away in the back, nursing his drink while he slowly ran his finger over a broadsheet, moving his lips as he read.

Viv turned and stopped short. An enormous, shaggy creature sat in the center of the shop, sprawled in a square of sunlight. Tandri stood on its other side, eyes wide.

The beast had to weigh ten stone and was as big as a wolf, but it looked like nothing so much as an enormous, shaggy, and slightly sooty housecat.

"It just . . . appeared," said Tandri weakly. "I didn't see it come in."

"What in the hells *is* it?" asked Viv.

The massive animal ignored them both but yawned, extended all the claws in its forepaws, and arched its back in a languorous stretch.

"Dire-cat," a voice piped up from behind Viv.

The elderly dwarf looked over from his paper. "Don't see 'em nummore, these days. S'posed to be lucky." He squinted. "Or mebbe unlucky. I forget."

"You've seen one before?"

"Aye. Used to be more around when I was wee. Good ratters." He coughed. "Also kep' the stray dog population down."

Tandri blanched. "Should we . . . try to move it?"

The dire-cat regarded first Tandri, then Viv, with green eyes like saucers. Slowly they drifted to slits, and the rumble of a distant landslide filled the room. Viv realized it was *purring*.

She thought of the thumps on the roof tiles and Laney's pilfered cake. She thought about the lines of verse and the Scalvert's Stone.

"Honestly," said Viv. "If I've learned one thing, it's that if a beast isn't angry yet, don't get it started. I think I'll leave it be. Maybe it will wander off? I'm pretty sure it lives around here."

Tandri nodded dubiously and edged behind the counter.

The elderly dwarf folded his broadsheet under his arm, hopped down, and strolled past the cat, giving it a scratch behind one of its enormous ears. "Aye, a good girl," he said. "Missed seein' 'em around."

"How can you tell it's a girl?" asked Tandri.

The dwarf shrugged. "Guessin'. But I ain't gonna lift 'er tail to find out for sure."

———+———

The dire-cat did not leave, but Viv did manage to lure it to a less central corner of the shop with a dish of cream. The animal approached with magisterial grace, surveyed the room, and then emptied the dish with a tongue as big as a spade. Then it resettled in a great, shaggy heap, the sound of its rumbling purr trebled, and it fell asleep. Tandri was visibly relieved to have the creature out of the way.

The café was empty again, in what Viv was beginning to suspect would be the slowest part of the day, although she was hopeful they'd get at least a visitor or two.

But the one who appeared at the threshold was the last person she wanted to see.

Fennus strode into the shop, hands behind his back, his perfume trailing like a cloak. His hair was pinned up fashionably, expression arch. The elf had always possessed a regal bearing. Viv couldn't understand how he managed to look down his nose at her, even though she was two heads taller.

She'd crewed with him for years, and neither had warmed to the other. Viv tried to chalk it up to personality conflict, but deep down, she knew that it was mutual dislike. Fennus always found ways to make her feel less-than with the barest twist of inflection or a carefully chosen word slipped like a knife between the ribs, so sharp you didn't notice the wound until you looked up from a lapful of blood. And Viv wasn't above a blunt riposte, even if it often came far too late.

She'd assumed she'd never see him again and would have been glad of it. The fact that he was darkening her doorway meant he wanted something. She very much hoped she was wrong.

Still, she forced a smile. "Fennus! Surprised to see you here."

His smile was even more false than hers, although it hardly marred his beauty. "Viv. I'd heard from Roon that you'd set up an"—he glanced around with a perfectly wrinkled brow—"*enterprise*. I thought I'd see for myself."

"And how is Roon?"

"Oh, well. Very well." He ran a finger along the counter top and inspected it.

Tandri watched the exchange with pursed lips and clearly noticed the electric buzz of tension. Leaning on the counter and adopting a smile, she addressed the elf. "Hello, there! I don't want to interrupt, but would you care for a sample? It's a grand opening promotion."

"*Grand* opening?" Just the slightest quirk to the first word, the tiniest caress of amusement. "Ah, is this that gnomish beverage you were so taken with?" He glanced at Viv with an indulgent smile. "No, not for me, thank you kindly. I'm just stopping in to see an old friend."

"A pleasure," said Viv.

It wasn't.

"Yes, so excellent to see you off to such a promising start." The elf surveyed the conspicuously empty dining area, maintaining his smile. He delicately rapped a knuckle against the coffee maker and cocked an ear at the subtle tone it generated. "It does indeed have the *ring of fortune* about it."

Viv froze.

Then suddenly, a furry bulk stalked past her to stand in front of Fennus, and the rocks-down-a-washboard sound of its purr became something altogether more menacing. The dire-cat's hair stood on end, making it look half-again as large, and it hissed louder than the coffee maker ever had.

Fennus eyed the animal uncertainly. "Is this thing . . . yours?"

Tandri leaned farther forward and surprised Viv with her tone of politely savage delight. "She is. A bit of a shop mascot."

He wrinkled his nose in distaste, and then his eyes flicked to Viv. "Charming. Well, I suppose I'll be on my way. I only wanted to deliver my congratulations. Best wishes, Viv."

She silently watched him leave, and Tandri came around the counter to hunker in front of the enormous cat, which was now licking one forepaw with regal deliberation and looking pleased with itself.

Tandri's prior apprehension forgotten, she scratched behind the dire-cat's ears, eliciting a deeper purr, and murmured, "You're a good girl, aren't you? You know a dickhead when you see one." She looked at Viv. "Old coworker? No love lost between you two, I guess."

"Something like that. Being the best of friends isn't a requirement for the work I used to do."

Tandri returned her attention to the cat. "Mmm, you need a name. How about . . . *Amity?*"

Viv snorted, unable to suppress a small smile. "Why not, since you're already such fast friends?"

"Not like you and *him.*" Tandri jerked a thumb toward the recently departed elf. "What do you think he really wanted?"

Viv didn't answer, instead thinking of what Fennus had

said. Her hand went to the folded scrap of verse she kept in her pocket.

Well-nigh to thaumic line,
the Scalvert's Stone a-fire
draws the ring of fortune,
aspect of heart's desire.

11

Despite a fitful sleep plagued with worries over Fennus, Viv eventually steered her thoughts to Hemington's parting comments about food. While she ruminated, Tandri blacked out the lines on the signboards mentioning free samples and limited supplies and adjusted the menu while she was at it.

When the regulars returned—plus a few new faces—Viv noted with pleasure that they paid for their drinks without complaint. Viv and Tandri shared a relieved glance and got down to business, enjoying the warm bustle behind the hissing machine.

Cal stopped in again, too, obviously relieved there was no silence to fill with idle observations. He groused when Viv refused his copper but hovered by the counter while he drank, nodding every once in a while as he watched them work.

Remembering the idea she'd been toying with, Viv asked Tandri to handle brewing duties halfway through the rush.

Tandri smoothly took up the orders while Viv went to find the rattkin, tucked away in one of the back corner booths, feet swinging, eyes closed, meditating over his steaming mug.

She slid in across from him, and his bright eyes opened to

regard her warily. He was wearing the same apron she'd seen him in every morning, whitened liberally with flour. Up close, pale powder flecked the fine hairs on his arms and face, as well.

"Hi, there. I'm Viv."

He nodded and slurped at his latte.

"Not too talkative?"

He shook his head.

"That's all right. But I wanted to ask you something. I noticed your"—she gestured at his apron—"well, the flour. And I wondered if you happened to know anything about baking?"

The rattkin stared at her, whiskers twitching, and gently set down his mug, then gave a slow triple nod.

"You *do*? So I have something of an idea. I'm thinking what this place might need is some . . . breads—or something baked—to eat." She squeezed an invisible loaf between her hands. "Snacks, I guess. Not something I know much about, though. But I thought, you, well, if you *did* know something about that, then . . ."

The rattkin raised a tentative paw to forestall her. Leaning forward over his drink, in a tiny, breathy voice, he said, *"Tomorrow."*

"Tomorrow?"

He nodded again. *Eagerly*, Viv thought.

She didn't know whether he had to be on his way or needed a few hours to think, but despite her curiosity, she wasn't going to press the matter. She rapped the table and stood.

"I'll look forward to it, Mister . . . ?"

He stared up at her, and in a solemn whisper, said, *"Thimble."*

"Thimble," Viv agreed. Then she gave him a nod and returned to the counter.

—◆—

The afternoon again became a desert of inactivity. Hemington returned and purchased a drink, a pained expression on his
face, and once more left it untouched.

Viv wiped down tables in the empty dining area, gathering
dirty mugs. Suddenly, Tandri's voice cut through the hush, her
tone icy.

"What are you doing here?" Tandri glared at a young man
who leaned on the counter top, gazing back at her in an overly
familiar way. His soft handsomeness hinted at money, and while
he wasn't wearing the split robes Hemington wore, Viv saw one
of the stag pins on his tailored shirt.

"Saw you through the window and just had to stop by," he
replied. "Haven't seen you in a while, Tandri. I'd almost think
you were avoiding me."

"And you'd be right."

"Well, I'm only here as a customer, so we can call this an
intervention of fate."

"You just said you saw me through the window. If fate inter-
venes, it'll be to turn you around and send you right back out."

"Now don't be that way. A succubus like you, you can *feel*
this"—he gestured between them—"this *attraction*, I know you
can."

Tandri looked stricken, and then her expression became deliberately neutral. "Kellin, there *is* no attraction. There never
has been. I think you should leave."

"But I haven't *bought* anything yet," he protested, a smile in
his voice.

"I don't think we have anything you want," said Viv, approaching the front of the shop and looming, arms crossed.

Kellin turned his attention to her, and his easy smile vanished, replaced by something sharper. "I don't remember involving you in this conversation."

Viv was mildly surprised he hadn't quailed at the sight of her.

"It's my shop," said Viv evenly. "I serve who I want, when I want. And I don't think I want to serve you. So, I'll ask you to leave."

Kellin stared at her hard for a moment, a sneer developing. "I don't guess you've met the Madrigal, yet. At some point, *everybody* around here serves them. Which means that sooner or later, you're going to be paying your dues to me."

"Oh, so you're his errand boy? I thought that was the man with the very fine hat."

He was about to retort when Amity emerged from behind Viv and strolled by with deadly grace. She settled beside Tandri and indifferently licked a massive paw.

Kellin blinked but recovered his sneer.

Viv couldn't decide if he was brave or stupid.

"I'll leave for now," he said. "But you'll be seeing me again."

He looked at Tandri again with that soft, proprietary smile. "But you and me, we'll catch up later. Looking forward to it. *Fate.*"

He left.

——+——

Tandri released a slow breath.

"What was that all about?" asked Viv.

"He was a student at Ackers. He had an . . ." Tandri searched for the words. "An unhealthy obsession with me."

"When you took classes there for . . . personal interests?"

"Yes."

"Guess he's working for the head of the local hoods, too. Seems education didn't lead to better things."

"Oh, I'm not surprised, at all," Tandri muttered darkly.

"We'll keep him out."

The succubus crouched next to the dire-cat. "Or maybe Amity needs a snack. Are you hungry, girl?"

Amity purred like a rockfall.

—◄+►—

That evening, Tandri left long enough to collect some blankets and a big goose-down pillow. She and Viv put together a make-shift bed in the back corner of the shop for the dire-cat. The next time Amity reappeared, she stalked over to the rumpled pile, patted it experimentally with one enormous forepaw, and then strolled away.

But they left the bed.

—◄+►—

Thimble rapped on the front door as the two of them prepared to open. In his hands he clutched a cloth-wrapped lump that trailed wisps of steam. Viv smelled something warm and yeasty and sweet, and thought she recognized cinnamon, too.

He scuttled indoors.

Tandri emerged from the pantry with a bag of beans and a carafe of milk, inhaling deeply. "What is that wonderful *smell*?"

The rattkin glanced anxiously between them, then slid his wrapped bundle onto the counter top.

Viv pointed at it. "May I?"

Thimble nodded hesitantly.

Carefully unfolding the cloth, Viv revealed a roll as big as her fist, almost *too* large to imagine eating. Soft bread wound in a spiral, with dark sugar and cinnamon nestled between the rings, and a thick, creamy glaze frosted the top and dripped down the sides.

Tandri was right. The scent was unbelievably amazing.

"You made this?" asked Viv, impressed.

"*Did,*" whispered the rattkin, again with the little bobbing nod, his hands clasped before his flour-dusted apron.

Viv and Tandri shared a glance, and then Viv delicately tore a piece from the enormous roll, sniffed deeply, and popped it into her mouth.

She closed her eyes and made an involuntary noise of pleasure. It was easily the most delicious thing she'd had in . . . well, maybe ever.

"Good gods," she murmured around the mouthful. "Tandri, try it."

Tandri peeled off a piece and obliged.

As she chewed, Viv could feel some kind of atmospheric shift around Tandri, a sultry radiance, and her tail lashed back and forth in elegant loops. Viv and the rattkin watched her chew, rapt.

When the succubus opened her eyes again, her irises were huge, cheeks flushed. She looked dreamily at the rattkin. "You're hired." Her voice had gone husky. Then she startled and glanced at Viv. The aura dissipated. "Wait, that is why he's here, isn't it?"

Viv turned to Thimble. "How would you like to bake these here every day?"

He nodded and shifted from foot to foot, as though he wanted to say something, but couldn't find the words.

"Four silver a week?" Viv prompted. She looked at Tandri to make sure there would be no objection.

The succubus nodded, eyes big, and made a yes-yes-get-on-with-it flapping with her hands.

Thimble nodded an affirmative, then he stretched out his nose, and for the first time, uttered more than one word in his silky whisper. *"Free coffee?"*

Viv offered a hand. "Thimble, you can have all the coffee you want."

12

When Thimble reported for duty, he had a much-stained scrap of parchment in his paws. He bobbed his way into the shop and slid it onto the counter top, patting it gently.

Tandri picked it up to scan. It was a list, written in a crabbed and slanting script. "Flour, soda, cinnamon, dark sugar, salt . . . These are ingredients," she said.

The rattkin nodded earnestly, pointing at the parchment.

"And some supplies," Tandri added as she finished reading. "Looks like some pans, bowls . . ."

Thimble scurried to investigate the area behind the counter top, then peered into the pantry, as well, tapping his lip with one claw as he took inventory. He gestured for the paper, and Tandri returned it to him with an amused smile.

Seizing a stylus from under the counter next to the cashbox, he stood on tiptoe to add a few more items to the list before nodding decisively. If Thimble could communicate without speaking, that certainly appeared to be his preference.

"And this is what you'll need to make more of those rolls? The ones with cinnamon?" asked Viv.

Thimble affirmed in the expected way.

"Any idea where I can get all this?" Viv asked Tandri.

"Not immediately, no. I'm sure I can find a baker, but . . ."

Thimble interrupted by pulling on Viv's sleeve and pointing to himself. "*I show.*"

"Oh. Sure. Well, no time like the present, I guess. Tandri, you're fine with holding things down 'til we get back?"

"Of course."

The rattkin shifted from foot to foot and stared longingly at the coffee machine.

"*Coffee first?*" he pleaded.

————+————

Thimble took his time with his drink, clearly appreciating every sip in what had become his favorite booth. The morning rush was in full swing before he finished and carried his mug to the front, where he waited by the door until the last customer in line had ordered.

"Guess we'll be going," said Viv, drying her hands and joining him.

Tandri gave her a distracted nod while frothing milk for a bleary-eyed Gatewarden.

Just as they prepared to leave, Amity drifted across the threshold like a low-lying thunderhead, and Thimble froze without so much as a squeak.

"Oh hells," hissed Viv, preparing to hoist the rattkin out of reach at the dire-cat's slightest aggressive twitch.

But Amity only blinked slowly, licked her nose, and then wandered past with marked disinterest.

The beast's visits were so infrequent and unpredictable, Viv hadn't spared a moment's thought for how the cat might regard their baker.

Or maybe Viv trusted the Stone, and there'd never been a danger from the start.

They left the shop, and Viv followed the rattkin as he scampered to the merchant district on the north side.

It took the better part of the morning to gather everything Thimble needed, and Viv found herself thoroughly lost on several occasions. When they visited the mill, she bought flour from the same miller she'd rented the cart from. For a few bits extra, he threw in some empty sacks to carry the jumble of bundles, sealed jars, and pieces of crockery remaining on Thimble's list.

The rattkin never hesitated, navigating unerringly through a warren of alleys and streets. They visited various shops, and several times, he rapped on the door of a private residence. In one notable case, they visited a bespectacled old man whose house swam with a heady mix of exotic scents. Each time, Thimble tapped his list to request an item of the proprietor, then looked expectantly at Viv until she paid.

List conquered, Viv limped awkwardly to the shop with two flour bags over one shoulder, bulging sacks clenched in a fist, and the rest tucked under the opposite arm. Her lower back was complaining again. Thimble marched before her, clutching an armload of wooden spoons. When they arrived, Viv sidled past Hemington and two other customers into the back and unburdened herself with a sigh of relief.

Thimble immediately set to unpacking and arranging his prizes in the pantry, struggling gamely under the weight of the flour sacks but declining any assistance with a sharp shake of his furry head. Viv shrugged and left him to it.

"Find everything?" asked Tandri.

"Sure *seems* to be *everything*." Viv groaned, cracking her spine.

Thimble popped up between them, shocking them both with his longest utterance yet.

"*Enough t' be getting on with.*"

Then he returned to his parcels with gusto.

——+——

After massaging away the worst of her back pain, Viv took over for Tandri as they served the latest round of customers. Behind the two of them, Thimble hummed tunefully to himself. A clatter of pans and bowls and wooden spoons was followed by much measuring and scraping and stirring.

He quickly appropriated the small table they'd been using as a drying rack, clambered up on the footstool, and began kneading out his dough. A mist of flour drifted around him as he worked.

While the dough rose, he approached with a nervous twitch of whiskers and whispered, "*Latte?*"

"Thimble, I'll keep a fresh cup in front of you all day, if you want."

His whole body wriggled with pleasure.

Later, after all the customers were served, Viv and Tandri watched curiously as he resumed his work. He smoothed out the dough with his new pin, spread a thick cinnamon filling across in a glistening layer, then carefully rolled it into a long cylinder. He sliced it evenly, peeled apart the rolls, and deposited them neatly in a pan.

While the dough rose a second time, he lit the stove, threw fistfuls of sugar into a bowl with butter and milk, and stirred vigorously to make a glaze. A pleasant yeast and sugar smell pervaded the shop.

Once the rolls had risen to his satisfaction, he hopped down to slide them into the side box, then sat on the stool, steepled his fingers, and patiently waited.

The scent that arose from the stove now was impossible to ignore.

"Good gods," murmured Tandri. "That smells amazing. I almost can't stand it."

Viv was about to agree but then looked up as she caught motion from the corner of her eye.

A carpenter, if the shavings in his hair were anything to go by, swayed in the entryway, his expression foggy. He sniffed hugely, then blinked. He just stood there for a minute, glancing quizzically around the shop and at the menu.

"Help you?" asked Viv.

He opened his mouth, closed it, and took another deep lungful.

"I'll 'ave . . . whatever it is you 'ave," he said.

He took the coffee Tandri brewed, paid dreamily, drifted into the dining area, and sat. He absently sipped his drink while staring off into the distance.

Tandri and Viv raised their eyebrows at each other.

"Eight hells, what *is* that smell?" asked a voice they both recognized. Laney approached the counter.

"Got a new baker." Viv cocked a thumb at Thimble.

"Still in the oven, eh? Well, miss, don't mind tellin' you that I'm r'lieved. Didn't want to speak ill o' the coffee, but bakin' is more liable to keep you afloat. An' I pride myself on my bakin', so, you c'n trust my judgement." She pressed a modest hand to her bosom.

Viv kept her face carefully neutral, thinking of Laney's cake.

"Well, won't keep you," continued the old woman. "But when you've some to sell, you set some aside for me, hear?"

"I sure will."

As Laney hobbled out of the shop, three customers entered behind her, and beyond them, Viv could see passersby slowing and glancing around curiously as they entered the cloud of scent that was pouring out the door.

It looked like the afternoon might not be so lean, after all, and they hadn't sold a single roll yet.

——+——

Viv and Tandri held a hurried conference. Viv thought they should charge two copper bits per roll, but Tandri laid a hand on her forearm, stared at her seriously, and said, "Four bits, Viv. Four. Bits."

They took down the menu slate. Tandri quickly added a new entry and, in economical strokes, an illustration of a pastry, complete with sinuous lines representing the incredible smell.

⌁LEGENDS & LATTES⌁
~ MENU ~

Coffee ~ exotic aroma & rich, full-bodied roast—½ bit
Latte ~ a sophisticated and creamy variation—1 bit
Cinnamon Roll ~ heavenly frosted cinnamon pastry—4 bits

❊

FINER TASTES FOR THE
~ WORKING GENT & LADY ~

"Four?" Viv asked again as she reseated the menu on the wall. "Really?"

"Trust me."

Thimble hopped off his stool, took up a thick dishtowel, cracked open the stove, and withdrew the rolls. They were enormous and golden and beautiful. The smell billowed out in a wave as he placed them on the stovetop and closed the door. Viv thought Tandri might have involuntarily moaned, and her own stomach growled noisily.

The rattkin drizzled them with the thick, creamy icing that he'd kept to the side, sniffed experimentally, and nodded in satisfaction.

Viv looked up to find Hemington staring with interest at the rolls. "What an incredible smell," he said.

"Well, you said you wanted something to eat. You can be first in line."

"Ah," said Hemington, looking embarrassed. "Well, you see, I have certain dietary restrictions. I don't exactly eat *bread* . . ."

Viv's brows drew low, and she leaned heavily on the counter.

"I'll just buy one though, shall I?" he said lamely.

"Thank you."

"Er. Indeed."

At Thimble's nod of encouragement, Tandri transferred the warm rolls onto a platter one by one and reverently set them on the counter.

As Hemington paid, Viv handed him a roll on a piece of waxed paper and leveled a glare at him. "If you don't eat this, it's possible Tandri or I may have to kill you."

The young man laughed, although the laugh became strangled when Viv didn't join in. He slunk back to his books with the roll balanced carefully on both palms.

Anyone who'd been in the dining area was already in line, waiting their turn, and within thirty minutes, every last roll was gone.

Tandri stared at the crumb-strewn plate, ran a finger through a dribble of glaze, licked it off, and looked bleakly at Viv. "I didn't even get to have one," she said. "I would've paid *more* than four bits."

"Well, you're in luck," said Viv. "Seems like you'll get another chance. And I don't like to think what Laney will do with that broom if we don't remember to set one aside for her, too."

Thimble was already busily mixing up a new batch, humming again, louder—and happier—than before.

13

With Thimble already elbow-deep in his baking before dawn—
and with Tandri strategically cracking the door ahead of time
to let the smell creep into the street—the opening crowd was
easily triple the prior day's.

Tandri and Viv brewed side by side, working both handles
in a flustered but energized confusion, nearly tripping over one
another to fill orders.

Thimble's cinnamon rolls disappeared in minutes, but he had
wisely already set more dough to rise while the first batch was
in the oven.

With the stove running full blast, the shop was hotter than
usual, and muggy from the steaming rolls. Both women sweated
through their shirts within the hour. The chatter of the crowd,
Thimble's clatter, and the hiss and rumble of the gnomish coffee machine filled the air with a dizzying madness.

As the morning crept toward noon, the crowd slackened but
never lapsed for more than ten minutes. The dining area sang
with a lively clamor, and the rumble of conversation pervaded.
Customers dallied longer, enjoying their baked goods and sipping

their drinks without hurrying, and for the first time, more sat at the big communal table than sought the relative solitude of a booth.

Viv leaned on the counter, studying their faces, and saw, at last, what she'd been too nervous to hope for. She found it in half-lidded eyes and a slow, deliberate swallow. In cupped hands around the warmth of a mug and the lingering enjoyment of the last taste. It was the echo of her own experience, and a pleasant flush of recognition washed over her.

"You haven't stopped smiling in an hour," said Tandri, startling Viv out of woolgathering during a brief lull.

"I haven't?"

"Nope."

They were both red-faced and too warm, but Viv couldn't help but notice how much more relaxed Tandri seemed today. Viv liked it.

"Just feels like everything lined up. I had the same feeling a few times before—like when I found Blackblood." Viv tipped her head toward the blade on the wall. "She just felt at home in my hands, and when I went to use her, well . . ." Realizing where that story went, she stopped short. "Anyway, this feels . . . right."

"It does."

"Still some kinks to work out, though."

"I think you can rest on your laurels for a day or two," said Tandri, with a wry smile.

"I don't know, we might boil to death in the meantime."

Thimble appeared between them, and they looked down. He glanced up at Viv and tugged at the hem of her shirt, pointed at the oven, then spread his arms wide.

"I . . . sorry, I don't know what you mean, Thimble."

His nose wriggled, and he whispered, "*Bigger. Would be better . . . bigger.*"

"The *rolls*? They're already as big as my head!"

He shook his head. "*Stove. Stove!*" Then he quailed. "*Sorry! Sorry!*"

Viv glanced over at the oven Cal had installed. Thimble had worked nonstop, and the rolls sold out almost as soon as they cooled. Perhaps demand would taper off a little, but she could certainly see how the pace might run the poor rattkin ragged. A bigger stove *would* make it easier to stay on top of things.

"I'd like to, Thimble, but I don't know how we could fit it in. It's already getting pretty tight back here."

Thimble looked downcast for a moment, but he nodded in reluctant agreement.

"If only they could keep longer," mused Tandri aloud. "If they didn't have to be fresh, then we could hold them in reserve and take some of the pressure off."

The rattkin stared at her, tapped his lower lip thoughtfully with a claw, and blinked a few times. He slowly meandered back to his dough, rolling out a fresh sheet, but Viv noticed that he paused every once in a while to stare into the distance.

—◄+►—

When Cal dropped by for the first time in days, Viv immediately handed him a cinnamon roll. He examined it curiously, then took a modest bite.

His response was entirely predictable.

"Hm."

But it was the good sort of *Hm.*

He nodded at the busy dining area while he chewed and swallowed. "Looks as though things are tickin' right along. And this . . ." He looked at the roll appreciatively. "This is mighty fine. Told you that stove might show itself worthy. Don't s'pose I could have one of those lattes to go with?" He examined the menu and slid six bits onto the counter top.

Viv slid them right back. "You keep those. And I've got some more for you if you can think of something to do about the heat in here. It's hot as the eight hells when the stove is going."

He chewed another bite, closing his eyes with a pleased sigh. "Well. I may have a thought, but might need a piece of time to see if it'll work. Somethin' I saw on a gnomish pleasure craft. Very clever."

Viv was intrigued. "Some kind of window?"

"Nope. Not a window," he said. "Don't want to get your hopes up if it ain't workable. You give me a day or two, I'll see what I can see. Try not to burn the place down between now and then." He favored her with one of his thin, but genuine, smiles. Then he took his drink and his roll and ambled into the dining area.

———+———

Later in the day, business held steady, with customers trickling in and out often enough to keep them occupied but not harried.

As Viv dried her hands for what must've been the eighth time after washing mugs in the basin, a big fellow with the look of a farmhand entered the shop. Viv was perplexed to see some kind of lute tucked under one arm. Thick sheaves of yellow hair kept falling over his eyes, and his hands were as enormous and rough as her own, which seemed odd for a musician.

"Help you?" she asked.

"Er, hello there. I wanted to ask if I . . . wait, um. Uh, hello," he stammered, starting over. "My name is Pendry. I'm a . . ."

His voice dropped very low, almost to a whisper. "A *bard?*" It sounded more like a question.

"Congratulations," replied Viv, in an amused tone.

"I was . . . was wondering if I could, maybe . . . maybe *entertain?* In here, I mean?"

Viv was taken aback. "I hadn't really thought about anything like that before," she admitted.

"Oh. Oh, well, um. That's . . . that's fine." He nodded hugely, his hair flopping against his cheeks.

She couldn't be sure, but she thought he might be *relieved.*

"Are you any good?" asked Tandri, coming around the counter and crossing her arms.

"I, uh. Well, I . . ."

Viv snorted and nudged Tandri gently in the ribs.

"Tell you what," said Viv, thinking of the Scalvert's Stone and that feeling of *snapping closed* she'd experienced, everything slotting into place. "Why don't you go ahead. You're not asking for anything but permission, right?"

Pendry looked a bit sick to his stomach. "Yes. I mean no. I mean . . . okay."

Then he just stood there.

Tandri made a shooing motion. "Go ahead, then." Her expression was severe, but Viv could tell she was trying not to smile.

The farmhand, or bard, or whatever he was, shuffled into the other room and looked around with barely suppressed horror on his face. He made his way to the back, head down, and turned slowly around. Nobody paid him much attention, and he simply stood there for a few minutes, strangling his lute, fidgeting with the tuning pegs, and murmuring under his breath.

Viv was pretty sure he was arguing with himself, and she peered curiously around the corner at him.

The lute was odd. She'd never seen one like it before. There didn't seem to be an opening on the front for resonance. Instead, there was a slab of some sort of slatelike stone underneath the strings, with silver pins embedded in it.

She almost thought he'd fold under his anxiety and slink back out of the shop, but he took a deep breath and began to strum.

The noise that emerged was unlike anything she'd expected, and all conversation cut short. There was a raw, wailing edge to the notes, *much* louder than any lute Viv had ever heard before. She flinched and saw others do the same as Pendry began playing in earnest. The sound the man produced wasn't *unmusical,* but there was something almost savage about it.

She wondered if maybe her trust in the Scalvert's Stone to draw what she needed here might have been a bit *too* blind, because if *this* was its doing . . .

Viv glanced at the patrons, who looked uncomfortable. A few rose as though they were preparing to leave.

She started to approach the young man, who, for a wonder, looked fully relaxed at this point, lost in the music. As she drew near, his eyes fluttered open, and he saw her. He glanced around the room and absorbed the shocked expressions of the people there, and abruptly stopped playing.

"Pendry?" Viv held up a hand.

"Oh, gods," he moaned, clearly mortified.

And he fled the shop, his lute held before him like a shield.

———✦———

Viv felt sorry for the kid, but the afternoon rush put him out of her mind. Demand for baked goods tapered off enough that

Thimble could rest, and eventually Viv sent the poor rattkin home. He was knackered, and Viv got the impression that if she didn't cut him off, he'd work himself into unconsciousness.

As she returned from clearing tables, she found Tandri standing by the front window.

"It's not Kellin again, is it?"

"Hm? No, nothing like that."

"What then?"

"That old man."

Viv leaned out the door to look. Seated at one of their tables was an elderly gnome wearing a curious bent cap, like a small sack, and dark spectacles. Before him was a mug, a cinnamon roll, and a chessboard with little ivory pieces on it. Nobody was seated across from him. Curled around the base of the table, however, was Amity, purring in a contented rumble. The huge cat remained an infrequent visitor and shunned the bed of blankets they'd made, so it was a surprise to see her in repose.

"Huh, Amity seems to like him." Viv shrugged. "I must be missing something though."

"He's been there for an hour. He came in a little after our would-be bard."

"And?"

"I can't figure out who's moving the other pieces."

"He's playing by himself?"

Tandri nodded. "But he never seems to move for the other side. Or at least, I've never caught him doing it."

"You managed to track that out of the corner of your eye?"

"I mean, at first, I didn't pay any attention, but now I can't help but keep glancing over."

"Well," said Viv. "We've had hell's own bard here, today. Why not a chess-playing phantom?"

"I'll catch him doing it *sometime*," Tandri said, nodding decisively.

Then two Gatewardens crowded through the door to buy out the rest of the rolls.

They promptly forgot about the gnome.

Thimble appeared before they opened the doors, another list clutched in his paws. It wasn't particularly long.

"Currants, walnuts, oranges . . . cardamom?" Viv asked, with a puzzled expression.

Thimble nodded ardently.

"I don't even know what that last one is. And the rolls are already perfect!"

The rattkin wrung his hands and looked aggrieved. "*Trust*," he whispered.

Viv held in a sigh. "All right, I'll take care of it. Tandri, you're fine while I gather . . . whatever this is?"

"If it means Thimble bakes more things, then I'll do almost anything you need," said Tandri.

Thimble beamed.

The morning was chill and damp as Viv headed back to the market district, doing her best to remember which shops Thimble visited during their first excursion. The currants, walnuts, and oranges didn't give her too much trouble, even if the oranges were a little rare this time of year. Viv asked about the last curious item at each stop, but the shopkeepers were as bewildered as she. She eventually retraced Thimble's steps to the elderly gentleman with the fragrant house.

After a few wrong turns, Viv located the place and rapped on the door. After some shuffling and muttering, the old man cracked it an inch and glared at her suspiciously.

"Uh, you might remember me," she said. "I was here with, um"—she held a hand at Thimble's approximate height—"little guy. Anyway, I'm looking for . . . cardamom?"

"Hmph. Running errands for Thimble, eh?" He opened the door a little wider.

"Guess so. I have to say he's one hell of a baker."

The old man glowered up at her through his spectacles. "Lad's a genius." Then he snatched the parchment from her hand and shuffled into the shadows of his house. Such a dense array of scents filtered out his door, it made Viv dizzy. Individually, they might have been pleasant, but taken all together, they were too much. She didn't know how the old man could abide it.

After some distant muttering, some clatters and bumps, and a few sharp expletives, the old man returned with a brown paper packet. He thrust it at her, along with the list.

"Two silver, four bits," he said.

"That much?"

"Somebody else offering you a better price?" His grin was wide and not entirely pleasant.

"Hm."

Viv dug through her coin purse and paid the man.

The door snapped shut in her face.

—◆—

Thimble received the groceries with a pleased squeak, carefully arranged them in the pantry, and returned to the rolls he had in progress.

Business was at least as heavy as the day before, and Tandri flashed a grateful smile as Viv joined her behind the counter to help manage the rush. Viv couldn't help her disappointment that Thimble didn't seem to have an immediate use for the fruits of her shopping, but the morning press soon chased it from her mind.

Only later, when the demand for rolls was more manageable, did Thimble retrieve the items from the back.

Tandri gently elbowed Viv. "I am *unbelievably* excited to find out what he's going to do."

"The old man I bought the cardamom from said Thimble's a genius," murmured Viv.

"I don't think I needed some old man to tell me that," Tandri replied with a chuckle.

"I'd say that's fair."

—◆—

The rattkin set to measuring and stirring and produced a thick, glutinous dough, to which he added chopped walnuts and currants. He then grated the skin of the oranges over the bowl. The cardamom, it turned out, were small, wizened-looking seeds. He diced them incredibly fine, crushed them with the flat of his knife blade, delicately scraped some of the dust into the dough, and set the remainder aside in a twist of waxed paper.

Tandri and Viv grudgingly took turns making drinks for customers as Thimble kneaded and formed long, flat logs. He laid them out on two pans, sprinkled them with fistfuls of sugar, and popped them into the oven. Then he tidied things away, humming all the while in his delicate, tuneful way.

The smell was promising—nutty and sweet and subtle. It put Viv in mind of winter solstice celebrations. When he eventually withdrew the flat loaves from the oven, she and Tandri loomed close, but he shooed them away. Slicing them, he arranged rows on pans and returned them to the oven.

"Twice?" asked Viv.

He nodded vehemently.

When he judged them done and set them out to cool, Viv studied them doubtfully. They smelled nice but resembled sad little slices of bread that hadn't risen.

Thimble insisted they wait until the pastries cooled, and then, with nervous ceremony, he handed one to each of them. Viv wrinkled her brow as she examined hers. It was hard, like incredibly stale bread. The old man *had* extolled Thimble's brilliance, and it was difficult to argue with the success of the cinnamon rolls, but she shared a slightly worried look with Tandri.

As they went to take bites, he waved anxious paws at them and urgently whispered, *"With drink!"*

Tandri dutifully brewed two lattes. They took experimental nibbles. And . . . those hard little slices *were* good. They crumbled nicely, and the nuts and fruit were elevated by an exotic, creamy sweetness that had to be the cardamom. Maybe not as good as the cinnamon rolls, but . . . pleasing.

The rattkin made an urgent dipping motion.

Viv shrugged. She dunked one end into her latte and took another bite. Her eyes went wide. She chewed, swallowed, and allowed herself a moment to appreciate this subtle, elegant comingling of flavors. "Oh hells, Thimble. That old man was right. You *are* a genius."

The real genius, however, wasn't apparent to her until Tandri pointed it out. "These will keep, won't they? Overnight, maybe for several days?"

He nodded and beamed at them both.

"We're going to need something to store these in. And Tandri, I think we're going to need to update the menu again. What do we even call these, though?"

"I think I might have an idea," Tandri replied. With a smile tugging at her lips, she retrieved her chalk from under the counter.

LEGENDS & LATTES
~ MENU ~

Coffee ~ exotic aroma & rich, full-bodied roast—½ bit
Latte ~ a sophisticated and creamy variation—1 bit
Cinnamon Roll ~ heavenly frosted cinnamon pastry—4 bits
Thimblets ~ crunchy nut & fruit delicacies—2 bits

❀

FINER TASTES FOR THE
~ WORKING GENT & LADY ~

The following morning, the Thimblets didn't start as strong sellers, but in the occasional absence of rolls, diners took a chance on them. As the day progressed, they were sometimes even a first choice.

Every so often, Viv found herself absently munching one and humming to herself.

—+—

The kitchen seemed to grow more sweltering each day, and Viv and Tandri were both anxious for Cal's return. When he eventually appeared, the hob produced a big, folded sheet of parchment, which he spread out on the counter top in front of them. It contained a few separate sketches with some measurements, but Viv had no idea what she was looking at.

"So, this is our solution to the heat problem back here?"

"Hm. It's an auto-circulator. Like I said, saw one on a gnomish pleasure craft. Would take me a few hours to fix it in place. Maybe even a whole day. Have to cut into the stovepipe a bit, and we'll need the ladder to hang it up there. Prob'ly need a hand from you. Heavy." He pointed at the ceiling.

"I'm happy to close for a day if it means we don't feel like we're *in* the oven back here."

Tandri blew out a breath of agreement.

"Ain't cheap, though," said the hob, looking apologetic. He tapped the diagram. "These I have to get from a gnomish artificer, and they come dear."

"How much are we talking?"

"Three sovereigns."

"Huh. That's only two months of telling the Madrigal to take a swim."

Cal's glare was severe.

"Only joking!" said Viv mildly, although she wasn't sure she was. "But yeah, let's do it."

She dug out four sovereigns and handed them over. "And for your time. No, don't hand one back."

"Hm. End of the week work for you?"

"Perfect."

◄━✦━►

When Cal returned at the appointed time, Viv already had a sign out front.

CLOSED

TODAY ONLY FOR RENOVATION

She'd already seen several morning regulars reading it with various expressions of disappointment. An irrational fear that they'd never return again seized her, but she squashed it as best she could.

The hob pushed a handcart loaded with a big, brass-barreled mechanism, multiple large, winglike blades, a smaller fan, like a windmill, and a long, leather band of some sort, resembling an enormous stropping belt.

Viv stared at the confusion of parts with hands on hips. "Huh. I had no idea how this was going to work from the drawings, and now I'm even more confused."

"Oh, it's clever," said Cal, grunting as he maneuvered the handcart through the doors Viv held open. "Trust a gnome to surprise you."

First Cal removed a section of the stovepipe, cutting it in half and installing the small windmill-like fan into a clever housing with a set of interlocking gears on the spindle. Viv helped him position and reaffix it into the primary stovepipe.

Viv retrieved the old ladder from the back alley and leaned it up against the wall. With some careful maneuvering, Cal ascended, and she stepped up behind him, hauling the brass mechanism. She managed to hold it in place against the ceiling with one hand, even *her* muscles straining at the awkward position and the weight held high above her head.

Cal installed it quickly with some gnomish screws, and Viv tugged on it to make sure it wasn't going to come down on their heads.

Viv ended up holding Cal above her so he could slot the big winglike blades into four arms that radiated from the barrel, making it resemble a much larger version of the contraption in the stovepipe. Then they strung the enormous leather belt around the spindle of the brass barrel and across to the exposed wheel housing in the stovepipe.

"Well," said Viv. "I *still* don't know how this works, but stone me if I don't want to see it in action."

Cal chuckled wryly and tossed some wood into the stove before setting it alight.

At first, nothing much happened, but as the heat built and the hot air rose, the belt began to move, very slowly at first. It never achieved a particularly high speed, but the big fan on the ceiling began to stir the air in a steady, cooling breeze.

"I'll be damned," said Viv.

"Hm," said Cal. "Maybe. Least you won't burn alive 'til you get to the hells, though."

15

"Gods, what a difference," said Tandri.

Cal's auto-circulator twirled lazily above them, and the cool downdraft was indeed a blessed relief. Thimble appeared to appreciate it just as much, if not more. Viv wasn't even sure if the rattkin could sweat. He'd probably suffered more than any of them, especially working near the stove, although he'd never complained.

Some morning regulars bemoaned the previous closure, but any grumbles were outweighed by their interest in the new gnomish gadget stirring the air.

Glancing around, Viv decided that she was extremely proud of the shop's interior. It felt *modern* and forward-thinking, but also cozy and welcoming. The combined aromas of hot cinnamon, ground coffee, and sweet cardamom intoxicated her, and as she brewed and smiled and served and chatted, a deep contentment welled up. It was a glowing warmth she'd never experienced before, and she liked it. She liked it a great deal.

A look around at the regulars confirmed they felt it, too. And yet, from behind the counter, there was a sweetness she alone experienced.

Because this shop is mine, she thought.

She caught Tandri slipping into a smile beside her.

Or maybe, it's ours.

———+———

Viv glanced up and saw Pendry, the hulking would-be bard, shifting from foot to foot, just inside the threshold. This time, he had a more traditional lute clutched in front of him. She thought he might accidentally twist the neck off with those big hands, he gripped it so tightly.

"Hi there, Pendry."

She waited to see what he'd say, a touch amused. It was clear what he *wanted* to say.

"I. Uh. Well."

Tandri shot her a mildly reproachful look, and Viv took pity on the poor kid.

"Want to give it another try?" she asked, carefully keeping her eyes on her work.

"Er. I . . . would . . . like that. But I promise, I'll play something less mod—I mean, more *traditional*, miss."

"Miss? Oof. Now I know why Laney hated that." Viv made a face.

"I'm . . . sorry?" he ventured, wincing.

She waved at him. "Go ahead. Last time wasn't *bad* exactly. Just . . . surprising. Break a leg."

Pendry looked stricken.

"I guess that's not a common saying around here?"

Tandri shrugged. "Sounds pretty martial."

"You're probably right."

Pendry blinked in confusion, then ducked his head and shuf-

fled into the dining area again. This time, Viv resolved not to
follow, in case it made his nerves worse than they already were.

She *did* cock an ear, and waited for a minute or so. Hearing
nothing, she laughed under her breath and shook her head,
starting a fresh pull of coffee.

As she passed it to a customer, and the hissing of the machine died down, the sound of the lute became gradually apparent. Much softer than last time, Pendry was playing a gentle
ballad with a pleasant melody. It had a catchy strumming pat-
tern, interspersed with delicate finger-picking.

"It's nice," observed Tandri. "He can play, can't he?"

"Not bad," agreed Viv.

A voice then joined the lute, high and sweet and soulful.

"Hang on," said Viv. "Who is *that*?" She ducked her head
around the corner and gawked. "Well, I'll be damned."

It was Pendry, his singing voice unaccountably melodious
and pure, a startling contrast to his bulk and blockiness.

> . . . *The price of what I meant to do*
> *Was higher when the day was through,*
> *And when I took a different road,*
> *I almost couldn't feel the load* . . .

"I don't think I've ever heard that before," said Tandri.
"Maybe traditional-*sounding*, but not traditional. I'd wager he
wrote that."

"Huh." There were no expressions of shock amongst the diners, and Viv even caught a foot or two tapping along. "Sorry I
ever doubted you," she murmured, partly to herself, but mostly
to the Scalvert's Stone tucked away beneath the floor.

"What was that?"

"Oh, nothing. Just another stroke of good luck."

———+———

Later, Hemington approached the counter and rather awk-wardly ordered one of everything.

"You want a coffee *and* a latte?" asked Viv, eyeing him with suspicion.

"Er. Yes." He paused and fidgeted for a moment. "And then, I had something I wanted to ask you."

Viv sighed. "Hemington, if you're looking for a favor, just ask. I don't want to brew coffee you're not going to drink."

"Oh, well, excellent," he said brightly.

"You're buying one of these though," she said, sliding a Thim-blet over to him.

"Um. Of course." He paid for it but didn't seem to know what to do with it.

"Well, what can I do for you, Hem?"

"To start, I'd appreciate it if you didn't call me *Hem*."

"I believe you're the one asking for a favor. In a shop where you don't actually want anything we sell . . . *Hem*."

He grimaced. "It's not that I don't *want* anyth—! Oh, *never mind*." He took a big breath and tried to start over. "I was *hoping* you'd allow me to lay a ward here, as part of my re-search."

Viv frowned. "A ward? What for?"

"Well, it's really my primary area of study. And with the non-fluctuating confluence of ley lines here, and the amplifying effect they have on thaumic constructions that align with the material substrate, it—"

"Maybe a more straightforward answer, Hemington?"

"Ahem. It will be *entirely* unnoticeable." He absently bit the Thimblet.

"But what will it *do?*"

"Well . . . it could do any *number* of things. That, in and of itself, isn't important. And it will *not* disrupt your customers, or anyone else. You shouldn't even see it!"

"Then why haven't you already done it?"

He looked affronted. "I would *never*," he said, with great dignity, spoiled somewhat by the bite of Thimblet that followed.

"What sort of ward?" asked Tandri, who had clearly been listening in. "Optical trigger? Anima proximity? Using a precision focus?"

"Er, anima proximity. And the focus could be anything. A pigeon?"

"Why would you want to track whether a pigeon flew over the building?" asked Tandri.

"Well, it was just an *example*," said Hemington. "As I said, what it does isn't important. I'd just like to study the stability, range, and accuracy of the ward's response."

Viv sighed in resignation. "If I don't have to hear any more about it, then go right ahead. Unless . . ." She looked at Tandri. "Unless I *should* care?"

She was nervous that this would somehow expose the secret under the floor, but objecting more strenuously might accomplish the same thing. If he had some means of investigating specifically for the Stone, she wouldn't know anyway, so perhaps it was best just to go with it, for now.

"It'll be fine," said Tandri.

"I *told* you it would be unnoticeable," huffed Hemington.

"Unnoticeable isn't the same as harmless," said Viv mildly. "But yeah, go ahead."

"I . . . thank you."

"How was the Thimblet?" she asked with a sly smile.

"The what?"

She pointed at his now empty hands.

He'd eaten the whole thing.

—◆—

Things had been going far too smoothly for far too long, and if Viv had been out in the wilderness or on a campaign or camped outside a beast's lair, a premonition of impending misfortune would have prickled along her spine.

While she and Tandri shut down for the evening, Lack appeared outside the shop with Tandri's unwelcome admirer, Kellin, and at least six or eight others.

As Viv stood blocking the doorway, she reflected that she really should not have let her vigilance lapse.

"What is it?" asked Tandri, dropping the mug she'd been cleaning into the wash-water and moving to look around Viv's side. She froze at the sight of Kellin, her eyes darting to the men and women behind him.

They bristled with enough knives to warrant concern. Viv found herself wishing that Amity would show up, but the dire-cat was frustratingly absent.

Viv wasn't particularly worried about the knives for *herself*, but Tandri's presence threw off her mental calculus of risk entirely. The succubus had witnessed her last encounter with Lack, but there was no Gatewarden present this time to uphold the illusion of law. Alone, Viv never feared for her own skin. With Tandri beside her, brute strength felt like no defense at all.

"Congratulations on your ongoing success," said Lack, doffing his hat and executing a half bow.

Viv couldn't decide if it was intended to be mocking or not.

"End of the month already, is it?" she asked grimly. "Could have sworn there were a few more days."

Lack nodded agreeably. "Indeed. You know, it's not readily apparent, but the trickiest part of my job is ensuring that things go smoothly. That there are no *problems*. You see, if there is blood, or bones get broken, or property meets misfortune, that's a *failure*. It's just not a foundation for good business. The Madrigal wants *good* business. Repeatable business. And diligence on my part is key to making that happen."

"Hi, Tandri," said Kellin, with a possessive smile in her direction.

Lack frowned at him.

Tandri glanced at Viv, eyes wide.

Viv tried her best to project confidence.

Lack continued, "I'm here to impress on you that I'm serious. That we *do* expect collection at the end of the month. And to reiterate that while I would prefer to count this as a success, a failure of . . . civility . . . will be more to your disadvantage than ours."

Viv clenched her fists at her sides. "Might be more of a disadvantage for you than you expect."

Lack sighed in an aggrieved way. "Look, there's no denying you're *very* physically capable. That's clear. But you have a business. You have employees. You're doing *well*. Would you really want to throw all that away on some sort of misguided principle? The world is full of taxes and allowances and concessions that keep things moving *forward*. This is just another one of those."

"Hate to see the place burn to the ground," said Kellin, with an extremely punchable grin on his face.

Lack's motion was liquid and savage as he snagged Kellin's

lapel and yanked him close to his face. "Shut *up,* you insuffer-able *shitweasel,*" he snarled.

From the speed of that motion, Viv instantly knew that she'd misjudged Lack's quality as a threat.

Kellin stumbled away, mouth gaping, chastened.

Lack straightened his overcoat and replaced his hat on his head. "Another week," he said. "I look forward to a *trouble-free* relationship in the future." He nodded to Viv, and then to Tan-dri. "Apologies, miss."

And then they left.

———+———

Viv was straightening up from her pack with the Blink Stone in hand when Tandri found her in the loft.

"Are you all right?" asked Tandri.

Viv was touched, swiftly followed by a guilty realization of who had been most threatened by the men in the street. How could she have failed to ask how Tandri felt? It was too late now, though.

"Fine." She winced at the shortness of her answer. "Just think-ing about my options." She stared at the Blink Stone in her palm. The succubus glanced curiously at it, but Viv didn't offer to explain.

Tandri swept her gaze over the barren room, empty except for Viv's bedroll, her pack, and some leftover construction materials stacked neatly in the corner.

"This is where you sleep?"

"I'm used to less," said Viv, suddenly embarrassed.

Tandri was quiet for a long moment.

"You know, you've built something pretty wonderful. Some-thing special." She held Viv's gaze. "And I know you're remaking your life. I can relate. I know what that feels like and what it means to want that." She gestured around the empty room. "But that down there is not your *whole* life. What you do with the rest of the time is at least as important. For someone who reads a lot, you don't even have any books."

Maybe Viv had neglected a few pleasures. That was hard to argue with, but she tried anyway. "I don't really need anything else, though. I could feel it today. It was *enough*. And I don't mean to lose it."

"*Is* it enough, though?" Tandri frowned and looked down. "What they want to take from you . . . the reason it's so . . . un-tenable. It's because they'd be taking everything you have. I'm just saying that . . . maybe, if you treated the rest of your life the same way you do the shop—invested in it the same way—then the cost would seem less."

Viv didn't know what to say to that.

"Whatever happens," said Tandri. "I think maybe you should pay a little attention to *this* room." Her smile was wan. "At least get a damn bed."

———◆———

Viv waited until she heard Tandri close the shop door behind her. When she entered the kitchen a short while later, the only sound was the thrum of the stove.

She opened the firebox door and stood for a long time, staring into the flames.

Viv glanced at Blackblood, freshly garlanded.

Then she tossed the Blink Stone in, closed the stove, and climbed the ladder to try—and fail—to find sleep in her cold bedroll.

16

It was three days before the old crew—minus Fennus—arrived at the shop. In the late afternoon, Roon was the first to duck inside the door. He raised his eyebrows at Viv behind the coffee maker and gave the busy interior a considering glance. Gallina stepped out from behind him, where she'd been hidden by his bulk, goggles up in her spiky hair, a wide grin splitting her face. Taivus slipped gracefully in after and inclined his head.

"Evenin', Viv," said Roon.

"Closing a little early, folks," hollered Viv. Boisterous complaints answered back.

Tandri gave her a startled glance, saw her expression, and then noted Roon and the other new arrivals. "All friends of yours?"

"Old friends," said Viv, cocking a thumb at the sword behind her.

"Is that *Blackblood?*" exclaimed Gallina, with a high laugh. "She looks like a solstice wreath!"

"That's her," said Viv, with a smile. "Give me a few minutes to empty the place."

It took longer than she'd have liked to encourage the last of the diners out the door, and Viv wished—not for the first time— that she had some way to let customers take their drinks with them. *Ah well. A problem for another time.*

She sent Thimble on his way, but when she opened her mouth to speak to Tandri, the succubus held up a hand, her tail lashing sharply behind her. "I'm staying."

Viv thought about that for a moment, then nodded and said, "All right."

—◆—

They sat on the benches at the big communal table. Tandri brewed coffees, and Viv set out a plate of cinnamon rolls and Thimblets.

"Thanks for coming," said Viv, when they were all seated and served. She toyed with the mug in front of her. "And I guess, first things first, this is Tandri. She's my . . . coworker. Tandri, you know Roon. This is Gallina, and Taivus." She gestured to each in turn.

"Twice charmed," said Roon around an enormous bite of cinnamon roll.

"A succubus, huh?" said Gallina, her chin propped on her hand.

Viv saw Tandri stiffen.

The little gnome must have, as well. "Nah, I don't mean anything by it, sweetie. Long as you don't ask *me* to *invent* anything. Pleased to meetcha. Love the look." The gnome waved tiny fingers at Tandri's sweater.

"Gallina tends more to, uh, wet-work," said Viv.

"I *do* like knives." Gallina produced one from nowhere to trim her nails.

Taivus nodded solemnly at Tandri and nibbled at the edge of a Thimblet. The stone-fey was as taciturn as ever, his watchful face framed in white hair.

"Nice to meet you all," said Tandri. She took a quick sip of her drink, and Viv could swear she was nervous.

Roon set his matching Blink Stone on the table between them as he polished off his roll and reached for a Thimblet. "So. Seein' the place, an' tastin' these, I'm inclined to think you didn't send for us because you're hopin' to sleep rough an' crush skulls again."

"You got me there," said Viv. "No, I'm not coming back." She stared at Gallina thoughtfully. "Before I get into that, though, I owe you an apology. All of you. I'm not proud of the way I left. You deserved better from me, after all those years. I was just afraid—"

"We know," said Gallina. "Roon told us." She squinted at Viv. "I was a little pissed, I don't mind sayin'. But . . . this is *nice*." She gestured expansively at the shop. "Happy for you, Viv."

"I didn't mind," said Taivus in a quiet voice, because if anyone understood avoiding a difficult conversation—or, indeed, *any* conversation—it was the stone-fey.

"Well, now that's out o' the way, let's get down to it," said Roon, with a big grin. "We're folk o' action, hey? Unless you just wanted to feed us. An' if that was the case, can't say as I'd complain." He started in on his second roll.

Viv took a big breath and sighed it out. "So . . . things are going well. *Really* well, better than I could've hoped. But. There's a local . . . *element*, that I need to deal with."

Taivus looked suddenly interested, and Gallina stood up on the bench and planted both hands on the table to get a better eyeline. "And you haven't sent 'em off with broken bones and better manners, yet?"

"Well, no, not so far."

"Then you want us to *help* with that?" Gallina's grin was eager and a little bloodthirsty.

"It's not as simple as that."

"Oh, this is the *simplest*," said Gallina. "Nothin' simpler!"

Viv flattened her hands in front of her and tried to think of the right words to use. "Here's the thing. I was hoping that . . . the *threat* of me would be enough. I even hung Blackblood on the wall as, I don't know, a sort of warning. I don't want to deal with this the way that the old Viv would have, because . . . because . . ." She struggled to articulate it.

"Because if she does, it ruins everything," said Tandri, joining the conversation.

Roon looked skeptical. "She's taken care of problems just like this a dozen times. Two dozen! Protectin' what's yours? There's no shame in that. Don't see how that would ruin anythin', except the face of whatever fool is tryin' to shake her down."

"That's not what I mean," said Tandri, with surprising heat. "Sure, it might be fine this time, for this *one* thing . . . but once it's an option, once she can pick that back up . . ." She pointed at the sword on the wall. "She loses what she won by building this place without it. Maybe next time, it's just a job to earn a little silver in a lean winter. Maybe a bounty in exchange for a shipping discount. And little by little, this isn't that coffee shop in Thune where you can get a cinnamon roll as big as your head. It's Viv's territory, and you don't want to cross her, and did you hear about the time she broke the legs of somebody who looked at her funny?"

"She *has* done that," whispered Gallina out the side of her mouth.

"That was before." Tandri stabbed the table with a finger.

"Right now, in this town, the shop is a clean slate. She should pay the Madrigal and let it be."

"Well, Viv," said Roon, who looked confused. "If that's what you're thinkin', then why are we here?"

Viv tossed up her hands helplessly. "I don't know . . . advice? Or I guess I thought . . ."

"You thought we might do it," finished Gallina. She archly inquired, "Were you gonna offer to *pay* us?"

Viv looked pained. "No, that's not what I had planned, I . . . I don't *know* what I should do." She made a frustrated growl deep in her throat. "The problem is I don't *want* to pay them. I don't think I can bring myself to do it. And no, I'm not trying to hire you to take care of the problem. But I thought, maybe . . . just a *show* of force."

"That's the sword on the wall, again," said Tandri. "And if you go too much further, you might as well use it and be done with it."

They all fell silent for a moment.

"The Madrigal," said Taivus.

"You know him?" asked Viv.

"I know of them," he replied.

"Then what do you think?"

Taivus was characteristically thoughtful and quiet, but they all waited without saying a word.

"It may be," he eventually said, "that this can be resolved without blood."

"I'm all ears," said Viv.

"It's possible I may be able to arrange a parley," he continued.

"Meetin' in a dark alley to talk terms seems like a sure way to get a knife in the back," observed Gallina.

"The Madrigal and Viv have more in common than you might think," said Taivus.

"Why do you say that?"

"I've met them before," he said. "I'm bound by certain oaths not to reveal overmuch, and I take those oaths seriously, but I have a . . . sense . . . that it would be worth the effort."

"And you could set this up?" asked Viv.

"I believe I could. I'll reach out to a contact in the city. We should know by nightfall tomorrow."

Gallina looked unconvinced. "I still think murderin' them in their beds would be safer."

"I assure you, it would not," said Taivus, dryly.

"And you really think the risk of this is better than just paying what they're asking?" Tandri crossed her arms, her expression severe.

Viv thought about that for a moment. "I don't think it's better." She sighed. "But I feel like I've cut all the tethers to the old Viv but one. And I can't bring myself to cut that last rope. I'm just . . . not ready yet."

Tandri's mouth tightened, but she said nothing further. There was a long and uncomfortable silence.

It was broken suddenly when Roon shot up from the bench. "What in the hells is that!" he exclaimed.

The dire-cat had appeared and circled behind them. She rubbed along the bench, purring like an earthquake.

"That's Amity," said Viv, with a relieved grin. She glanced over at Tandri, grateful that the tension was broken, or at least deferred.

"Why d'you need us when you've got a damned hell-beast on staff?" Roon cried.

"Aww, you're just a sweetie, aren't you?" cooed Gallina, scratching Amity's back vigorously with both hands. She could have easily ridden the dire-cat.

"She's a fair-weather watchcat." Viv chuckled. "Shows up when she feels like it."

"She's hungry, too," observed Gallina, offering the enormous creature a roll. Amity swallowed it whole.

After that, the conversation moved on to other, less delicate matters, and Viv brought out more drinks while Roon polished off the remaining baked goods.

—+—

Dusk was long past when they finally filtered out the door, leaving Viv and Tandri behind to close up shop.

They quietly cleaned together, scrubbing and wiping and sweeping. As Viv dried her hands and turned to the front of the shop, Tandri was standing in the entry with an unreadable expression on her face.

"I'm sorry," the woman suddenly said.

"For what?"

"It wasn't my place to say those things. To speak for you. So, I apologize."

Viv frowned and looked down at her hands for a moment.

"No, you were right. You were right about how it *should* be. How I think I want it to be. I don't know if I can do that yet. But—" She looked back at Tandri. "I hope that someday, I can. So. Thank you."

"Oh." Tandri made a small nod. "That's all right, then. Good night, Viv."

She quietly left the shop.

"Good night, Tandri," Viv said to the closed door.

17

Viv and Tandri worked quietly and companionably, with no mention of the prior evening. Viv worried it might become tense between the two of them, but it hadn't. The morning was calm and easy, and she allowed herself not to think about the Madrigal or the end of the month or how it would feel to take Blackblood in hand and cut any brewing problems off at the knee.

It was nice.

Pendry showed up again around midday, lute at the ready, and with less cringing dread about him, Viv thought. She jerked her head toward the dining area with a smile, and he shuffled around the corner. A slightly more energetic, but still folksy ballad arose shortly after, twinned with Pendry's sweet, earnest voice.

Even nicer.

Later, Tandri nudged her and murmured, "He's back."

"Who is?"

"The mysterious chess player."

The elderly gnome was indeed unfolding a wooden board onto the table out front. After carefully setting out the pieces, clearly reproducing a game in progress, he strolled into the shop.

He peered over the counter top, and in a voice like rumpled velvet said, "One latte, please, m'dears. And one of those delightful confections." He pointed at the glass jar of Thimblets.

"You bet," said Viv.

As Tandri was brewing his drink, her tail did a few quick back-and-forth slashes, which Viv was coming to recognize as one of her anxious gestures. Eventually, the woman couldn't stand it anymore, and asked with exaggerated casualness, "So . . . waiting for someone?" She indicated the chessboard through the window.

The little old man looked surprised. "Not at all," he replied and took his drink and pastry, bobbed a nod, and returned to his table. Within moments, Amity had appeared as if by magic and curled up under his table again.

Tandri scrunched her mouth into a frown. "Damn it," she said, under her breath.

Viv chuckled to herself, and with no customers waiting, brewed another coffee and strolled into the other room to watch Pendry play. He'd taken one of the outdoor chairs and moved it inside to sit on, which seemed a bold move for him. Viv approved.

Eyes closed, he lost himself in his playing, fingers flying, crooning another song that Viv didn't think she'd ever heard before.

When the tune concluded and he took a brief break, she walked over and handed him the drink. "You're good." She glanced around. "No hat or box for coins?"

He looked surprised. "I, uh, hadn't thought of it."

"You should."

"I . . . okay," he stammered.

"So, that music you were playing the first day. It was . . . unusual."

He winced and looked like he was going to apologize.

"Not bad," she said quickly. "Just, different. Maybe you should give it another try, now that you've warmed them up a little." She gestured with her head at the diners behind her.

"It's something I was . . . experimenting with. But maybe it's a bit much." He still looked a little green around the gills.

"You weren't always a musician, huh?" She pointed at his blunt and weathered fingers, so much different from the callused fingertips of a lifetime lute player.

"Uh, no. No. The, uh, family business was—is—a little different."

"Well, keep at it. And maybe bring that other lute back when you feel like it." She nodded and left him goggling after her.

—◄+►—

"Hello again, Cal. Good to see you," said Tandri.

Viv turned to find the hob on the other side of the counter, where he eyed the interior critically, as though fearing it might collapse at any moment.

"Place seems to be holdin' up all right," he declared.

She almost expected him to test a wall by kicking it. "Your usual?"

"Hm." He nodded.

Tandri smiled with genuine warmth as she started the grinder. It grumbled for a moment, there was a sputter and a long whir, and she cut the switch. "Oh hells, the bean hopper is empty."

"I'll get a bag," offered Viv.

"No, I'll take care of it." Tandri briefly touched Viv's arm and headed for the pantry.

When Viv looked back at Cal, he flicked his gaze up from her arm to meet her eyes. She found his thoughtful look puzzling.

He cleared his throat. "Everythin' seems to be goin' along just fine, it appears," he said, with more delicacy than usual.

Viv squinted at him. "Fine enough. Although I don't mind saying I wish I saw more of you. Drinks are on the house anytime you drop by."

Cal snorted but couldn't hide a smile. "Playin' on my contrariness so I pay double?"

"Triple, if I can get it, you stubborn old goat."

She managed to get a laugh out of him at that, but then caught him looking over her shoulder toward the pantry.

"Goin' along just fine," he repeated. "Make sure to stop an' see it, hm?"

Viv started to ask what he meant when Tandri reappeared. "Sorry about that. Won't be a minute," she said, as she flipped the hatch and poured beans with a rattling hiss.

When Cal got his cup, Viv grudgingly accepted his copper, but then slid a roll in front of him with a triumphant smile. He grumbled good-naturedly but took both.

———+———

Gallina appeared in the late afternoon, alone.

"Was hopin' to catch up some before we head out tomorrow," she said, standing on tiptoe to fold her arms on the counter. "Just us two."

"Sure! That would be good, honestly. Let me just close things up early here first."

"It's all right," said Tandri. "No need to close. You go ahead."

"You sure?"

"Absolutely. I'll handle everything later. It's not *that* busy." Tandri shooed her off.

"Thanks," said Viv, with a grateful smile.

As Viv and Gallina strolled away from the shop, Viv asked, "Anything you had in mind?"

Gallina looked up at her and cocked an eyebrow. "I'm hungry. You're the local. What's good?"

"Can't say I've really taken in the sights. Although, maybe I *do* know a place."

Viv led her to the fey eatery she and Tandri had once visited.

"Oooh, this *is* fancy," said Gallina, with a twinkle in her eye.

"Oh, I'm pretty cosmopolitan, now." Viv snorted, remembering what Tandri had said.

They ordered and ate and talked about old times. Viv began to feel like they'd sailed back into the easy waters of friendship again.

As they picked at the crumbs of their meal, Gallina's expression grew speculative. "You know what *I* think of all this," she said, circling her hand, her tone sharp.

"You think I should knife them in their beds," said Viv, smiling a little.

"I do," replied Gallina seriously. "Before they decide they wanna take more from you than they planned. And I don't care what Taivus says, meetin' this Madrigal, you're gonna go and stake yourself out like a goat in front of a cave."

"Worse comes to worst, I can take care of myself."

"I know you *can*. I just wanna make sure you *do*." She produced four slim knives like magic, and slid them across the table toward Viv. "I want you to take these with you. Fine, leave Blackblood wrapped up in flowers or whatever, but don't be dumb."

Viv was simultaneously touched and a little exasperated.

She put one big hand over the weapons and pushed them back toward Gallina. "If I give myself that breathing room, I might just take advantage of it. I don't want to have the excuse."

"Oh, eight hells, Viv." Gallina crossed her arms and pouted. Then she whisked the knives away.

"Not going to stab me with one of those?"

"Maybe later." She sighed hugely. "Whatever, I guess. But now you owe me somethin' sweet for bruisin' my feelin's so bad."

"I'll see if they've got a dessert menu."

—◄+►—

Gallina walked Viv back to the shop.

"So, what's a girl gotta do to get a sack of those sweet rolls?" she asked.

"Didn't I just buy you dessert?"

"Thing about gnomes, we got the metabolism of humming-birds," said Gallina, with a huge grin.

"I'll see what I can do."

Tandri was in the middle of shutting things down and waved at them both.

Viv wrapped the last three rolls in wax paper, tied them with some string, and grandly handed the packet to Gallina.

"Should last me the walk to my room," she said, with a nod and a wink. Then she sobered. "Look, I don't know if I should say it, 'cause I don't want to set you jumpin' at shadows, but Fennus . . ."

"What about him?"

"I think you should just keep an eye out."

"Did he say something?"

"No, not exactly, but . . . I don't know if you had some

arrangement with him or somethin', but . . . he's been strange lately. So maybe it's nothin'. But. I gotta listen to my little voice, I guess."

"I'll be careful," said Viv, remembering Fennus's visit and his parting remarks.

It does indeed have the ring of fortune about it.

—+—

Viv helped Tandri finish closing up. As she washed and dried the last mug, Tandri leaned on the counter. "Good visit?"

"It was," said Viv. "I've known Gallina for years. Not my finest moment, leaving the way I did. But I think that's smoothed over now."

"That's good."

Tandri's tail did its side-to-side lash.

"But?" prompted Viv, knowing there was more.

"You should be careful. When you take the meeting."

Viv chuckled. "You don't live as long as I have, doing what I did, without taking precautions."

"I think that's what worries me. Precautions."

Viv stared at her levelly. "Gallina offered me knives. I made her keep them."

"I . . . that's good. I mean, it's not my place to . . . ah, *shit*." Tandri hung her head, and her glossy hair fell forward. She looked up again. "You know, part of what I am—*who* I am—I have a . . . sense about things."

"A sense?"

"As a succubus. We pick up more of intentions, emotions. And also . . . secrets."

Viv had a sinking feeling that she knew where this was going.

"Look, I know that there's more to all this than what you'll say. And that's okay! Again, it's not my place, but . . . it makes me think this is more dangerous than just some crime boss wringing out protection money."

Viv thought about the Scalvert's Stone, but she hadn't gotten any sense from Lack or his goons that *they* knew about it. And why would they? The Stone's lore was obscure, and it was hardly sitting out for all to see. She'd been careful.

"I . . . do have something I'm playing close to the vest," admitted Viv. "But I can't figure any way that the Madrigal could know about it, and even if he did, the odds he'd care are low, I think."

"Like I said," said Tandri, "I can sense things. From you. And from all of them yesterday, something unsaid. And I have a bad feeling."

Viv thought about Gallina's warning about Fennus and wondered exactly what he *had* said to the rest of the crew.

"I'll be careful," said Viv. "That's all I know to do, at this point."

"I hope that's enough."

The shop was fully squared away, and after glancing around, Tandri nodded to herself and, after a long silence, said, "Well . . . good night."

As she turned to go, Viv blurted, "Hey, so, you want a walk home? What with that Kellin guy, and your . . . sense of things, maybe it'd feel safer?"

Tandri thought about it for a moment, then replied, "That'd be nice."

◆—◆—◆

The night was dark and cool, and the smell of the river had a fresher, earthy flavor that was pleasant. The street lanterns cast yellow pools in the blue of the evening shadows.

They strolled in a relaxed silence, with Tandri leading the way, until they came to a building on the north side that was clearly a grocer's on the bottom story.

"Up there," said Tandri, gesturing to a side stairway. "I'm sure I'll be fine the last few steps."

"Of course," said Viv, suddenly awkward. "See you tomorrow, then?"

"Tomorrow."

After watching her ascend and slip into the building, Viv walked around Thune for several hours before returning to the darkened shop, where the last embers in the stove had gone cold.

18

Viv handed Laney one of her own plates with a fresh and steaming roll on it—something she'd been doing for a few days now. Laney always left a clean plate on Viv's counter before closing with four shiny bits on it, and every morning, Viv returned it less the coins and plus a pastry.

"Well, *thank* ya, dear!" cried Laney, taking the plate with eager hands. "You tell that rattkin lad if he wants to trade recipes sometime, I've got some corkers."

"I'll be sure to let him know," Viv replied, wondering what Thimble would make of Laney's cakes.

"Jes' so proud to have you as a neighbor."

Viv glanced back at the shop. "I hope so, because it looks like you might be stuck with me."

Laney nodded. "Good to see you settlin' in. All that 'twas needed was a partner."

"A partner?"

The old woman's eyes grew distant. "My ol' Titus used to say we filled each other's gaps. 'Course, when he said it, it sounded *dirtier*."

While Viv puzzled over that, Laney wafted the steam from the roll to her nose. "I don't mind tellin' you, this beats the smell of horse apples, any day of the week." Her eyes disappeared in the dried-fruit crinkle of her grin.

"I'd always hoped we'd clear the high bar set by horseshit."

Laney burst into cackling laughter, and Viv returned to the shop, shaking her head.

Taivus was waiting beside the door, gray as morning smoke and just as quiet. He wordlessly handed her a folded scrap of parchment.

Viv thanked him, and he nodded, then ghosted down the street.

She unfolded and read it.

FREYDAY, AT DUSK

CORNER OF BRANCH & SETTLE

COME ALONE

UNARMED

Her meeting with the Madrigal was set.

—◀+▶—

"I don't like that you're going alone," said Tandri.

"It's not really up for negotiation." Viv set the crossbar across the big doors and moved to douse the wall lanterns.

"I could watch from a distance."

"Even if they didn't notice you—which they would—it wouldn't do any good. The Madrigal isn't at this address. Likely they'll cover my eyes, and we'll walk far from there. If you followed, they'd *definitely* notice."

"Aren't you worried?"

Viv shrugged. "Not much point."

"That's exasperating."

"I learned to stay loose and level a long time ago. Things always turn out better that way, usually for everybody."

The shop was fully shut, and they stood outside as Viv locked the door. The sun was coming down slow but sure, and the light burned red.

"Go home," said Viv gently. "I'll tell you everything tomorrow."

"If you're not here in the morning, then what should I do?" asked Tandri grimly.

"I'll be here. But if I'm wrong . . ." Viv handed her the spare key to the front door, and after a second's thought, she unstrung the one around her neck. "And this one's for the strongbox."

Tandri turned them over in her hands. "This isn't exactly reassuring."

Viv grasped her shoulder and could feel the tension there. "It'll be fine. I've been in worse scrapes, and have the scars to prove it. And I don't expect to have any new ones tomorrow."

"Promise me that?"

"Can't promise, but if I'm wrong, I guess you can clear out the cashbox."

Tandri gave her a thin smile. "I expect the door to be unlocked tomorrow when I get here."

◄═╉═►

Viv didn't have to wait long on the corner of Branch & Settle, far south of the shop. She could see why they'd chosen it. The intersecting streets were intermittently lit, and the corner itself was overlooked by a big, splintered heap of a warehouse.

A familiar face emerged from a darker scrap of shadow, and doffed his hat.

"We're well on our way to becoming fast friends, it seems. It won't be long 'til you find yourself using my name."

"I guess you can put in a friendly word for me, then," said Viv. She looked around but didn't see anyone else. She knew they were there, though. "How's this going to work?"

"Follow me," said Lack. He gestured at a small doorway into the warehouse.

She did, and once they stepped inside, he produced a hood.

"A blindfold won't do?"

Lack shrugged. "You'll breathe just fine."

She sighed and tugged it on. Only a little of the warehouse's dim light filtered through the weave. Lack's hand found her elbow, and she didn't flinch at his touch.

He steered her through the building, and then she heard a metallic shriek. Viv felt the boards under her feet jump as he flipped open a pair of doors in the floor with two dusty bangs. He led her down a set of creaking stairs, touching the top of her head to warn her of the frame so she didn't crack her skull as she descended.

She smelled earth, at first, and then the growing scent of the river. They passed through pockets of coolness and cross-breezes, and they turned several times. Sometimes, the floor was stone and gravel, and other times dirt or wood.

Eventually, they ascended another set of stairs, rising into the smell of wood oil and cleaner and fabrics and something more floral that Viv couldn't quite place.

"All right," said Lack.

Viv removed the hood from her head and took in what was before her. "Well, I guess I wasn't expecting that."

The room was cozy. A pair of huge stuffed armchairs sat before a small, tidily bricked fireplace with an ornate folding screen, the low twinkle of flames showing behind. Polished tables flanked the chairs, one holding a tea service heavily illustrated with twining plants. A large, gilt-framed mirror hung above the fireplace, and red velvet drapes bordered big, paneled windows. Enormous bookshelves towered against the walls, positively crammed with thick volumes. Crocheted doilies covered a long, low table, and a luxurious carpet was soft underfoot.

A tall, elderly woman sat ensconced in one of the armchairs, her silver hair in a severe bun, her face regal but not unkind. She was crocheting a fresh doily and took her time completing a round before absently looking at Viv.

To Viv, it was blindingly clear from her bearing, and from the deference Lack showed, that this was, indeed, the Madrigal.

"Why don't you take a seat, Viv," said the woman. Her voice was dry and strong.

Viv did.

Before she could speak, the Madrigal continued.

"Of course, I know a great deal about you. That's at least half my business, knowing. And connecting. But I confess, I *was* surprised when Taivus reached out. Of course, he went by a different name when I knew him." She glanced up from her crocheting. "Did he mention how he knew *me?*"

Her expression was mild, but Viv sensed a great blackness beneath that question. "No, ma'am."

The Madrigal nodded, and Viv couldn't help but wonder what might have happened if she'd answered differently.

"Taivus's appeal might not have been enough for me to agree

to meet you," she said, "if it hadn't been for another mutual acquaintance."

"Another?" Viv was confused.

"Indeed." The movement of her crochet hook was hypnotic.

It only took another moment for Viv to catch on, and it should've taken less. "Fennus?"

"He *did* provide me with some interesting information. And as I said, knowing is my business."

"So he had a tale to tell. Something about a scrap of an old song, maybe, and a new visitor to the city?"

"All of which is why you're here, not because of some monthly dues." She fluttered a hand as though they were of no consequence. The woman's mouth pinched. "Also, I'll be frank. Despite what you might think, given the circumstances, I don't have much use for *assholes*."

Viv couldn't stop herself from snorting. "You agreed to meet me out of *spite*."

She thought she caught a twinkle in the Madrigal's eye. "Let me be straightforward. At my advanced age, I've found that the fast cut bleeds less."

That wasn't exactly Viv's experience, but she understood the sentiment. If this woman wanted directness, she'd oblige. "What do you want to know?"

"You have a Scalvert's Stone?"

"I do."

"Somewhere on the premises, I imagine?"

"Yes."

The woman nodded appreciatively. "I've read a few of the verses and myths. Fennus supplied some, as you've guessed. But my own resources are extensive."

"You could *take* it from me." Viv had a twist of nausea but also a wild feeling of boldness. Almost like the old days.

"I could," agreed the Madrigal. She looked sharply at Viv. "Would it do me any good?"

Viv thought about that for a moment. "Hard to say. Based on what I know, location matters. And I'm not entirely sure it works."

"My dear, there was a derelict livery at that address, ruined by an impotent moron with a drinking problem, and in a few months you—a woman who deals mostly in blood—have rebuilt it into a successful business that is gathering attention across Thune. Let's not be coy."

"I guess I've seen enough coincidences that I find it easy to doubt. But you're probably right."

"I'm rarely wrong. It's been known to happen, but I don't like to let on."

"So. Are you planning to take it from me?"

The Madrigal put her crocheting in her lap and stared hard at Viv. "No."

"Can I ask why not?"

"Because the information available is open to interpretation. I'm not convinced I'd benefit."

Viv frowned thoughtfully.

The Madrigal continued, "Now, about those monthly dues."

Viv took a deep breath. "Begging your pardon, ma'am. But I'd rather not pay."

The Madrigal resumed her crocheting. "You know, you and I aren't so different." A side of her mouth quirked up. "Well, you're certainly taller," she said drily. "But we've both journeyed between extremes of expectation. I've simply traveled in the opposite direction. I feel a certain kinship with that sort of ambition."

Viv remained respectfully silent until the Madrigal continued. "There are precedents to maintain, however. Now, I have a proposal for you."

"I'm listening."

After the Madrigal made her offer, Viv smiled, agreed, and reached out to shake her hand.

19

"A *Scalvert's* Stone?" asked Tandri, returning Viv's keys.

They sat across from one another at the big table the following morning, long before Thimble was due. Tandri had unlocked the door and slipped inside in the wee hours, not that Viv had been asleep. As promised, she was recounting the meeting, and she omitted nothing. "Ever heard of them?"

"I haven't. I mean, I suppose I know what a scalvert is. Mostly from children's stories."

"They're large and ugly and mean. Lots of eyes. More teeth than you'd like. Hard to kill. And the queen of a hive grows a stone, here." Viv tapped her forehead.

"And it's worth something?"

"Not to most people. But I came across some legends. Heard it in a *song* first, if you can believe it."

Viv fished the scrap of parchment from her pocket and slid it across to Tandri, who unfolded it and read.

Her eyebrows rose. "The ley lines. No wonder you twitched every time Hemington mentioned them."

"You noticed that, huh?"

"Draws the ring of fortune, aspect of heart's desire . . ." Tandri looked up at her. "So it's, what, a good luck charm?"

"A handful of long-dead people thought so. I'm not sure that's *exactly* what they meant, but the idea comes up again and again. There's a lot of old mythology around the Stones, but you don't hear about them much these days. Probably because there aren't a lot of Scalvert Queens around and even fewer people willing to kill one."

"Well, you've certainly piqued my interest. Where does one hide a maybe-magical luck stone?"

Viv rose from the bench, motioned for Tandri to do likewise, and slid the big table aside a few feet. She squatted, dug sand from around the flagstone, and pried it up and out with the ends of her fingers.

She carefully scooped aside earth, revealing the Stone, which glistened as though wet.

"Been here since the first day," said Viv.

Tandri squatted to examine the Stone. "I have to say, my mental image was a little more spectacular. And you think it's responsible for *all* this?" She gestured at the surrounding building.

Viv thought it might be responsible for a lot more than the *building* but didn't elaborate.

"I've had my doubts, but the Madrigal sure seems to think so."

"But, she let you leave. Why hasn't she already *taken* it?" Tandri's expression was dubious. "In fact, why aren't her men here *right now* tearing this place apart?"

Viv carefully set the flagstone back in place and brushed sand in around it. "I'll get to that." She slid the table back into place, and they both sat again. "You remember Fennus?"

"Difficult to forget. And . . ." She glanced at the scrap of verse on the table, brow furrowing as she thought back. "It's obvious now that he knew you had it."

"Yep. And it sounds like he made sure the Madrigal knew, too."

"Why, though? Pure maliciousness? You left on terms that bad?"

Viv sighed. "My guess is that I made a stupid mistake, telling him it was all I wanted from our last job, which I had a hand in finding in the first place. He was probably suspicious afterward and did a little digging of his own. He must have figured I was trying to cut them out of something big. Or more importantly, cut *him* out."

"If *he* wants the Stone, I don't understand why he'd tip off another interested party."

"Why confront *me* over it, if he could leave that to someone I'm already striking sparks from? Just like him, honestly, to stand back and let someone else bleed. Maybe I'd panic, and he'd catch me moving it, saving him the search. Failing that, it's always a good idea to let your enemies soften each other up first. Wait until the dust settles, and poke through the ashes. Could be he gets what he wants without a hair out of place."

"All right, but that doesn't explain why the Madrigal hasn't taken it."

Viv chuckled ruefully. "Well, I can't be positive it's the *only* reason, but it sounds like he just rubbed her the wrong way."

"That's it?"

"I mean, he is an enormous dick."

"I don't get the impression he's going to give up that easily, is he?"

Viv frowned. "Definitely not. In fact, he's probably much more dangerous now." She glanced at the door and couldn't help imagining Fennus with his ear pressed to the keyhole. "I'll take care of it, though."

There was a long silence while Tandri tapped her lower lip, her tail making lazy loops. At length, she said, "Setting that aside. What about the protection money? What about the Madrigal's little enforcer squad?"

Viv spread her hands. "We came to an arrangement. Her idea."

"An arrangement?"

"Well, there *is* going to be a payment, of sorts. Weekly, in fact."

Tandri's brow wrinkled in consternation.

"I guess she likes Thimble's cinnamon rolls."

———+———

When Thimble arrived at his usual time, he was laboring under the burden of a wooden box about two feet long and one foot wide. Viv took it off his hands, and he directed her with a paw to the pantry, where she set it down and removed the lid. Inside, packed in straw, was . . .

"Ice?" she asked.

The rattkin gestured at the cold-pit, where they kept the cream and several baskets of eggs. "*Colder. Keeps longer.*"

"Where did you get it, though?"

"Must be from the gnomish gasworks?" said Tandri.

Thimble nodded enthusiastically.

"I don't know what that is?"

"It's a big building on the river, steam-and water-powered.

I'm not clear on the mechanics, but somehow they can produce ice."

"Huh." Viv glanced over at the coffee machine. "Guess I'm not surprised. How much did this cost you, Thimble?"

He shrugged.

"Well, from now on, we'll pay for it. You hear?"

He nodded agreeably and began transferring the chunks of now-melting ice into the cold-pit.

She glanced across the room. "Actually . . . this gives me an idea."

——◆——

Viv slid into the booth across from Hemington, who looked up distractedly from his research. She pushed a mug over to him.

He blanched and then quickly mustered a smile. "Why, thank you. But as I've said, I don't really like—"

"Yes, I know. Hot drinks." She nudged it closer.

He pulled it the rest of the way, and his eyebrows shot up as he examined the contents. "Cold?" A few small chunks of ice bobbed in the coffee, and sweat pearled on the mug. He took a tentative sip, licked his lips, and gave the drink a considering look. "You know, that's not bad."

"Great," said Viv, lacing her fingers together and leaning forward on the table. "I have a little favor to ask of you."

His gaze immediately became suspicious. He made to slide the drink back, but then had another quick sip. "A favor?"

"Actually, it might help *you*. You've already set up your ward here, right?"

"I have. But I assure you, it's—"

She waved a hand at him. "I'm sure it's fine. Haven't noticed. What I want to know is, can you set *another* one?"

"Another?"

"Yes. For a person. A *specific* person."

Hemington pursed his lips. "Well, certainly. You understand, I'd need some very *precise* information and materials to manage that, but, yes, that's something I could do. You have someone in mind?"

"I do," said Viv.

By the time they'd finished talking, Hemington had drained his mug and was crunching the ice between his teeth.

———◆———

Viv joined Tandri behind the machine. "So. I'm pretty sure we have a new drink to add to the menu. But we're going to need regular deliveries of ice, I think."

Tandri smiled at her. "Still room on the board."

Then her smile fell away.

Viv glanced at the door, and there stood Kellin, again wearing an expression that begged to meet a fist.

He eased up to the counter and leaned on it in a familiar way that made Viv's skin itch. "Hello, Tandri."

Tandri didn't respond, and Viv waited, unsure whether the woman wanted her to intervene or not.

Kellin didn't seem to notice—or didn't care about—Tandri's icy glare and continued, circling one finger on the counter top. "It's so nice to be able to see you whenever I want. I'd really like for us to see *more* of each other, and I think that now—"

"Please, leave," Tandri said tightly.

He looked annoyed at being interrupted. "You know, there's no call to be rude. I'm just making a friendly gesture. If you're free this evening, then I could—"

"She *asked* you to leave," said Viv. "Now, I'm *telling* you to."

The kid glared at her with undisguised loathing. "You can't tell me a shitting thing," he spat. "Just try to lay a hand on me, and the Madrigal—"

"Oh, didn't you know?" Viv interrupted him. "The Madrigal and I had a little meeting. *She* and I came to a bit of an under-standing. Did nobody tell you?"

Kellin laughed, but he couldn't help sounding—and look-ing—a bit unsure, especially at her special emphasis on the word *she*.

"Right," continued Viv, "and one thing I remember partic-ularly well from our little chat was how much she hated *ass-holes*. You know, some people might consider *any* of her crew to be assholes, just because of the nature of the business. But *I* don't think that way." She gestured at Blackblood on the wall. "I've got respect for people who have to get their hands dirty to get things done. That's just *work*. No, it takes something special to be a real asshole, and I think she and I are of the same mind."

She held his gaze, then crossed her arms.

"*You* aren't an asshole, are you, Kellin? I think she'd be pretty disappointed if that was the case."

He opened and closed his mouth several times, tried to gather his dignity, and then turned and strode stiffly out of the shop.

Viv didn't say anything to Tandri, and went right back to her work, but out of the corner of her eye, she caught the barest curve of a smile on the woman's lips.

◄━✦━►

At closing, they took down the menu again, and Tandri revised it.

ᵔ LEGENDS & LATTES ᵔ
~ MENU ~

Coffee ~ exotic aroma & rich, full-bodied roast—½ bit
Latte ~ a sophisticated and creamy variation—1 bit
Any drink ICED ~ a refined twist—add ½ bit
Cinnamon Roll ~ heavenly frosted cinnamon pastry—4 bits
Thimblets ~ crunchy nut & fruit delicacies—2 bits

❖

FINER TASTES FOR THE
~ WORKING GENT & LADY ~

As Viv watched Tandri chalk in some snowflakes with a flourish, she felt that old crawling sensation on her back and couldn't help but glance over her shoulder. She half-expected to find Fennus's humorless smile at the window.

An old saying came to her unbidden:

The poisoned cup foretells the poisoned blade.

20

As Viv returned from a lunchtime break, thumbing through a chapbook she'd bought, she paused near the table out front. She glanced at the one-sided chess game in progress, then at the little old gnome studying it. "This seat taken?" she asked.

"Not at all!" He smiled at her and gestured toward the chair.

Viv slid it out and sat, placing her book on the table. She offered her hand over the top of the board, mindful not to upset the pieces. "Viv," she said.

"Durias," replied the old man, shaking her forefinger with his tiny, knobbly hand. He carefully sipped the drink before him. "I must say, I *do* enjoy your wonderful establishment. Real gnomish coffee? Never thought I'd taste it again. In my day, you couldn't get it so easily, even in the bigger cities like Radius or Fathom. And to find it here? Well. A rare pleasure."

"That's good to hear," said Viv. "Glad it passes muster."

"Oh, indeed. And these pastries?" He waved one of Thimble's confections. "An inspired pairing."

"Can't take any credit for that, but I'll pass it on."

Durias crunched into the Thimblet and closed his eyes in appreciation.

"So," said Viv, shifting in her seat. "You don't have to answer, but my friend in there is going crazy over your chess game." She pointed at Tandri, who was looking at her suspiciously from behind the counter.

"Really?"

"She swears you never move the other pieces. She's been trying to catch you doing it and says she never has."

"Oh, I definitely move them." The gnome nodded.

"You *do?*"

"Certainly. But I did it a long time ago," he said, as if that made any sense at all.

"I'm sorry?"

"You know," said Durias, without clarifying in any way whatsoever, "I used to be an adventurer like you. I'm *also* a retiree, now."

"I, uh . . ."

"You've found a very peaceful place here. A special place. You've planted something, and now it's blossoming. Very nice. A good spot to rest. My thanks to you for letting an old-timer shade under the branches of what you've grown."

Viv's mouth hung open. She hadn't a clue how to respond to that.

The moment passed as Durias cried, "Ah, *there* you are!"

Amity stalked around the corner and deigned to allow the gnome to scratch behind her enormous ears. She stared balefully at Viv, then curled around the base of the table. The gnome rested his feet on her back, where they were lost in tangles of sooty fur. "What a marvelous animal," he said, with real admiration.

"Certainly is," murmured Viv. "Uh, well, I didn't mean to interrupt your game. I'll let you get back to it."

"Not at all!" said Durias. "You go tend to what you're growing."

When she returned to the counter with her book, Tandri eyed it approvingly, then whispered, "So . . . what's going on with the chess game? Did he say?"

"He did say. But I'm not sure he answered," Viv replied.

———+———

Around noon, Thimble scampered off after making a series of gestures that neither Viv nor Tandri could interpret. He obviously had some errand in mind, and Viv waved him on his way.

He returned later with a small parcel bound in twine, and when there was a lull at the front, he placed it on the counter, delicately untying it. He folded away the paper to reveal several rough, dark slabs and chunks of something brown that gleamed with a soft waxiness.

"What's that, Thimble?" asked Tandri.

The baker broke off a sliver, popping it into his mouth and gesturing for them to do the same.

Viv and Tandri each snapped off a small piece. Viv sniffed hers. The earthy smell was slightly sweet—almost coffee-like. She put the fragment on her tongue, and when she closed her lips, it melted, spreading throughout her mouth. She tasted dark bitterness, but with subtler flavors of vanilla, citrus, and in the far back, a hint of something that reminded her of wine. It was bold, both creamy and harsh, but alluring.

Honestly, Viv doubted you could eat very much of it. That bitterness would overwhelm you. But the old spice-seller was right. The kid *was* a genius, and she couldn't wait to see what he had planned.

Tandri thoughtfully rolled the taste around in her mouth. "Okay, I'll ask again, because I have to know. What *is* this?"

He leaned forward, whiskers aquiver. *"Chocolate."*

"You've got something in mind?" asked Viv.

He nodded and produced another of his lists. Shorter than before, but with a few requested pots and pans.

Viv squatted to stare him in the eyes. "Thimble, anytime you have any big ideas, you can assume I'm on board, all right?"

His velvety face wrinkled in a pleased expression that squeezed his eyes nearly shut.

——+——

It didn't take long for Viv to gather Thimble's requested items. When she returned to the shop, she drew up short on the threshold, a sack over one arm.

Kellin was back, standing stiffly before the counter.

Viv's expression hardened, and she prepared to drop the sack, pick him up by the back of the neck, and haul him bodily into the street.

Tandri caught her eye, though, and gave a small shake of her head.

The succubus passed a folded waxed paper sack across to the young man, who moved as though to snatch it, but mastered himself, reaching for it gently.

"For the Madrigal," said Tandri.

Kellin nodded jerkily, like a marionette, and said in a strangled voice, "Thank you, Ta—*miss.*"

He turned with the sack in hand, startling when he saw Viv. Recovering quickly, he rushed out the door.

"Huh," said Viv, watching him go. "I'll be twice-damned."

——+——

As they prepared to lock up, Tandri went into the pantry and returned with a linen-covered handbasket that Viv hadn't noticed before.

"What's that?"

Tandri opened her mouth to speak, then fidgeted the basket to her other arm, and finally said, "What . . . do you have planned for the evening?"

"Planned? Nothing. I'm usually bushed and turn in early. A bite to eat first, maybe."

"Oh, good. Er. I mean . . . I thought that, given how things went, we should . . . celebrate? If you'd like."

Viv wasn't sure she'd ever seen Tandri properly nervous before. She had to admit, it was charming.

"Celebrate? I guess I hadn't thought about it. Sure, the Madrigal isn't a big worry, now, but I don't think it'll take Fennus long to figure out a different angle to—" She saw Tandri's expression grow pained and caught herself, suddenly feeling very stupid. "Um. I mean, yes. A celebration sounds good. What did you have in mind?"

"Nothing fancy," said Tandri. "There's a little park above the river, west of Ackers. Sometimes, I go there in the evenings. Used to, I mean. The view is nice, and I, um, I packed some things. So. A sort of picnic. Ugh, that sounds childish." She winced. "And not like a celebration, at all."

"It sounds wonderful," said Viv.

Tandri recovered some of the pieces of a smile.

—◆—

It *was* a nice view. The spot wasn't so much a park as a groomed area featuring a statue of some long-robed Ackers alumnus, whose countenance was undoubtedly more imposing in stone than it ever was in life. Cherry trees and hedges ringed him, and he presided over a little rise above the river. The vantage provided a lovely sunset panorama of the university's copper steeples. Little twirls of smoke dotted the rooftops, like freshly extinguished candles.

They sat on the grass, and Tandri unpacked some bread and cheese, a small crock of preserves, some hard sausage, and a bottle of brandy.

"I forgot glasses," she said.

"I don't mind if you don't," replied Viv.

"It's really . . . not much."

Viv opened the brandy, took a swig, and passed the bottle to Tandri. "Feels like a celebration to me."

Tandri took a solid glug, as well, while Viv sliced the sausage and slathered some preserves on the bread.

They ate and drank and talked about nothing much as some birds came to roost in the cherry trees. The sun drew down, and the chill of the river crept up in a slow, shivering wave.

They shared an easy silence in the waning light, and then Viv asked, "Why'd you leave the university?"

Tandri looked at her. "Not, 'why did you go in the first place?'"

Viv shrugged, "I wasn't surprised by that, at all."

The other woman looked back out over the university steeples and thought for a while.

Viv guessed she wouldn't answer and regretted asking.

"I wasn't born here. I *fled* here."

Viv almost said something, but waited.

"Nobody was chasing me, if that's what you're wondering. I was fleeing . . . the trap of what I am. This," Tandri touched the tip of one of her horns, and her tail lashed. "I thought, a university? That's a place where ideas are challenged. Where what you do matters, not where you came from, or *what* you came from. A place where logic and math and science would prove that I'm more than what I was born to. But it seems I take that with me wherever I go."

"You attended, though."

Tandri nodded grimly. "I did. I scrimped together the tuition, and I was granted admission. Nobody stopped me. They took my money, absolutely. There are no bylaws keeping someone like me out."

"But?"

"But . . . it didn't matter, not really. What's the saying? They followed the letter of the law, but not the spirit?" She sighed. "The spirit was unenlightened."

Viv thought about Kellin and nodded.

"So, I fled. Again."

They allowed the silence to resume, and Viv passed Tandri the brandy.

She drank more deeply, and when she wiped her mouth, she looked over at Viv. "No pearls of wisdom?"

"Nope."

Tandri's eyebrows rose.

"But I *will* say . . ." Viv glanced over to regard Tandri solemnly. "Fuck those *motherfuckers*."

Tandri's surprised laugh startled the birds from the cherry trees.

◄─╂─►

Viv carried the basket while walking Tandri home again, this time all the way to her room. Neither was unsteady—they hadn't finished the brandy—but they were both pleasantly warm and liquid.

Tandri opened the door at the top of the stairs, and after a moment's hesitation, ushered Viv inside.

Viv stooped to keep from banging her head on the low ceiling. The tiny, single-room apartment featured a tidy cot, some shelves bursting with books, a tasseled carpet, and a small vanity.

"Stayed here when I went to Ackers," said Tandri, waving a hand at the room. She took the basket from Viv and set it on the vanity. "I just . . . never bothered to move."

She looked up at Viv, who could feel the warm glow that sometimes peeked out when Tandri was at her least cautious. But she didn't think it was responsible for the prickling warmth that burned deeper inside herself. The brandy, surely, was the culprit.

"Viv," began Tandri, but her gaze dropped and she lost what she was going to say. Viv didn't let her find it again.

"Good night, Tandri." She was very conscious of the size and roughness of her hand as she reached out and squeezed Tandri's shoulder. "And thank you. I hope I never make you flee."

And then, before her friend could say anything else, Viv left, quietly closing the door behind her.

21

Viv and Tandri moved through the morning routine, easing around one another with low murmurs, careful not to touch, each exquisitely aware of the space the other occupied. Viv acted with unthinking economy—brewing, serving, greeting, and registering very little.

Neither of them noticed Thimble's industry with his new cookware and ingredients until the smell of melting chocolate permeated the shop.

At a tug on Viv's shirt, she looked down to see their baker anxiously clasping his flour-caked hands together. "Oh. Hey, Thimble."

On the back table, golden crescents cooled in neat rows atop several racks. Thimble selected one and offered it to her. She took it with a nod. Flaky and yellow, the pastry's buttery layers folded over in gentle curves. The smell was gorgeous.

She took a bite that almost melted in her mouth, at once rich with butter and impossibly light. Comparing these to a loaf of bread was like comparing silk to burlap.

"This . . . is incredible," she managed. It was so good, in fact, that she only hesitantly followed up with, "But, this can't have the . . . what was it?"

"Mmm. Chocolate," supplied Tandri, as she pinched off another corner and popped it into her mouth. She made a small sound in her throat and closed her eyes as she chewed.

Thimble made a get-on-with-it gesture with his hands, his impatience evident. Viv shrugged, took another, bigger bite, and found the molten core of chocolate inside. The taste was *nothing* like what she'd sampled yesterday—sweeter, deeper, richer. Creamy and decadent, with a subtle spice.

"*Eight hells*, Thimble!" she managed. Her mouth sang with the flavor of it. "How do you keep *doing* this?" She stared at the pastry in surprise, and then immediately had another bite.

Viv glanced over to find Tandri transfixed, chocolate smearing her lips, eyes huge and luminous.

"Thimble. You might not know this, but I, that is, *we*"—Tandri's tail swept in a head-to-toe gesture—"we respond *strongly* to all kinds of sensations. Including taste. And, well."

Viv experienced that warm pulse again, and Thimble must have, too, because he blinked and shivered.

"Whatever this is . . . it's just about incapacitating." The succubus sighed appreciatively.

"You were right before, Thimble," said Viv. "We have *got* to get you a bigger kitchen."

Tandri considered the available space. "Two stoves? Push out the wall?"

"I'll ask Cal." Viv glanced back at their chef. "In the meantime, what do you call these?" She polished hers off, licking her fingers for every last tender flake and chocolaty smear.

The rattkin shrugged and took one himself, testing it with a squeeze and nibbling one end.

"Leave it to me," said Tandri, around another huge bite.

⟨LEGENDS & ⟨LATTES⟩
~ MENU ~

Coffee ~ exotic aroma & rich, full-bodied roast—½ bit
Latte ~ a sophisticated and creamy variation—1 bit
Any drink ICED ~ a refined twist—add ½ bit
Cinnamon Roll ~ heavenly frosted cinnamon pastry—4 bits
Thimblets ~ crunchy nut & fruit delicacies—2 bits
Midnight Crescents ~ buttery foldover with a sinful center—4 bits

❖

FINER TASTES FOR THE
~ WORKING GENT & LADY ~

—◆—

The quiet tension between her and Tandri had evaporated, and Viv almost thought she'd imagined their hazy morning dance. Thimble's crescents predictably sold out within the hour, and he was already at work on a new batch.

Viv preoccupied herself with the restrictions of their small kitchen. What might Cal suggest, once she had the chance to ask for his thoughts? She kept glancing at the auto-circulator above and thinking that the answer might be nothing she expected.

"The usual, Hem?" she asked, when he stepped up to the counter.

Hemington leaned closer. "I *do* wish you wouldn't call me that," he said in an undertone.

She smiled, her eyes on her work. "Mmm. Is that a yes, then?"

"What I *wanted* to say is that the ward is nearly set. And yes, an iced coffee, please."

"Oh, it is? On the house, then."

"It should cover the premises and a few additional feet in a rough circle."

"How will I know if it's . . . gone off?"

"That's the last detail." He held his left hand out on the counter. "I'll need yours, please?"

Viv didn't hesitate, and placed her much larger one down, mirroring him. He tapped with the first two fingers of his right hand on his left, and made several curling gestures and complex twists. A blue light flared. Before the glow faded, he touched palm to palm with Viv and there was a brief fizzing, like beer bubbles against one's lip.

"That's it?" she asked, as he broke contact.

"That's it. If the ward is triggered, you'll feel a sort of gentle tug in that hand. It should be enough to wake you."

"A gentle tug, huh?"

"Now, bear in mind, the ward only functions once. I'd have to reset it if it were triggered, but . . . well, there it is."

"Once should be enough." She slid his drink across to him. "Thanks, Hem."

He opened his mouth to object but shook his head instead. "You're welcome, Viv." He nodded and took his drink back to his table.

"What was that about?" asked Tandri.

"Just a little insurance."

—◆—

The following afternoon, Pendry reappeared in the shop, this time with his original, bizarre lute. Viv nodded encouragingly, glad to see him.

"So. Um," he said. "I'll *stop* if you don't like it. Or if . . . if anyone complains." He sucked his breath through his teeth as though bracing for a blow.

"It'll be fine, kid. Here, start with one of these." She handed him a Midnight Crescent, and he took it with a confused look. Pointing to his instrument, Viv said, "Also, I have to ask. What exactly *is* that?"

"Oh. This? Well, um, it's . . . it's a thaumic lute? It's . . . well, they're sort of . . . new." He pointed at the gray slab with silver pins beneath the strings. "See, the auric pickup sort of gathers in the sound as it . . . uh . . . well, when the strings vibrate, there's an . . . um . . . Actually, I don't know how it works," he finished lamely.

"'S alright," said Viv, and waved him in. "Knock 'em dead. Figuratively, please."

Blinking, he wandered into the dining area while taking a tentative bite of the pastry, and Viv smiled.

No sound arose for several minutes, and she figured he was finishing his food. Then she forgot about him as a line of customers formed in front of the counter.

When he finally began to play, she glanced up in surprise.

The lute wailed that same ragged, buzzing tone, but the music he played was more delicate than before—subtly picked with the slow lope of a ballad. An additional *presence* underpinned, as though the notes reverberated in a larger space, with a thicker, warmer feeling. Also, she could swear the result was quieter than his first, aborted attempt.

Viv didn't know much about music, but now that she'd grown used to the kid's occasional visits, the leap to this confident, modern sound didn't seem so far anymore. He'd been bridging the gap this whole time, and taken the obvious next step. Pendry's altogether unexpected style was . . . *right*. Especially here.

She and Tandri exchanged bemused smiles. Viv noticed that Tandri's tail was subtly, metronomically swaying behind her.

Viv figured that was endorsement enough.

—◆—

As the week wore on, Viv lived in constant anticipation of phantom tugs at her right palm. Hemington had explained that it would be gentle, but she imagined it as a fishhook embedded in her flesh that would yank sharply, jerking at her hand.

Nothing happened, though.

Her skin tingled as she envisioned it, but eventually the feeling of wary expectation faded.

—◆—

Laney dropped by with increasing frequency, making *many* offers to trade recipes with their baker. Viv always deferred to Thimble. The little old woman's exasperation with his gestures and anxious blinking left Viv both amused and a smidge guilty for foisting her off on him. She also thought his hand signals were at their most cryptic *only* when confronted with Laney.

The old woman always bought something, though.

—◆—

The dire-cat appeared with more regularity. Viv sometimes felt the prickle of Amity's regard and turned to find her perched in the loft like a sooty gargoyle, surveying the diners with disdain.

Tandri tried using treats to tempt the animal into claiming the bed they'd made for her, but Amity only ate them, made very deliberate eye contact, and then sauntered away with her tail high.

Viv discovered she didn't mind having a watchful monstros-
ity around. Not one bit.

———+———

Viv and Tandri settled back into a comfortable equilibrium.
There were no further picnics or walks home. Viv harbored a
wistful ache that she didn't examine too closely, and an almost
cowardly relief that Tandri didn't mention their evening at the
park.

They stayed busy, and the days brimmed with good smells
and unexpected music and companionable work. Her hopes for
the shop had been exceeded in every regard.

That was enough . . . wasn't it?

———+———

Tandri startled Viv by dropping some of her art materials on
the table, including a bottle of ink, a slim brush, and one of the
mugs.

"I have an idea," she said.

Viv looked up from wiping down the machine. "I'm listening."

"So, I think about this a lot. My first drink—I have it while
I work. I take a sip when I want, and I make my cup stretch
through the morning. I love that."

Viv nodded. "Yeah, sure. I do the same."

"Your customers . . . They don't have that."

"*Our* customers," said Viv, but nodded again. "Okay. I'm with
you."

"Well, what if they could take it with them?"

"I've wished for that before, but . . ." She shrugged. "Never
figured out a way to do it. So if you *have* . . ."

"We sell them a mug. And . . ." She turned the cup. In Tandri's flowing script, she'd written *Viv*. "We add their name. They can leave it here behind the counter if they like, but they own the mug. They can be on their way with a drink in hand, whenever they want. All they have to do is bring it back."

"I think that's perfect." Viv rubbed her neck. "Honestly, I feel like a bit of a fool for not thinking of it myself."

"You probably would have, eventually." There was that warm pulse again, increasingly recognizable.

Viv was suddenly awash in an old feeling of fraught potential. A critical instant that hinged on the movement of a blade, the placement of a foot, a moment of trust extended or withheld. Failure to act was as much a decision as any other.

"You know, Tandri, this place is . . . really becoming as much yours as mine. You're *making* it yours."

Tandri looked dismayed, "I'm sorry, I—"

Viv winced and scrambled to explain. "That's not what I mean! I mean, it wouldn't be what it is *without* you. I'm *glad* it's becoming yours. And I want to make sure you know that . . . that . . ." She fumbled her words and fell silent.

Into that confused pause, Tandri murmured, "You don't have to worry. I'm not going anywhere."

Viv suddenly found herself lost and alone on a dark road, abandoned by whatever guiding light had led her this far. "I . . . that's . . . good. But what I wanted to say was . . ."

Really, what did she want to say?

Had she grown so complacent that she'd trust the outcome of this conversation to some mythical *stone*? Wasn't Tandri more important than that? Didn't she demand Viv's truest words, offered unambiguously?

The darkness bristled with dangers, some perhaps even worth risking.

Tandri straightened and forced a quick smile. "So. I'll just add this to the board then, all right?"

"That's . . . yeah. We should definitely do that," Viv lamely replied.

Tandri backed away for them both, and Viv couldn't decide if she was relieved or disappointed.

22

Thimble squeaked for emphasis, pointing at a woodcut print in the gnomish catalog Viv had spread on the counter top. The rattkin stood on a stool to get a proper view.

The stove depicted in the advertisement was twice as wide as theirs, with dual extra-large ovens and fireboxes and a back panel with temperature-control gauges and knobs. Viv found it difficult to make out much detail from the woodcut, but the look was very modern, and the listed features set Thimble's eyes sparkling with longing.

"You're sure?" She raised her eyebrows at the price.

She'd come to Thune with a nice nest egg, but renovations, equipment costs, and specialty food orders had whittled it down. The beans she regularly ordered from Azimuth came dearly, too. A new stove would nearly wipe out her remaining funds, although she was pretty sure they'd recover it in a few months, given the popularity of Thimble's baked goods.

The rattkin nodded decisively, but at her expression, he hesitated, and then reluctantly indicated a less expensive model farther down the page.

"No, Thimble," she said, pointing at him. "The best deserve the best, and that's you. I'll have Cal make sure we can install it, and I'll put in an order."

Her gaze snapped up when she heard a familiar voice speaking to Tandri.

"Here for this week's delivery. And . . . let me see, one of the lattes, please, my dear." Lack stood opposite, humming as he stared at the menu board.

While Tandri brewed his drink, Viv retrieved the reserved sack of rolls from underneath the counter and, after a moment's thought, added two of Thimble's crescents, as well. She gave the man a slight nod as she passed the bag over. "Let me know what the Madrigal thinks of this week's tribute."

"I'll do so." Lack returned the nod, accepted his drink, and went quietly on his way.

—◆—

"Is . . . Will there be music today?"

The girl was young and looked a little breathless and windblown.

"We're never sure," said Viv with a shrug. "Pendry comes and goes."

"Oh." The girl seemed disappointed, but covered it quickly.

"Anything I can get you?"

"Er, no, thank you. So . . . you don't know when he might be back?"

Viv thought she was trying—pretty unsuccessfully—to downplay her interest in the answer to that question. "Afraid not."

After the girl left, Tandri arched a brow. "That's the third one this week."

Viv gazed thoughtfully after Pendry's admirer. "You thinking what I'm thinking?"

"You pin him down. I'll make the sign."

——+——

The next time Pendry darkened the doorstep, Viv thought his bearing was a little more assured. He nodded cheerfully, comfortable enough to head to his impromptu stage without permission.

"Hey, Pendry," she said, catching him before he disappeared around the corner. "Got a second?"

"Uh . . . sure."

The old worry started to creep back into his expression, so Viv forged ahead. "You still don't have your hat out for coin, do you?"

"Well . . . no. I just . . . just like to play. It feels sort of like . . . begging? To ask? If my da ever heard tell of me—" He broke off, grimacing hugely.

"What if I paid you? More like a wage, maybe."

He looked surprised. "But . . . why would you? I . . . I . . . already . . ."

"Well, I'd need you to be a little more regular, of course."

"Regular?"

"Say, four times a week? Every other day. And at the same time, every time. Maybe five in the evening? Six bits a session. How's that sound?"

Pendry looked disbelieving. "Well, I'd . . . you'd really *pay* me? To play?"

"Yep. That's about the size of it." She extended a hand.

"Yes, ma'am," he said, pumping it vigorously with his own.

"Oh, and Pendry . . . ? You should still put your hat out."

By the end of the day, another sign hung outside the shop, painted in Tandri's flowing script.

~ Live Muƒic ~
Mornðay, Tauðay, Vintuƒ, Freyðay
Five in the Evening

———◆———

Viv started awake at a painful tearing sensation in her right palm, the skin splitting and peeling away. She was up in an instant, the bedroll thrown open, searching her hand for the wound that must be there.

Her flesh was smooth and undamaged.

The feeling persisted, though, lancing up her forearm. Viv's instincts had not yet entirely fled her, despite the months of inaction, and she lunged for Blackblood's accustomed resting spot beside her bedroll. Of course, it wasn't there, instead hanging uselessly on the kitchen wall, tangled in garlands.

Hemington's ward.

Fennus.

The elf *must* have heard her flinging the bedding aside, the creak of the boards. Mustn't he?

She crept to the ladder, anyway, hunched and shifting her weight carefully from bare foot to bare foot. The tugging, ripping feeling in her hand abated. She heard nothing from below. When she peered over the edge, a scant bar of moonlight blued the dining area.

The chandelier loomed almost in front of her face, and beneath she could see the softened silhouette of the big table, the dark slabs of the booths surrounding it, the sketchy strokes of the flagstones. Her night vision wasn't particularly good, but she held her breath, staring hard for any hint of motion.

A minute passed.

Another.

Then the ghost of a scent, something foreign under the pervasive aroma of coffee. A faint but recognizable perfume—floral and ancient.

He was cloaked and hooded, but it was him.

Not so much as the rustle of cloth betrayed his presence, but Fennus had always been impossibly stealthy, usually to the advantage of their party. Now on the receiving end, Viv marveled at his noiseless advance with a grim new respect.

She had to squint hard to track his motion, but she saw him pause at the end of the big table. The glimmer of one pale hand appeared, gently resting on its surface. The Scalvert's Stone lay hidden directly below. His head tilted inside his cowl, as though listening, or using some elven sense Viv didn't share.

There was no point in waiting.

She leapt, landing heavily.

There was no point in stealth, either.

"Hello, Fennus," she said.

He didn't even have the grace to appear startled. Turning smoothly toward her, he folded back his cowl, and a pale, yellow light burst into being in his cupped left hand. His face was illuminated from below, as infuriatingly mild as ever.

The elf nodded to her as though he were greeting her at his own doorstep. "Viv. I'm intrigued that you heard me," he said, in a tone that was anything but interested. There wasn't a shred of shame, either.

"Had a little help." She shrugged. "I don't suppose there's any point in asking why you're here?"

"Of course not. And I imagine the guilt has been preying on you."

"Guilt?" Viv asked incredulously. "What in the eight hells do you mean, *guilt?*"

The elf sighed, as though her obtuseness disappointed him. "You didn't deal fairly with us, Viv. I had my suspicions from the beginning, you know. You were so *evasive.*"

"It was a fair cut," said Viv levelly. "Especially for what amounted to rumor and chance. The scalvert's hoard was plenty to balance the scale."

"I don't agree," he replied silkily.

She found his patient, reasonable voice incredibly irritating.

Then his lips wrinkled in uncharacteristic annoyance. For the first time, his mask of cold indifference slipped. "You were hardly subtle. All that muscle, and not half the wit for guile. Was it taxing for you, the plotting and planning? *Clever Viv,* untangling a fabulous mystery! Why, you must have thought you were the first! How amusing. Then with the Stone in hand, off you scurried, as fast as you could, afraid you'd let something slip if you lingered too long. Or perhaps the shame sent you packing?"

"Shame?" Viv laughed. "You're full of shit, Fennus."

"Am I? Tell me then, do the others know?"

"That I made a fool's bet based on a few lines from a song? No. But not because I was *ashamed,* Fennus. *Embarrassed* is closer to the truth."

He gestured expansively at the building. "A fool's bet? It seems not."

Viv ground her teeth. "A deal's a deal, and I kept my end of the bargain. You really *need* it, Fennus? What do you think it'll do for you? Or are you defending a *principle* by creeping around in the night to take what's mine?"

"Mmm, a principle? Something like that," he murmured. His eyes flicked to her greatsword on the wall. "When you put that blade away, never believe you exchanged it for scruples."

"I figure I've talked enough. Do what you're going to do, and I guess we'll see what happens."

"Oh, Viv, it's a shame that—"

Fennus leapt suddenly, gracelessly backward as an enormous, sooty shadow lunged over the table, narrowly missing him with a swipe of fearsome claws. Amity landed with predatory grace and whirled on the elf with a hitching snarl.

"Gods-be-damned *thing*!" spat Fennus.

The dire-cat stalked toward him with slow, deliberate steps, her muzzle bunched up above impressive fangs. Viv hadn't even known the beast was in the building. How had she *missed* her?

Amity's growl throbbed louder, and then Fennus ghosted past with a nimbleness even the cat couldn't match. In an instant, he was out the door and had vanished into the night.

The dire-cat stared after him for a moment, then lazily blinked her enormous green eyes. She padded back to the pillow and blankets in the far corner, circled on them, kneaded them with her claws, and then settled back down to sleep again.

Viv cautiously knelt and stroked the big cat's fur. The vibration of her purr rattled all the way up to Viv's shoulder.

"When in the eight hells did you start actually sleeping here?" she wondered aloud. *And why didn't I see her before?*

Either way, Viv was going to make sure there was extra cream on hand. And maybe a nice joint of beef.

———◆———

Despite the sure knowledge that Fennus *couldn't* have disturbed the Stone—he plainly hadn't had time—Viv couldn't sleep without reassuring herself.

She checked up and down the street before shutting and relocking the front door. Pushing aside the table, she squatted and turned over the flagstone in order to stroke the Scalvert's Stone where it lay.

The shop, Tandri, Thimble, Cal . . . and now Amity. The way each week seemed to flower into the next, budding into the fulfillment of a heretofore unknown need? Up 'til this moment, speculation over whether her fortune was due to the Scalvert's Stone had been almost academic. Why probe a good thing too closely?

Now, the question seemed like it always should have been . . . what would happen if she *lost* the Stone? If it truly was the root of everything she had grown, then if it were cut away, would the plant wither and die, or could it continue on? And if so, for how long?

She thought about the last few months. And she especially thought about Tandri, and the spartan room upstairs.

Maybe her friend was right. Maybe the shop wasn't her life. Maybe she *should* be prepared to lose it.

Without it, though, what was she, really?

She could only arrive at one answer.

Alone.

23

"He was *here?*" asked Tandri. "In the middle of the *night?*"

They opened late. Tandri insisted. Viv said nothing at first, but the other woman quickly sensed that something was amiss—her innate talents at work—and demanded to know what was wrong.

"He came for the Stone, then. Did he get it?"

"He didn't."

The succubus waited for her to elaborate, and when she didn't, Tandri slapped a palm on the counter, hard. "What happened? *All* of it, this time, please."

So Viv told her in as much detail as she could remember.

"We should find a way to hire the cat, too," muttered Tandri, when she had finished.

"Leg of lamb in the cold-box, for when she shows up," said Viv with a faint smile. "She was gone this morning. No idea how she got out."

"So, this ward that Hemington set. It's spent now. You'll need to have him reset it."

"There's no point," said Viv. "Fennus won't try the same thing twice. It'll be something else. I don't know what, but I'll just have to be wary. I'm pretty good at that . . . at least, I *used* to be."

"How far will he go to get it?" asked Tandri, eyes narrowed.

"Honestly? I don't know. Further than this, though."

Tandri paced the room, tail whipping from side to side, drumming her fingers against her chin. "The Stone. If it *was* gone, what would happen?"

"I've been asking myself the same thing. I think we're at the point of assuming it works. Things have gone so *well*, and the Madrigal seemed pretty sure of it, too. It's not like I have any basis for comparison, but still."

"What's the most you could lose?"

Viv stared at Tandri and didn't voice her first thought.

Instead, she hedged. "I don't know. Maybe everything? Maybe nothing. Maybe I should stow it somewhere else, just to find out. Maybe I should throw it in the river and forget about it." She gave an exasperated sigh. "Or, maybe I should sleep next to my sword again."

"Stop it," Tandri said sharply. "Self-pity doesn't look good on you."

Viv grimaced. "Sorry."

Tandri stopped pacing and looked suddenly uncomfortable. "And I think it may be a *particularly* bad idea to get rid of it, anyway."

"What do you mean?"

The succubus hummed like she didn't want to answer, but then she relented. "Well . . . there's a concept in thaumistry. It's . . . it's called *Arcane Reciprocity*. It's why thaumistry is so controlled and why we don't use it in warfare, at least not to kill." She sighed. "Are you familiar with the idea that when we treat pain with medicine, we're really just delaying it? That when the treatment is done, you suddenly feel all that deferred suffering, like it was stored up for later?"

"I've heard that, but not sure I believe it. I've felt a *lot* of pain," said Viv with a wry smile.

"So," continued Tandri, "in thaumistry, it's sort of like that, only measurable. An effect caused by arcane power has a reciprocal effect that is . . . *expressed* when the power is removed. Everything has to balance out. Once the power stops, something *pushes back.* Advanced thaumistry is all about redirecting the blowback."

"Then, you think if the Stone is taken away, maybe there's some sort of . . . backlash. Like bad luck?"

"I don't know for sure," said Tandri. "Is the Stone even thaumistry? Do the same principles apply?" She winced. "It's just *maybe* a possibility. But if it's true, the real question you . . . *we* have to ask isn't how much there is to lose. It's how much more there is to take after that."

Viv stared at Tandri and clenched her jaw.

"More than I want to give up."

———◆———

Viv tried to think of some other place inside the building to store the Stone—one more secure—but eventually resigned herself to the fact that it really didn't matter. If Fennus had found it in the first place, a new hiding spot wouldn't be a secret for long. Since she'd surprised him once, he'd assume his intrusion would be detected, so she couldn't imagine him creeping in at night a second time. She needed to figure out how he'd come at her next.

Or through whom.

Waiting for a blow to fall was not something that Viv was

used to. She'd spent a lifetime ending threats before they man-
ifested, not bracing herself for a knife in the back. Constant
wariness wore at her, and she became increasingly snappish and
impatient.

The first week was the worst, and she apologized more than
once to Tandri and Thimble for being short with them. A
few times, Tandri gently moved her aside and took over at the
counter when Viv didn't realize she was glowering menacingly
at a customer. Viv was both embarrassed and grateful.

But inevitably, time dulled the edge of her anxiety, reducing
it to the occasional startle at an imagined sound in the night
and furtive glances toward the Stone's resting place throughout
the day.

At the same time, Pendry's scheduled performances became
something of a pleasant hassle. A regular audience began to
build for his appearances. Quite a few of the attendees didn't
actually buy anything, but Viv was fairly certain that some of
his fans were converting to actual customers.

To manage, they sorted out a way to add overflow seating.
Viv bought more tables that they stored in the alley, and on
performance days, they set them in the street and threw the big
doors wide.

The kid, for his part, was slumping less, smiling more, and his
bulk finally seemed to fit the space he occupied.

Once or twice, Laney made her way across the street to make
a few tart complaints about the noise, but since they were usually delivered around a mouthful of Thimble's baking, the sting
was somewhat lessened.

Amity even appeared during performances, weaving between
startled customers and settling beneath the big trestle table.

Regulars learned to be protective of their treats, since she casually swallowed any unattended pastries in her path. Her lashing tail was a menace to mugs.

Viv never once considered shooing her away.

———+———

Three weeks had come and gone since Fennus's nighttime intrusion, and while Viv couldn't pretend the threat had passed, she did relax back into her routine. Her mood improved, and she hadn't apologized for a waspish remark in a fortnight.

Cal took to dropping in more regularly, and Viv caught him in huddled conference with Tandri once or twice. He made a few loud and pointed observations about the quality of the locks, and Viv assured him she'd look into replacements.

When the Madrigal strode into the shop, Viv stood open-mouthed for a moment.

"Good evening," the woman said.

"Evening, um . . . ma'am," she managed. "Can I help you?" Viv had the good sense not to speak her name, at least, but *ma'am?* She cringed inwardly.

The Madrigal's dress was understatedly elegant, and she carried a handbag over one arm. Viv spotted at least one of her men, subtly shadowing her from the street. And if there was one, at least two more lurked out of sight.

The woman's eyes glittered with cold, curious regard.

Gods, what if I'd made an enemy *of her,* thought Viv. She could hardly believe she'd ever spoken so bluntly to her face.

"I've heard so much about this establishment," the Madrigal said. "At my age, I don't get out quite as much as I once did, but the opportunity presented itself, and I simply had to see."

"Well, we try to make sure we're good neighbors," said Viv, asking as subtly as she could manage if there'd been some misstep on her part.

"Indeed, I'm sure you are. Not everyone is so neighborly, though, I fear. And that element can sometimes be quite tenacious."

She pointedly held Viv's gaze, then crisply opened her handbag and reached within. "Ah, yes, and I'd like one of those crescent pastries, please, my dear."

Numbly Viv took the coins and handed over the foldover, wrapped in waxed paper. She lowered her voice. "Tenacious?"

The Madrigal sighed, as though it was all so disappointing. "It would be such a shame if anything untoward were to happen to such an excellent neighbor. A touch of vigilance over the next few days might be warranted. It's my fervent hope that these worries of mine are misplaced because"—she took a delicate nibble of the crescent roll—"these really are quite excellent. Good night, dear."

She nodded regally, turned, and left in a rustle of gray silk. Her man vanished from sight, as well.

Tandri eyed the woman's departure with suspicion, having caught the unspoken interplay. She shot a knowing glance at Viv, who subtly shook her head in answer. A sick feeling bubbled in her stomach.

—◆—

After closing, Tandri finally asked, "Was that her? The Madrigal?"

"Yeah."

"She gave you a message."

"Yeah. More of a warning. I don't know why she bothered to let me know, but Fennus is going to move soon."

"And what are we going to do about it?"

"Well, I could always kill him," said Viv.

Tandri just stared at her.

"Joking," muttered Viv.

Was she, though?

"The problem is, I actually stopped to consider it," Tandri confessed. "He is such an asshole."

"After that big speech you gave a month ago?"

"Yeah, well. Nobody's perfect."

Viv sighed. "Now, we're back to square one. Trying to guess what he'll do next."

"No, we're not. Because we know he wants the Stone enough to come here himself."

"We can't be certain he'll try the same thing again. In fact, I can almost guarantee he won't."

"Well," said Tandri. "One thing *is* certain."

"What's that?"

"You're not staying here alone."

———◆———

"I don't know why you're still arguing," said Tandri as she double-checked the locks.

Up to her elbows in soapy water, Viv scrubbed rather aggressively at a mug. "It just doesn't make any sense. What difference could it possibly make for you to be here?" she grumbled.

The light dimmed as Tandri began extinguishing lanterns. "You're right. With Hemington's ward gone, what difference could I *possibly* make? I'm only gifted with exceptional sensitivity to hidden emotions across an unbelievable range. How on earth could that be of *any* use?"

Viv set the mug down more forcefully than she'd intended. A crack spidered up the side, and she gritted her teeth. "I still don't like it."

"Since you can't refute my point, I guess I don't care."

Viv turned around to look at her, crossing her arms sullenly.

"Don't be such a baby. We'll make a pact. If mortal danger threatens us, I promise to hide behind you. Deal?"

Viv stared back, feeling increasingly foolish, until she relented with a sigh. "Deal."

—◆—

Exhausted, they stood together at the top of the ladder.

"I thought I told you to buy a bed." Tandri grimly surveyed the still-barren loft.

Viv had Amity's seldom-used blankets and pillow under one arm. "Well, I was a little distracted. Nighttime intruders, and all."

Tandri rolled her eyes. "Give me that."

She seized the bedding, shaking the dire-cat hair out of the blanket and pillow before busying herself unfolding Viv's bedroll and assembling a larger place to bed down.

Viv watched with a growing feeling of embarrassment and trepidation.

"Well," said Tandri, her hands on her hips. "At least with the stove running, it shouldn't be that cold. I can't believe you live like this."

"I'll be fine alone, really. There's no reason you shouldn't sleep in your own bed."

"Stop it. We already had that argument." After a moment's hesitation, she shucked down to her smallclothes, slid quickly under the blanket, and turned her back to Viv.

Viv extinguished the lantern and then did the same, tiptoe-
ing as if Tandri were already asleep, then snorting at her own
ridiculousness. She pulled the blanket—still smelling strongly
of dire-cat—over one shoulder. Even with her back to Tandri,
she could feel the woman's warmth.

"Good night, Tandri," she said, too loudly.

"Good night."

Viv stared ahead into the darkness.

"Is that your tail?"

"I'm just getting comfortable." Tandri's reply was tart.

After some strategic adjustments, she fell still.

There was a long silence.

Viv cleared her throat. "I'm glad you stayed."

Tandri's breathing was slow and even, and Viv thought she
might already be asleep. But then came a murmured reply. "I
know."

After that, for the first time in ages, Viv fell asleep almost
instantly and did not wake until morning.

24

When Viv's eyes opened, she could tell from the coldness behind her that Tandri had already risen. She was amazed she hadn't woken when the succubus left. Viv wouldn't have thought it possible.

She smelled freshly brewed coffee and dressed slowly, needlessly delaying. Then, she became annoyed with her own dithering. Before Tandri, she'd never been hesitant in her life. Was she really going to pick up the habit, now? She descended the ladder with great deliberateness.

Tandri sat at the big table, staring over the top of a mug that curled a ribbon of steam. As Viv joined her on the bench, the woman slid over another mug, still hot.

"Thanks," murmured Viv.

Tandri nodded and took a slow sip.

There was a relaxed curve to Tandri's back, and her tail made slow, lazy motions behind her. Viv's tension released, and she swallowed some of the good, hot drink. The warmth of it settled into her whole body. The gabble of Thune's waking noises, muted by the walls of the shop, surrounded them peacefully.

They enjoyed their coffee, slowly and quietly. Viv was reluctant to break the meditative, mutual silence, but after dallying like a coward in the loft, she felt a need to act decisively.

"Did you sleep all right?" As a bold conversational gambit, it left something to be desired.

"I did. Floor notwithstanding."

Viv smiled. "Someday, I'll get around to that bed."

—◆—

When they'd finished, Viv rummaged for cheese in the cold-box and grabbed a few linen-wrapped pastries from the pantry. Tandri joined her in the kitchen, and they engaged in the well-worn routines of the morning—firing up the stove, lighting the lanterns and chandelier, filling the machine's oil reservoir, checking the cream, and arranging the mugs. They picked at the food and moved about one another in slow synchrony.

Then Viv opened the door, and the gentle spell was broken like a soap bubble.

The noise of the day overtook them both, the murky threat of Fennus receded, and the warm other place they'd occupied all morning became more and more dreamlike. The smells of Thimble's baking and the clatter of his cheerful labors filled up the kitchen as they greeted regulars. Chatter rumbled from the dining area, and the clink of mugs and plates skittered below it.

Cal dropped by, and Viv showed him the stove she planned to order for Thimble. He read the measurements carefully and squinted at the wall and the stove, while Thimble rummaged in the pantry.

"Hm," Cal said, stroking his chin with a thumb. "Well, s'pose you could fit it there, but goin' to be mighty crowded. May be that you'd best make do with what you have. Auto-circulator keeps up now, but with two fireboxes? Could be you're back where you started and sweatin' when you'd rather not. Might be you have to look for a bigger place, an' leave this one behind, if you're set on it?"

That was frustrating, and of course, moving wasn't an option. Viv glanced at the back room, from which Thimble hadn't emerged. She didn't look forward to seeing his disappointment when she told him. "That's a real shame. But I guess I have one other thing you might help with."

Viv led Cal into the dining area. "We've got a bard that comes in and plays back here." She gestured toward the far wall between the booths. "I'm thinking maybe a little . . . stage? Something higher up, with a step."

"Sure. Sure," said Cal, happy to be able to agree to something.

They talked details, and he tipped his cap and went on his way, carrying a hot to-go mug and a Thimblet with him.

—◆—

All too soon, the day was done.

"We're not going to argue about the sleeping arrangements again, are we?" asked Tandri archly.

"Never let it be said that I don't learn from my mistakes."

Tandri hummed.

"Although maybe you can keep your tail to yourself this time." Viv smiled, her back turned as she put away the last of the mugs.

Tandri laughed softly. "Dinner?" she asked, as though they often ate an evening meal together.

Viv glanced over at Amity, curled up under the trestle table. For a wonder, the beast had stayed in the shop the whole day. It was reassuring. "I should definitely eat something besides

Thimble's baking," said Viv. She slapped her stomach. "My clothes are feeling a little tight these days."

Tandri snorted and opened the door.

They locked up and strolled to the High Street, found a place that neither of them had visited before, and had a meal together. They talked about Laney's latest wheedling attempts to extract recipes from Thimble, how to break the news of the scuttled oven plans to their baker, and about Pendry and a few of his more ardent admirers.

"His biggest fan was back again yesterday. Early, so she got a good seat," observed Viv.

"The one with the hair?" Tandri gestured, miming wind-blown curls.

"That's the one. I don't think Pendry's noticed yet."

"Hmm. Well, people tend not to notice what's in front of them until it nearly knocks them down."

Viv was about to reply with an offhanded quip, but something about Tandri's expression made her reevaluate.

Eventually, she managed, "I guess that's true."

The conversation moved on.

After dinner, the two of them returned to the shop and snuffed the lanterns and candles. The rumble of Amity's purr echoed from under the table.

"I can't believe she's still here," said Tandri.

"I'm sure she'll be gone before dawn."

Viv hoped not, though.

"Maybe Cal will decide to sleep over, too, tomorrow? We're short of blankets, though." She waited for Tandri to ascend the ladder first.

They revisited that serene, gentle quiet they'd briefly shared that morning, and undressed. Viv found herself looking away as Tandri did.

They fell asleep back-to-back, comfortable and easy and warm.

——+——

Yowling shocked Viv awake, along with a heavy thud against her belly. Her eyes flew open as Amity's enormous skull butted her again.

"Wh-what?" Tandri mumbled.

"Get up!" Viv sprang to her feet, inhaling deeply. There was a smell in the air she couldn't quite place, acrid, but still faint.

The dire-cat lashed her tail and paced anxiously to the top of the ladder. Viv spared a thought for how impressive a leap that must have been. Then it dawned on her that she could see the animal *far* better than she should have been able to. At first, she thought the faint light was from the moon, but the color was all wrong.

It was a pale, corpse-fire green. And it was growing brighter.

"What's that *smell?*" said Tandri, as she snatched up her clothes and held them against her chest.

Viv didn't bother with hers. "Nothing good." As she rushed to the ladder, the dire-cat leapt down first. Viv grabbed a rafter and leaned out, grimacing when she saw tongues of spectral green flame licking at the frame of the big double doors and spreading fast. Strangely, there was almost no smoke. Then, with a thick, crackling sound, the flames sheeted up the doors like a waterfall in reverse.

"Shit! Hurry! It's fire! The bastard lit the building on *fire!*"

"We have to put it out!" cried Tandri.

Viv hoisted the woman off her feet. Tandri gasped in surprise and almost dropped her clothes as Viv scooped her other arm under Tandri's legs and leapt to the floor below.

Tandri grunted, rattled by the impact.

Viv set her down and looked around the corner into the kitchen. That door was also aflame, and little ribbons of fire crept up the wall behind the stove and over toward the pantry.

A piercing snap resounded from above as the pressure in the room changed, and then green poured across the ceiling like blood down a blade. She heard brittle, sharp cracks as the roof tiles burst like popping corn.

"That isn't normal fire," said Tandri, raising her voice to be heard over the roar of the flames, her eyes wide and panicked.

A normal fire smoked, but this one burned clean and pungent as incense.

"It isn't. We have to get you out of here. Now."

"Me? What about us?"

Amity yowled plaintively, then hissed like a teakettle. She crouched near the big table, shying away from showering sparks.

Viv had already waited too long. Much longer, and her options would dwindle to zero. There was no telling how hot this unnatural fire might burn or what might extinguish it. If, indeed, anything would.

She dashed to the water barrel in the kitchen, the heat already intense from where the wall burned. The metal on the stove was beginning to throb red. Steam rose from the barrel. Much hotter than a regular blaze.

Viv scooped up a few of Thimble's mixing bowls, dredged them one by one through the water bucket, and tossed the water toward the front door, now alive with sheets of flame.

The water had absolutely no effect. It hissed and evaporated before it even reached the wood, which had already charred, spiderwebbed with throbbing lines of orange.

"Shit!"

When Viv turned, she saw Tandri had discarded her clothes and gathered an armful of mugs. She hurled them one by one at the front window, trying to shatter it—but the mugs burst on impact, leaving the glass unmarred.

She turned to Viv. "How do we get out?"

"This way."

Viv sprinted back to the dining area and the big double doors, the heavy wooden crossbeam still in place. Snakes of green fire crawled all along its length, with curtains of flame dripping from above to meet those rising from the floor.

Viv wrapped both arms around one of the big benches, lifted, and heaved it over to the door, squinting against the heat's blinding intensity. She hooked one end of the bench under the burning crossbeam and jerked upward, hard. The beam lurched, but fell back into its brackets, showering the floor in a spray of green sparks that skittered and hissed like water on a skillet. Several struck Viv's bare feet and arms, stinging like hornets. The pain was incandescent, and she smelled her own flesh charring.

She heaved upward again, once, twice, and on the third attempt, the crossbeam was bashed free and slammed to the flagstones, along with another cascade of green sparks.

"Stand back!" shouted Viv. She readjusted her grip toward the center of the bench, lifted it fully, and then charged forward, hammering into the right-hand door and continuing past, leaping over the fallen beam. A rush of cool night air met her, and she let the bench carry her forward out of the shop, where she hurled it away. It rolled and clattered into the street, where she could already see the shadows of neighbors emerging.

Viv turned and saw Tandri framed in a hellish green window, the flames from the fallen crossbeam leaping higher.

A shadow to Tandri's right materialized and then launched itself through the flames. Amity landed in a smoking sprawl on the cobbles. She spared them a brief, terrified glance, and then fled down an alley.

Viv's gaze snapped back to Tandri. The woman held one arm, grimacing in pain, tears streaking her cheeks.

Taking a deep breath, Viv sprinted back into the building, leaping through the flames, which seemed almost liquid as she passed through, like boiling water. And then she was inside. Hauling Tandri into her arms again, Viv dove back through the green wall of heat.

"Stay here," she said, depositing Tandri in the street.

When she turned back, the entire building was engulfed, the fire spreading with supernatural speed across every surface. She winced at the sharp reports of more roof tiles popping, and clay shards rained down, peppering onlookers with fragments and dust.

"You can't go back in there!" Tandri yelled over the rushing howl of the flames.

Viv sucked in a lungful of air and charged back into the building.

She could smell her hair smoldering as she landed inside. Viv spared a glance for the flagstone under the table. Something seemed wrong—was it tilted out of place?

No time for that. Not now.

She scrambled for the kitchen, vaulting the counter top. The pantry boiled with flames behind her, heat pressing on her like a physical thing. She yanked the lockbox out and slammed it on the counter. She leapt over again and tucked it under an arm in a single motion, then sprinted for the doors. With a roar, she hurled it out into the street, trying her best to aim away from where she thought Tandri was standing. It struck on a corner with an ominous crack, and tumbled, but blessedly held.

She rushed back to the kitchen.

Viv spared a glance for Blackblood on the wall, the garlands already a glowing ruin of cinders. Then she heaved the coffee machine off the counter with both hands and walked deliberately back toward the open door. Sparks from above peppered her shoulders, her hair, little lightning-strikes of pain. Part of her braid caught fire, but she couldn't spare a hand to put it out. She grimly advanced, muscles straining under the awkward load. She came to a stop in front of the flaming crossbeam and wished she'd had the presence of mind to shove it aside with the bench to clear a path. But it was too late for that, now. Too late for anything else.

She took one enormous step over the burning beam, holding the machine before her. Fire licked her thighs, cooking her skin, the pain exquisite along both legs, and then she was over.

Staggering into the street, Viv gently set it down and groaned. Her back shrieked in agony, a pain that she hadn't known for weeks.

As she turned back toward the building, the lintel above the big doors collapsed, and the doors themselves folded inward in a huge gout of green, landing with the booming sound of explosives. The mullioned window exploded outward in chunks and needles of glass. Everyone shielded their faces with their arms.

They stood, stunned in the street, baking in the heat rippling from the building. The roof began to creak and snap, and in a shuddering slope, it collapsed, tiles pouring into the room below, where they glowed bright red in the pools of green flame.

Standing in their smallclothes beside the tumbled lockbox and the coffee maker, Tandri's hand found Viv's and gripped it tight. She coughed, her eyes watering.

Viv stared into the shop, her face set. The big table began to sag to the side, half buried under cherry-bright tiles, to crumble over the place where the Scalvert's Stone lay.

She squeezed Tandri's hand back. "At least we didn't lose everything."

Tandri looked bleakly at the machine and the lockbox. "You shouldn't have risked it."

Following her gaze, Viv turned fully to Tandri and leaned down until their foreheads met, shoulders slumping under the weight of loss and terror and exhaustion.

In a low voice, so low she was sure Tandri wouldn't hear it over the roar of the flames and the rising clamor of people and the ringing of watch bells, she murmured, "That wasn't what I meant."

25

Gatewardens appeared soon after the blaze began, lanterns in hand, and bellowed at the growing crowd in the street. Viv only dimly registered their presence until one of them approached, directed to her by some neighbor. She numbly answered his questions and forgot her answers almost immediately. When he disappeared, she returned her attention to the wreckage.

Ignimancers from Ackers—recognizable by their robes and pins and air of scholarly annoyance—were able to contain the spectral flames and prevent the spread to the neighboring structures, but there was nothing they could do that would have changed the outcome for the shop itself, so they let it burn.

The flames raged until nearly dawn, and Viv and Tandri remained in the street, watching the shop reduced to cinders. The walls collapsed and fell in fits and starts, a slow crumbling, and then a sudden rush, as timbers tumbled inward in corkscrew ribbons of sparks.

Tandri huddled by Viv's side. They were blasted dry, like they'd been scoured by a desert wind. The skin of Viv's face was raw, the burns on her thighs angry and throbbing. Laney hobbled over to them at some point, bringing blankets to cover up with. It was too hot, and Viv shed hers almost immediately, although Tandri kept one wrapped around her shoulders, held together in front with a fist.

By degrees, Tandri slumped against Viv's arm, exhausted. The succubus didn't suggest they leave, but she did murmur at some point, "When you're ready, we'll stay at my place."

Viv couldn't bring herself to acknowledge the offer.

Despite the heat on her flesh, a coldness drew down from Viv's skull to the soles of her feet, like every day she'd spent in Thune was leaching away, leaving a growing emptiness, the most physical manifestation of despair she had ever known.

Was this what Tandri had spoken of? What had she called it . . . *Arcane Reciprocity?* Was this what that *felt* like? Or was it just plain old, everyday hopelessness?

She didn't know. And she supposed it didn't matter.

Tandri tried once more, still indirect. "Aren't you tired?" Her voice was hoarse. While the smoke from the spectral flames had been sparse, their throats still burned from it.

"I can't leave," said Viv. "Not yet."

Her eyes stayed fixed on a place in the heart of the ebbing destruction, where the Stone once rested.

She had to know if it was still there.

As dawn glimmered, the green flames sputtered and died, as if they fed on the night as much as on earthly fuel. The heat was still intolerable, though, and the blackened spars and charred and glowing tile could not be approached.

Eventually, Tandri persuaded Viv to sit on Laney's stoop, and together they watched the dawn bloom fully. Now, the blackened wood *did* smoke in a more natural way, as though the arcane fire had consumed it until then. A black, noxious cloud of soot grew and spiraled skyward, where it was torn apart and scattered by a breeze from the direction of the river.

Laney stood behind them, leaning on her broom. After a while, Viv asked in a ragged voice, "Laney, do you have a bucket or two you'd lend?"

The old woman did, and Viv took one in each hand. Still barefoot and in her undershirt and short linen pants, she strode to the well, filled them both, and grimly tossed water onto the ashes of the space where the big doors had once been. It splashed and hissed now, without the green flames to burn it away before it could fall.

She took the buckets back to the well, refilled them, and did it again. And again. And again, forging slowly inward toward the ruin that had once been the big table.

Viv didn't count the trips, and her feet left bloody prints on the cobbles. Ashes caked her legs up to her stinging thighs.

Tandri waited on the stoop and didn't try to dissuade her. It would have been pointless.

The heat was still intense, and sometimes Viv poured a bucket over herself before she returned. The water always wicked away soon after she re-traversed the spattered trail she was blazing. At every splash, the ashes became briefly muddy, until the blackness quickly dried and cracked again.

In the street, the crowds had thinned some, although the murmuring onlookers that remained stayed far away from Viv as she deliberately forged ever inward.

Sometime during this endless, numb repetition, Tandri briefly disappeared and returned with Cal and a small wagon drawn by a sturdy pony. They enlisted the help of some nearby folk and loaded the coffee machine and the lockbox into the wagon, and Cal took it away again.

Viv hardly cared.

At last, she reached the place. Barely any wood remained of the table, and what did was powdery and burnt through in a patchwork. The first bucket of water that struck it made it wither and crumble away like salt.

Viv knelt and pawed away the ruin, her fingers scorched by embers hiding beneath. She stood and kicked at the cinders with her bloody feet until the flagstone beneath was exposed.

She breathed heavily, inhaling smoke and coughing raggedly, staring at it. One more trip with the buckets washed away some of the accumulated ash and cooled the surface of the stone. She took a blackened twist of metal and levered up the edge, flipping it into the crumbled remains of the table in a plume of gray.

Dropping to her knees, Viv sorted through the startlingly hot earth beneath with her scorched fingers.

There was, of course, nothing there.

When Viv returned to the street, she moved as though underwater, weightless, sound distorted and far away. She stared bleakly at Tandri, then stumbled toward her.

Before she reached Laney's stoop, Viv was surprised to see Lack shoulder past the people fringing the street. He carried folded sets of clothing and two pairs of cloth shoes. He said nothing when he passed the bundles to Viv and Tandri, but Viv saw the flash of a fine gray dress between a few of the folk behind him. The Madrigal caught her gaze, nodded solemnly, and then walked away down the street, stately and unhurried.

"Thank you," managed Tandri in her cracked voice, but it was all Viv could do to reach out and take what Lack offered without dropping it.

Lack murmured something to them that Viv didn't register, and then she stood staring at the clothes with only dim comprehension.

After that, Viv didn't remember sitting, but she must have done so at some point. She stared dully ahead, vision blurred as her eyes watered from the smoke.

A familiar voice whispered, *"Oh no. . . ."*

Viv blinked in recognition. She turned her head and squinted at the unfocused shape of Thimble. Tandri knelt before him in quiet conference, with Laney's blanket puddling around her.

Viv closed her eyes, and when next they opened, he was gone, and she didn't know how much time had passed.

Tandri was suddenly beside her again. "He's here." She gently put a hand on Viv's shoulder and turned her, and there came Cal, again, with the pony and the wagon. Tandri led her to it and gently urged her into the back, where Viv lay with feet dangling off the boards, staring up at the sky and the black ribbon of smoke that bisected it.

She distantly heard Cal and Tandri speaking on the buckboard as the cart clattered away over the cobbles. The smell of the burnt shop receded a little—but never completely. Viv reeked of it. The ashes fluttered away from her in the breeze of their passage like snow blown upward.

At last, the wagon stopped, and someone guided her up some stairs, and then she was inside Tandri's room. The woman sat her in a wooden chair that creaked under her weight. Tandri disappeared, only to return with a wet towel. She scrubbed Viv as gently as she could manage, although the nap of the cloth was like sandpaper where she was burned, which was almost everywhere.

Afterward, Tandri managed to get her undressed and into

the clean clothes that Lack had provided, and then she settled her into the lone bed in the room.

Viv resisted closing her eyes, resisted letting go of consciousness, but the next time she blinked, she was gone into a dreamless black.

———+———

When she slowly woke, Viv felt more present in her own body, but her bleakness had redoubled. Her eyes flickered open, and the blanket of Tandri's bed rasped against her skin, painful on her burns. At first, she closed her eyes again, craving the oblivion of sleep, but it eluded her.

"You're awake," said Tandri.

Viv turned her head, and the muscles in her neck ached. *All* of her ached. Her feet sizzled with pain.

Tandri was seated in the chair with a blanket pulled up to her chin. Her eyes looked bruised, hair singed. The tracks of tears were still clear on her smudged cheeks.

The smell of the fire filled the room. They were both still redolent of it.

"Yeah," whispered Viv. She didn't think she could manage more than that. She realized how parched she was, and that was something tangible. She needed water.

Tandri seemed to sense it. She stood and shuffled in her blanket over to the vanity and brought a full pitcher.

Viv managed to prop herself up and drink it all, greedily, in a few enormous gulps.

"Thank you," she said, not even bothering to wipe the wetness from her chin. It was icy relief on her tender skin. And then, because she felt it needed to be said, "I'm sorry."

"For what?" Tandri frowned at her in a tired way. "Saving me from the fire? The one I was such a big help in preventing?"

"I guess we should both be thanking the cat."

Tandri chuckled soundlessly at that, although it looked like it hurt.

"I have to go back," said Viv.

"Now? Why? Whatever it is, it'll keep. There's nothing there to recover."

"There's just something else I have to see."

Tandri stared at her, then sighed and shrugged. "Let's go then."

"You should sleep. I kept you out of your bed."

"I couldn't sleep without knowing where you were, anyway," replied Tandri. "Sleep will keep, too, I suppose."

Viv groaned as she sat fully upright, pushed herself to her feet, and then found and slipped into the cloth shoes that the Madrigal had provided. She hissed through her teeth as her soles protested, but she mastered herself.

Outside Tandri's room, she saw it was late afternoon, tending toward dusk. She must have slept for seven or eight hours.

The walk back to the shop was very slow, and she stepped carefully. Pain that she had shrugged off hours ago became insistent and sharp. She thought about what Tandri had said just a day ago about reciprocity. Pain that was ignored, magnified on its return.

Absolute devastation.

The heat had died down a great deal over the course of the day, although it was still uncomfortably warm. No walls stood. Hills of ash and the stubs of burnt spars and tumbled stone marked the perimeter, and slumped piles of gray and black resembled a blurry map of what had once been the interior.

Viv left Tandri in the street and waded in, carefully choosing her steps. She made her way behind where the counter had once stood and cast her gaze over the wreckage there.

At last, she found it. Viv tentatively reached out, careful of potential heat, but it was cooler than she expected.

She withdrew Blackblood from the pile, and black grit sifted away from its warped, tortured length. The leather that had bound the grip was, of course, burned away to the tang. The crossguard was curved and melted, the blade twisted, and a mother-of-pearl sheen rippled across it like oil. A crack ran from one side all the way down to the fuller, the steel destroyed by the incredible heat of the unnatural fire.

Viv held her sword in both hands, head bowed.

She'd forsworn her old life, crossing a bridge to a new land, and now knelt in its ruin.

This was the bridge burning away behind her, leaving her in a desolation.

She tossed the blade back into the ash and took the only path that remained.

26

She slept in Tandri's room, waking intermittently to attend to necessities, although Viv insisted on taking a blanket and lying on the floor. She was used to it anyway. Her awareness of Tandri's comings and goings was hazy at best.

On what she thought might have been the third day, a knock came at the door. Viv heard Tandri moving to open it, a quiet exchange of words, and then someone entered. She heard them pad across the floorboards.

"Hm."

Viv opened her eyes and half-turned over. Cal stared down at her with his arms crossed, and she felt suddenly foolish . . . and *angry* . . . lying there and exposing her weakness to him. In years past, she would have cursed herself as a fool for giving a foe such an advantage. Such carelessness would have killed her a hundred times over.

But Cal was not her enemy.

The hob drew up the chair and sat, his legs too short for his feet to reach the floor. He clasped his hands between his knees, looking away and giving her a moment to push into a sitting position.

"Cal," she rasped, and nodded. She didn't feel as though she'd slept, at all.

"First thing to get a handle on is cleanup," he said without preamble. "Then materials. Then labor. Need more'n me and you, this time."

"What are you talking about?" she asked, and there was an edge of irritation in her voice.

"Rebuildin', o' course. Ash is cooled. We'll get it shifted. Maybe eight, ten trips to the midden. Hired hand or two'll speed it up fine."

"Rebuilding?" Viv stared up at him. "Cal, I don't have the coin for that. And even if I did, I don't think it'd matter."

"Hm. Tandri told me. The Stone." He shrugged. "Maybe worse odds now, but didn't figure you were one to duck at a soft blow like that."

Viv flicked a glance at Tandri, who stared back with a level expression.

"Still doesn't change things," she said. Her battered strongbox sat to the side, where they must have placed it while she slept. She reached over with one huge hand and dragged it closer. Viv took the key from around her neck and unlocked it, flipping back the lid. Maybe seven sovereigns, a handful of silver, and a scattering of copper bits lay within. The platinum was long gone.

"I saved for *years*," she said grimly. "Bounties. Blood work. Most of it's gone, now." She glared balefully. "As gone as the shop and everything else. There's almost nothing left. Less than what I started with, by *leagues*."

She looked at Tandri, who winced at her tone of voice. "What did you call it . . . *Arcane Reciprocity?* Well, *here it is*, this is the backlash." She felt her teeth bared, her fangs huge in her jaw, her burnt and barely healing skin tight over her skull, her brain throbbing.

A part of her understood that she was hurting them, wounding these people who were friends. That some older, crueler self was emerging, crawling from the wreckage of who she thought she had become. That newly ruined part of her cried out for her to stop, to let it be for now, but the crueler self was ascendant, its opponent too weakened and diminished to intervene.

"It's fucking *gone*," she snarled. "I spent my chance, and I can't earn it back." She held Tandri's gaze and deliberately said, "This is the part where I do what desperate people do. This is the part where *I* flee."

Tandri jerked as if struck.

Savage satisfaction burned through Viv, followed by a wave of nausea.

"Give it time," said Cal, in his gritty, patient voice.

"What fucking difference would that make?" she roared.

In the next moment, Viv slumped, staring down at her hands, limp in her lap. "You should go," she whispered hoarsely.

She heard him quietly rise and leave.

For a while, she thought Tandri had left, too, but then Viv felt her draw near, crouch in front of her, and stroke her burned cheek.

Tandri's forehead touched hers, an echo of days ago. "Do you remember what you said, in the street? After the fire?" she murmured, her breath light on Viv's nose and lips.

"No," she lied.

"You said, 'At least *we* didn't lose everything.'"

Tandri paused.

"And I said you risked too much for the things you saved," she continued.

Another, longer pause, her breathing slow and sweet.

"But I knew what you really meant."

Viv didn't notice her own tears until Tandri's lips brushed her damp cheek.

She opened her eyes and stared into Tandri's, so close to her own.

The woman held her gaze steadily, face composed, but eyes wet.

Viv felt a warm weight in her center, and for a moment, they were enclosed again in that bubble of calm rightness they'd once shared.

Then the savage, older Viv clawed her way to the fore, whispering, *It's what she is. You've felt this before. She keeps it hooded like a lantern until she needs it, and then she lets it loose, and you fall under her spell.*

But even as that bleak thought spread through her mind like the spectral flame, it evaporated just as swiftly in the light of dawn.

Tandri's warm, pulsing aura, the one that had touched her a few fleeting times, was absent.

There was no arcana, no force, no trick.

No magic to it, at all.

There never had been. Not even once.

She saw in Tandri's face, composed though it was, that she was awaiting some judgment. Preparing herself for it, to be struck, ignored, or accepted.

And terrified of all three.

Viv's hand rose and carefully tucked Tandri's singed hair behind one ear.

With a sharply drawn breath, she tipped her head forward, and brushed her lips against Tandri's, light as a whisper.

Then she wrapped her arms around her and tried not to squeeze too hard.

Tandri squeezed back.

———+———

Cal was wrong. It took thirteen trips to the midden to clear away the debris. Viv didn't know where he'd rented the cart and pony from and was too ashamed to ask. It was the work of a week to shovel and hoist the ashes and cracked tile and stone into the back of the wagon.

The oven was a mangled wreck of slag that flaked apart when she tried to drag it from the debris. Cal kept aside a few stones and bricks that might prove useful, stacked to one cleared end of the lot.

Mopping her brow with a forearm, Viv looked down at him. "I still don't see how I'll afford the stone and lumber for this, much less the labor. Is there really any point in clearing it all away?" The acid was gone from her voice, replaced by a stoic flatness.

He cocked back his hat and tugged at one of his long ears. "Hm. What'd you say to me at the docks? '*You do it even when some might say it's wiser not to*,' I think? Well. Guess I'll just say . . . maybe be unwise a little longer."

Viv couldn't think of a response to that, so she got back to hauling and lost herself in the demanding physicality of the work.

She was taken aback when Pendry showed up on the second day with no lute in evidence. With a nervous little nod, he pitched in to help. Viv had to admit, his big, rough hands looked perfectly natural hauling stone. When she began to offer to pay him, he stopped her.

"No," he said and shook his head. And that was all.

Tandri intermittently appeared and disappeared with water or bread and cheese, and Viv tried not to stare after her too hard, or to think overmuch about that single, stolen kiss.

———✦———

Cal arrived with a cartload of bricks and river stone.

"Where's this from?" asked Viv, squinting at him as he climbed down from the buckboard.

"Well. Those'ns come from the quarry. And those'ns from the river. Gonna have to leave you two to unload 'em. Ain't tall enough for this."

Viv and Pendry shifted the stone into piles on the lot.

Cal stacked a few of the bricks and planks to form a make-shift table and bent over a roll of paper with a stylus and a ruling stick. Tandri huddled over it with him.

As Viv approached them, breathing hard, Cal looked up. "Figured if we're goin' to all the work, best build it back better, hm? Two ovens shouldn't be a problem with a bigger kitchen, I figure. So. Take a look."

Viv stared down at his neatly drafted plans.

"That kid needs a dipper of water," said Tandri, holding a hand over her eyes as she looked across the lot at Pendry. "I'll be back."

When she was gone, Viv looked back at Cal and pointed at the paper. "Is this the loft?"

"'Tis."

"There's something else I want to change," she said. And then hesitated. "If . . . if you're willing?"

"I'm waitin'."

So she told him.

———+———

When Cal showed up again with lumber and sacks of nails, Viv forced him to take most of her remaining funds. He didn't protest, but she wondered how he'd been paying for *any* of it. At some point, she simply allowed herself not to worry about it, which was both unnerving and freeing.

As construction commenced, Thimble made a habit of joining them at noon, bearing sacks of food—warm meat turnovers in flaky pastry, good hearty loaves of bread, and once, his cinnamon rolls. Everyone stopped their labors and companionably ate those, seated on the growing lower wall of brick.

Laney sometimes tottered across the street to offer advice. She'd tut over the fire and usually managed to abscond with a roll.

It turned out that Pendry was quite the stonemason, though nobody but Viv seemed particularly surprised. "Oh sure," he said, cheeks red and rubbing the back of his head. "It's the family business."

They were sheathing the half-wall of brick in river stone when Hemington picked his way onto the lot, having traded his books for a satchel of tools.

"Good afternoon," he said, seeming a little embarrassed.

"Hem," said Viv, surprised to see him.

"I thought . . . well, I thought you might appreciate a little ward-work in the foundation." He chuckled awkwardly. "Some warded inscriptions to proof against fire might not go amiss, perhaps?"

"I didn't know it was possible. If I said *no*, I think everyone here would curse me for an idiot," replied Viv.

"That's true, we would," said Tandri, rising from where she'd been mixing mortar. She smiled at Hemington and raised a brow at Viv. Her cheeks were streaked with gray, and she wore a rough work shirt, rather than her customary sweater. Viv thought she looked pretty radiant.

"Well, then," said Hemington. "I'll just get to it, shall I?" He withdrew a collection of instruments from his satchel and went to the four corners of the foundation, then the midpoints of each outer wall, where he busied himself etching and inscribing and doing whatever it was he did. Viv figured she could probably ask Tandri for details later.

She reflected that if the Scalvert's Stone *had* drawn something to this place, it might still be there.

27

They had the building framed in another week.

Partway through, a cart filled with clay tiles drew up to the shop-under-construction. Viv looked at Cal, who shrugged.

She walked over, nodding to the driver. "What's this?"

He was a big man, scraggly beard, beefy. The fellow beside him was well-muscled and lean. She had a feeling she'd seen them somewhere before, but couldn't immediately place them.

"Delivery," the driver said, helpfully.

"Yeah, but who from?"

"Can't say," he said, with no particular animosity.

"And no payment expected?"

The man shook his head and climbed down with his partner. They set to piling the tiles in stacks in front of the lot.

And then she remembered. She'd seen them in Lack's gaggle of hoods, all those weeks ago. She allowed herself a surprised grin, thinking of fine gray dresses. Then, shaking her head, she got back to work.

Covering the roof was rough labor, but Cal rigged a pulley system, and Viv doggedly hauled up buckets of tile. It took a week
before it was all fully laid, and then they began work on the
walls with some relief. Pendry still showed up every other day or
so, and Tandri was a fine hand with a mallet and nails.

Other help came and went, and Viv was never really sure
from what quarter. Whether Cal hired them or the Madrigal sent them or they just happened to wander by and lend a
hand—she stopped trying to guess.

Viv could see the skeleton of the shop fleshing itself in wood
and stone, now with a proper staircase to the loft, the pantry
relocated, and framing for more windows along the front.

Pendry bricked up a proper double chimney along the east
wall where space awaited the stoves. He lined the new under-
ground cold-box, as well.

Thimble arrived daily with one warm delicacy or another,
and Viv caught him eyeing the more generous kitchen footprint
more than once.

Even Amity appeared from time to time. To the relief of everyone, she seemed none the worse for wear, although her perpet-
ually sooty fur made it hard to tell. Like a great, gray ghost, she
weaved her way between bare studs, gazing around in a proprietary way before disappearing, once more.

—◆—

It was three more weeks before the walls were finished and plas-
tered and whitewashed, the stairs and railing completed, the
counter, booths, and table rebuilt. Summer was waning, and
the teeth of autumn gnawed at them, morning and evening.

The lumber and materials kept manifesting, and Viv told

herself when it was done, she'd ferret out the source from Cal and pay her benefactors back just as soon as she could afford it.

She kept sleeping on Tandri's floor, albeit with a bedroll and pillow. Viv felt guilty for staying, yet simultaneously reluctant to leave. She made a few tentative attempts to move to an inn or to rent a room with her meager remaining funds, but each time Tandri told her she was being foolish, and Viv didn't have much interest in arguing.

—◆—

Viv stood with Tandri and Cal in the waning light of another hard day's work, staring up at the face of the shop and the dark sockets of its glassless windows. As she was debating whether to temporarily tack cloth over them, she sensed someone approach.

When she looked down, Durias, the elderly, chess-playing gnome, greeted them with a nod. She wasn't surprised when Amity padded up behind him and loomed like a sentinel, half again his height.

"Glad to see you've decided to stay." He smiled up at her. "It would've been a shame to be robbed of such a fine cup of coffee."

"No thanks to me," said Viv. She nudged Tandri gently with one arm, and she thought the woman might have leaned into it, just a little. "It's these two who made sure of it." She indicated both of her friends.

Tandri continued to stare at the shop thoughtfully. "Maybe the Stone never did anything," she murmured.

"Hm," concurred Cal.

"Stone?" asked Durias, his bushy white eyebrows high on his forehead.

Viv didn't suppose there was any reason to be evasive. "A

Scalvert's Stone. I feel like a twice-blasted fool about it, but I once heard—"

"Ahh, yes," interrupted the old gnome, with a nod. "I'm very familiar. There's a reason there are so few, these days—scalverts. Unfortunate. Nearly hunted to extinction, they were."

"Really?" That got Viv's undivided attention.

"Been many a year, but too many old legends and songs mythologized them. 'The Ring of Fortune,' and that foolishness." He shook his head sadly. "Like lodestones for luck or wealth, or so many believed."

"And they aren't?" asked Tandri.

"Well," replied the gnome, tugging at his mustache. "Not the way folk hoped."

"So . . . it *was* for nothing, then." Viv shook her head bitterly. "Hells, all it managed was to get the place burned down. If I'd never kept it here, Fennus would've left well enough alone. We could've avoided all this."

Durias tipped his head and pinched his face in a speculative way. "I wouldn't be so sure of that."

"But you just said—"

"I said 'not the way folk hoped.' Didn't say it didn't work at *all*."

"What'd it do then?" asked Cal.

"That old song was a bit misleading. The Stones never granted fortune, but they *were* . . . gathering points, you might say. You'd find few who know it, these days, but 'the ring of fortune' is an old sea-fey phrase. It means . . . a *destined cadre,* I suppose. Individuals brought together, like to like. Which can *be* fortunate, of course. Sometimes, nothing's more fortunate than that! But that wasn't what most were seeking. Although maybe they should've been, eh?"

Viv murmured, "Draws the ring of fortune, aspect of heart's desire."

His speculative look sharpened. "Yes . . . well . . . it seems to have worked out well, here, I think."

Viv looked from Tandri to Cal, and back at the shop.

"Getting late!" said Durias. He doffed his little sackcap. "Must be getting on, with the cold setting in. My old bones complain if I'm not at a fire by dusk. I don't think it's too early for congratulations, though? Or maybe it is, I do tend to get a little muddled over timing."

"Congratulations? On rebuilding?"

"That, too! That, too. No, I was referring to . . . well. Never mind. Sometimes, I'm not sure which go-round this is. Could be I'm polishing the stone before the cut! A good night to you all!"

He turned and disappeared down the street, and after a moment, the big dire-cat slunk after him like a too-large shadow.

—◆—

A few days later, after the doors and windows had been fitted, two enormous crates arrived on a large wagon, and with them, some unexpected visitors.

Roon and Gallina sat side by side on the buckboard.

"Are those what I think they are?" asked Viv. Gnomish print rimmed the edges, and they certainly looked the right size to contain two new ovens.

"Depends, I guess," said Roon, easing downward and dropping the last foot to the cobbles. Viv went to give Gallina a hand, but the gnome flashed her a sharp look and leapt to the street with great grace.

"It was your girl behind it," said Gallina, glancing toward

Tandri, who emerged from the shop, still too far away to hear their conversation.

"My *girl?*" Viv echoed in a low voice.

Gallina shrugged and looked smug.

"You brought them!" said Tandri. When she saw Viv's face, she faltered a little, her steps suddenly uncertain.

"Did you order these? Tandri, how in the eight hells did you get enough—!"

"Little donation from us both," interrupted Roon, nodding at Gallina. He patted the flank of one of the pair of horses.

"Tandri sent a letter. Let us know what happened," said Gallina.

Viv looked at Tandri, thinking of the Stone. "Everything?"

Tandri took a breath, and firmly said, "Everything."

"So you *both* know about the Scalvert's Stone?" she asked her old comrades.

"Who gives a shit?" Gallina waved a hand like it was irrelevant.

Viv supposed it was.

"Fennus," Roon snarled with sudden savagery.

"Have you seen him, then?" asked Viv.

"Not in weeks," replied Gallina. "Didn't part on the *best* of terms. Man's always been a bit of a prick, but this?" The gnome shook her head angrily.

"Can't abide a welcher," supplied Roon. "Anyhow, help me wrestle these down, eh?"

Viv and Roon unloaded both crates and left them for Cal to unbox in the morning.

Roon left to stable the wagon. Viv couldn't help but be amused, given that they stood in front of an old livery.

"So," said Gallina. The three of them leaned against the crates while Viv caught her breath. The little gnome withdrew a dagger from one of the myriad places she stowed them and toyed with it idly. "Fennus. I know you didn't wanna dirty your hands before, and *I admit*, that seems to've worked out fine. Sort of. Apart from this shit. But." She leaned around Viv and waggled her blade at Tandri. "I know you're all . . . *nonviolent*, but ya can't tell me it wouldn't be a good idea to take just a finger or three. Can ya?"

Tandri snorted and made a show of stretching her back. "Don't ask *me*. I'm too sore to be objective."

Viv stroked her chin. "You know, if that old man was right, we might not have to."

"Old man?" Gallina frowned at them.

"This grandfatherly gnome. You know the type. Very mysterious. He said the Stone doesn't work the way I thought it did. What'd he say about it . . . ?"

"It draws like to like," recited Tandri.

"Yeah. Well, maybe the same happens for Fennus, if he keeps it."

"More than one Fennus in one place?" Gallina made a face.

Viv shrugged. "Maybe it's more like caging a bunch of starving wolves together. Sooner or later, one of them is going to eat the weakest. And maybe they all kill each other, in the end."

"Can't say I'm not disappointed we won't get those fingers, though," said Gallina.

"I'll see if I can make it up to you when we reopen."

"Maybe one of them rolls," the gnome mused aloud.

Viv rapped a knuckle on the lid of a crate. "Gallina, I think I can get you a whole sackful."

28

Autumn deepened, and reopening day approached, although the final two weeks crawled by. The days brimmed with minor tasks that took longer than seemed possible—refitting lanterns, hanging a replacement chandelier, staining and lacquering the table and counter tops, installing the ovens, and mounting a pair of new auto-circulators.

Viv also made a few special orders with a loan from Gallina. She extracted a half-joking promise that the gnome would menace her with knives if she wasn't repaid in two months. Viv felt she'd exceeded the bounds of friendship in every possible direction with everyone she knew, at this point, although she had a few ideas on how to rectify that.

When Thimble beheld the new pair of ovens, the expanded pantry and cold-box, and the more generous back counter space, he was overcome. He scurried from one end of the kitchen to the other, inspecting all the new cookware that Tandri had assembled, peering into the oven doors, and running his hands lovingly over the stovetops.

He stood before Viv, hands clasped in front of him, and gave
her a little ducking bow.

"*It's perfect*," he whispered, and his oil-drop eyes brimmed.

She hunkered down before him, "I told you, the best deserve
the best."

He threw his arms around her upper arm and gave it a brief,
startling hug, and then disappeared into the pantry.

Viv found her throat unaccountably thick.

—◄+►—

The morning before the reopening, Tandri was already gone
from her room when Viv awoke, which was unusual. Her heart
twisted, but her concerns eased when she saw the note that
Tandri had left on the vanity.

Errands to run. Will see you at the shop later.

Honestly, it couldn't have worked out better, since Viv wanted
to take delivery of a few shipments without the others around.

—◄+►—

When she unlocked the door to Legends & Lattes, it was empty
and quiet, the smell of wood stain and lacquer still strong. The
autumn chill had deepened, so she started a fire in one of the
stoves and idly watched the auto-circulators begin their slow
revolutions. The old coffee machine gleamed on the counter
top, only marred by a few scratches and dings from its uncere-
monious rescue months before.

She ascended the staircase, running her hand along the rail.
She paced through the new rooms, still chilly, but she could feel

the heat beginning to creep through the floor from the kitchen below. A new set of windows let the morning light pool at a slant in the western corners. Cal had really outdone himself.

There was a knock on the shop door, and she descended to find two younger dwarves, still with shortish beards, stamping their feet and rubbing their hands in the brisk air.

"Delivery?" The taller of them pulled a folded sheet from a cloak pocket. "And . . . assembly?"

"Been waiting for it," said Viv. "I'll get the other doors."

She opened the big bay doors to the dining area and helped unload and move the cargo up the narrow staircase with only a little cursing and grunting amongst them.

Unbundling their tools, the dwarves briskly and efficiently assembled what they'd brought. Viv signed the delivery receipt and bid them stay warm.

She spent another hour upstairs, fussing and fidgeting, before deciding she'd break something if she didn't stop.

On the ground floor, Viv clipped a barrier rope across the base of the staircase. Then she pulled a fresh sack of beans from the pantry and one of the new ceramic mugs. She lost herself in the meditative act of priming the machine and grinding and brewing. The hiss of steam and the smell of fresh coffee permeated the shop, and with the warmth of the stove and the frost riming the edges of the front windows, something clenched and watchful inside Viv released for the first time since the fire.

She leaned on the counter over a fresh chapbook, sipped her coffee, gazed at the blurs passing in the street, and gloried in a suspended moment of contentment.

The spell was broken when the front door banged open, letting in a curl of icy wind and revealing Cal standing on the threshold.

He was bundled in a long coat and gloves. Behind him, Viv could
see the first flakes of an early snow drifting down.

"Hm. You're here. Good."

He stepped back outside before Viv could reply.

"I've got my end," he said to someone in the street, and when
he reappeared, he and Tandri had either side of something large
and awkward and wrapped up in paper and twine.

They leaned it against the counter and stood back.

Tandri's face was flushed with the cold, and she hurriedly
closed the door behind them.

"Over next to the stove, you two. Looks like winter's setting
in early." Viv came around the counter and stared at the big
parcel, hands on hips. "What's all this, then?"

"Well," said Tandri, rubbing her hands briskly. "Something
you can't open the shop without." She smiled at Viv, but the
smile was a little anxious. "You should . . . you should probably
open it now."

Cal nodded, too, stripping off his gloves and tucking them
into a pocket.

Viv knelt and, after fumbling with knotted twine for a few
seconds, cut the ties with her pocketknife. Rough brown paper
shucked away from what lay beneath.

It was the shop sign.

"I thought it burned in the fire," she whispered.

"Saved it," said Cal. "Or most of it, I s'pose."

"Hang on . . . is this . . . ?"

Diagonally, where the embossed silhouette of a sword had
once been, a metal one was mounted. Steel. There was a unique
mother-of-pearl sheen to it that she recognized.

"It is," said Tandri, moving to stand behind her. She had her
arms crossed tensely in front of her. "I . . . took it after you . . .

well, I thought that . . . maybe you didn't have to be fully rid of it. Not yet." Then, in a rush, "I was just thinking that you don't have to forget who you *were* . . . because that's what brought you *here*."

Viv ran a finger over Blackblood's new incarnation, cut down to an icon of her former self. Then, she just stared at it.

"Do you . . . like it?" asked Tandri. "If you don't, we can unmount—"

"It's perfect," said Viv. "I can't believe you saved her."

She rose and embraced them both, blinking back tears as she did.

—◆—

On reopening day, the snow persisted, icing Thune from steeple to cobble. Gray skies bloomed with pink, which limned the clouds to the east, promising more pre-winter flakes.

The refurbished sign hung proudly from the swing arm above the door, snow frosting its nooks and crannies.

Viv and Tandri arrived first to feed the stoves and fill the new water tubs. Lighting the lanterns and candles filled the shop with a welcoming glow. By the time Thimble slipped in the door, the dairyman had delivered their cream and butter and eggs. The rattkin set to mixing and kneading, forming balls of dough to rise before assembling ingredients for his icings, humming to himself all the while.

Cal showed up, kicking snow from his boots and blowing from the cold, and Tandri brewed him a fresh cup. He took it to the big, new table and curled his fingers gratefully around the warm mug, while they speculated on the size of the opening crowd and jokingly wagered over how quickly the rolls would sell out.

Surveying the kitchen for anything out of place, Viv caught sight of the rail they'd built along the back wall. "Ah, hells! I almost forgot!"

She disappeared into the pantry and returned with a big square of slate, which she slid onto the counter, and presented Tandri with a new set of colored chalk.

After a moment's thought, Tandri set to work.

Viv and Cal crowded close to watch, until she gave them both the side-eye, and they quickly found other tasks with which to busy themselves.

Tandri straightened and stood back to examine her handiwork. "Help me get it on the wall," she said.

Viv lifted it into place.

⁓❭LEGENDS & ❭LATTES ⁓

re-est. NOVENDER 1386
GRAND REOPENING

~ MENU ~
Coffee ~ exotic aroma & rich, full-bodied roast—½ bit
Latte ~ a sophisticated and creamy variation—1 bit
Any drink ICED ~ a refined twist—add ½ bit
Cinnamon Roll ~ heavenly frosted cinnamon pastry—4 bits
Thimblets ~ crunchy nut & fruit delicacies—2 bits
Midnight Crescents ~ buttery foldover with a sinful center—4 bits
Inquire About Traveling Mugs
❖

WHAT FLAMES COULD NOT CONSUME,
NEVER SHALL BE EXTINGUISHED

⸺◆⸺

When they opened the doors, there was already a line down the street, despite the cold. They ushered everyone inside, letting the line curl back into the dining area, and the shop rapidly warmed. Cheerful conversation drowned out the hiss of the machine, and eager customers with red cheeks and coats undone offered congratulations as they gratefully took their hot drinks and shuffled to find seats.

"Early for you, isn't it?" greeted Viv, when Hemington stepped up to the counter.

"Yes, well," he replied, looking with real appreciation around the shop. "It's all rather exciting, though, isn't it? I've missed this place, I don't mind saying."

"Not just your research, then?"

He sighed. "Whatever phenomenon was happening here, it's passed. The ley lines fluctuate as normal. I can't help but wonder if that fire had something to do with it. Did they ever find the arsonist?"

"Afraid not," said Viv.

"A shame. Still, this is all so much more comfortable."

Viv nodded. "Iced coffee, then?"

He deliberated for a moment, and then, with some embarrassment, said, "You know, given the weather . . . perhaps I'll have . . . a hot one."

She cocked an eyebrow at him. "*You*, Hem?"

Hemington coughed. "Ah. And one of those rolls."

She smiled and didn't give him any further trouble over it.

⎯✦⎯

"Whoo! Cold out." Pendry pulled the door closed behind him. He wore half mittens, and he'd tucked his cloth-wrapped lute under an arm. A boxy, black device dangled from his fingers by a strap.

"Let's get you something hot to drink," said Tandri, already starting a latte.

"Yes, please!" He stepped to the right and caught his first glimpse of the stage at the end of the dining area. A tall stool awaited him, and a dark curtain draped the wall behind it. "Oh, wow," he breathed. "For me?"

"Don't trip on the way up," teased Viv. "Before you get settled, though, I have to know. What's that?" She gestured at the box he carried.

"Ah. This! Well, it's a, uh . . . they call it an . . . arcane amplifier? It, uh . . . it makes . . ."

". . . makes things louder?" finished Viv.

"Sometimes . . . ?" He looked pained.

"Make sure the glass stays in the windows, that's all I ask. We just put this place back together."

He nodded awkwardly, took his drink, and disappeared around the corner.

At the first opportunity, Viv checked in on him. She smiled to see the kid flanked by stone he'd laid himself.

Pendry warmed up with a catchy bit of finger-picking. The box sat a few feet away, and his music filled the room in a way that was *present* without intruding—enfolding rather than bludgeoning. When Pendry sang in his plaintive, sweet voice, she smiled and withdrew.

She turned to find herself face-to-face with the Madrigal, clad this time in a rich, red winter cloak with a fur ruff.

Viv was caught off guard for a moment, at a loss for words.

"Congratulations," said the Madrigal, inclining her head slightly. "I'm pleased to see the progress here. Your establishment is a real credit to the Redstone district. It would've been such a shame for it to disappear after such promising initial success."

Viv recovered enough to stammer, "Uh, thank you, ma'am." Thinking of all the deliveries and the unexpected laborers, she leaned closer. "And I mean that, truly. *Thank you.*"

The Madrigal glanced significantly toward the coffee maker and the piles of pastries on tiered serving trays, and Viv sidled around the counter to begin brewing her a cup.

Tandri turned, startled at the sight of the woman, and immediately began selecting rolls and Thimblets.

"A shame the arsonist wasn't apprehended," said the Madrigal. "I do hope they don't return."

"Doubt they will." Viv pursed her lips as the Madrigal seized her gaze. "I figure they got what they came for. No reason to come back."

The Madrigal nodded as she took her drink and a bulging sack of baked goods and departed.

She didn't offer to pay this time, which was an honest relief.

◄─+─►

When Durias made an appearance that afternoon, his cheeks pinked with the cold and snow in his neat, white beard, he was without his chessboard.

"Well," he said, his hands tucked into his coat. "Just like I remembered."

"Pretty close, anyway," said Viv. "We made a few improvements."

He seemed startled. "Oh, yes, I suppose that's true, looking at it from your end."

"Get you something to drink?"

"Oh my, yes, please. And one of those as well," he said, standing on tiptoe and pointing at the chocolate crescents.

"Have you seen the dire-cat around?" Viv asked as she made his drink.

"She comes and goes as she likes," replied the gnome. "But I daresay you'll see her sometime soon."

As Viv slid him his drink and pastry, Durias said, "It'll work out just fine, you know."

"So far." Viv looked around the busy shop with a small smile. "It seems to be."

"Oh, certainly, the shop," said the gnome. "But the rest of it, too."

"The rest?"

"Indeed." And he took his order, toddling off into the dining area.

Tandri leaned around her and looked after him. "Do you think he's cryptic on purpose?"

Viv shrugged, thinking about his one-sided chess game and about her arrangements upstairs. "Couldn't say. Don't think I'd ever want to play faro with him, though."

29

At day's end, Viv gently ushered the last customer out the door and into the brittle cold. She locked up behind them and turned back to her friends, spread throughout the shop.

Thimble fussed with a rack of cooling baked goods, Tandri was wiping down the machine, and Cal examined the hinges on one of the big doorjambs.

Viv simply watched the three of them for a moment, the soft, low bustle such a contrast to the cacophony of the day. The chimney pipes thrummed, and the icy wind sang under the eaves.

She quietly unclipped the cord across the stairs and went up to collect a leather scroll case, which she brought to the counter.

Tandri halted in the middle of scrubbing out a mug to look at her askance.

"Can I have the inkwell?" asked Viv.

"Sure." Tandri dried her hands and retrieved one from under the counter. She gave the scroll case a speculative look.

Viv cleared her throat, suddenly nervous. "Can I get everyone up here for a minute?" she called, overloud.

They gathered together, gazing at her curiously.

She took a big breath.

"I'm . . . not really good at speeches. So I won't try to make a good one. But I wanted to thank you, all of you." Her eyes suddenly stung. "This . . . all this . . . This was a gift you gave to me. And I . . ." She grimaced at Cal, and then at Tandri. "I didn't deserve it. The things I've done in my life . . . I don't have any right to this kind of good fortune.

"But more than this place, I don't deserve you. If there was any justice in the world, I'd never have met you, much less have even a scrap of your regard. And for a while . . . I thought maybe I'd cheated fate to have you near me. That I was bending the rules—forcing some impossible streak of luck—and any moment, you'd find out who I really was, and then you'd be gone."

She breathed out, slowly.

"But what a stupid thing to think. Unfair to you. Did I think so little of you? Did I think you *couldn't* see who I was, really? Was I foolish enough to believe I could make you see something other than what was there?"

She looked down at her hands for a moment.

"So. I might not deserve you. And you might forgive too much. But I'm damned glad to have you."

It was quiet, and she held each of their gazes in turn.

The silence stretched, during which Viv became increasingly uncomfortable.

"Hm," said Cal. "As speeches go . . . wasn't too bad."

Tandri snorted, and Viv's tension evaporated as though it had never been.

"Uh. Well, with that out of the way . . ." Viv opened the scroll case and withdrew a roll of foolscap. "These are writs of partnership. One for each of you. This shop isn't mine. It's yours, too. You built it. You made it work, and it'd be nothing without you. All you have to do is sign."

Tandri picked up one of the sheets and quietly read it over. "This is an equal partnership. When did you have this done?"

"A week ago," said Viv, rubbing at the back of her neck. "I mean . . . the ad I posted mentioned 'advancement opportunities,' so . . ."

"Ain't right for me to sign it," said Cal.

"Of course it is!" said Viv in surprise. "What in the hells do you mean?"

"Don't work here," he continued. "Just don't make sense. Ain't fair to the rest."

"Cal," said Viv, sliding a sheet across to him. "When I say that you all built this place, in your case, you *literally* did. There's nobody who deserves it more."

"Sign it," said Tandri. "And if you want to be persnickety about it, I know who to bother when things break."

"Or when Thimble decides *this* kitchen is too small, too," added Viv.

Thimble squeaked supportively.

And with much grumbling on Cal's part, and much chivvying from the rest . . . eventually, he made his mark.

———◆———

"One last thing," said Viv, and from the pantry she retrieved a small brandy bottle and four fine glasses. She set them in a line and poured a careful measure from the bottle into each.

"A toast. To all of you."

"To what the flames could not consume," murmured Tandri, and they all nodded solemnly.

They drank . . . and Thimble coughed and had to be patted on the back several times.

Then they quietly gathered their things to leave.

"Tandri," said Viv, quietly. "Stay a minute?"

Cal gave them a glance, then nodded to himself, and left behind Thimble.

———◆———

The two of them stood together in the warm center of the shop, with winter stealing in around it, the brandy glowing like coals inside them.

"There's . . . something I wanted to show you," said Viv, almost too low to hear. Then she quickly turned and went to the stairs, beckoning for Tandri to follow.

At the top of the stairs, a hallway split the upper story, with a door to the left, and one to the right. Viv strode to the one on the left and opened it, stepping inside.

Tandri peered in after her and gasped. "You bought a bed!"

"I did," said Viv.

The room was also furnished with a small dresser and table and a wardrobe.

"Even a rug!" said Tandri, nodding appreciatively. "Well, it's bound to be an improvement over my floor."

Viv closed her eyes and took a slow breath. "There's one other thing I want to show you," said Viv, with a cold flush of terror.

Tandri gave her a wry smile. "You didn't make a room for the cat, did you?" she asked, which did nothing to quell Viv's nerves. Quite the opposite, in fact.

Viv didn't trust herself to reply, so she went to the door across the hall and opened it, as well. Tandri's brow creased as she stepped inside. This room, too, was furnished with a bed, a vanity, and a wardrobe. A set of art supplies—ink and chalk and stencils and parchment—sat atop the vanity.

Tandri drifted to the center of the room, where she stood very still.

In the silence that followed, Viv couldn't breathe.

"Who is this room for, Viv?" she asked, quietly. Her tail made a cautious, flickering S behind her.

"For you. If you'll have it."

And there was a pulse of that warmth, that hooded self which only shone forth when Tandri was at her most unguarded.

She turned to look back at Viv.

Tandri didn't answer, instead closing the distance between them. Wrapping her arms around Viv, cheek to chest, she released all of her restraint.

For the first time, Viv faced the totality of Tandri's essential self, and was struck by the eloquence and delicacy that was revealed.

It was easy to see how one might mistake her nature for something purely sensual, how one might glean only what they most desired from that densely twined rush of feeling.

Hers was a potent dialect of emotion, rich with meaning, comprehensible only to those intimately aware of its subtleties.

Tandri didn't have to say yes.

The language was understood.

And when her lips found Viv's, no doubt could have survived.

EPILOGUE

Fennus strode, cloaked, through the webwork of Thune's south-ern alleys. Snow flicked in little curls from the slanting roofs above.

He was extremely cold and extremely irritated.

He'd stayed well clear of the city since the fire—a thaumic construction of which he'd been quite proud. He was even a little relieved that Viv had survived unscathed. He hadn't explicitly wanted to cause her injury. Or at least, nothing *too* extreme.

Roon, Taivus, and Gallina had been less than gracious about it, but he was sure that in time, their misplaced outrage would fade. And if it didn't, he supposed that might not be such a trag-edy, all things considered.

Rumors of the shop reopening had drawn him back, along with the increasingly insistent doubts he'd been harboring since procuring the Scalvert's Stone. Fennus simply *had* to investigate.

The shop was, indeed, rebuilt, and it looked at least as suc-cessful as before, if not more so. Which begged the question, had the Stone any worth whatsoever? If it wasn't responsible for Viv's string of fortunate turns, then what could *he* expect of it?

Had all of this really been for nothing?

If Viv had been a fool to place her faith in it, then what did that make him? A twice-damned fool?

It really was quite vexing.

Set in a small medallion, Fennus kept it tucked beneath his tunic, next to his skin. The silver of the setting was cold against his flesh.

He rounded a corner, heading toward the docks, when the light at the other end darkened. Someone else had stepped into the narrow, twisting alley.

His neck prickled as another presence fell in behind him.

"I'd heard you might be back in the city," said a voice he vaguely remembered.

Turning, Fennus placed it. That lackey of the Madrigal's named . . . *Lack*, amusingly enough. The enormous hat really was in poor taste.

Fennus smiled thinly. "Only briefly. I'd ask if I could help you, purely out of politeness, but I'm afraid my schedule won't allow it. I'm also not feeling particularly polite, at the moment."

"Oh, we don't need too much of your time," said Lack. "But the Madrigal was quite interested in that stone you were kind enough to mention. And I've heard tell it might have a new owner. That'd be you, wouldn't it, sir?"

Fennus's eyes narrowed. "If you're all the Madrigal sent, she's less perceptive than I gave her credit for." Faster than thought, he drew a slender white rapier from his side, luminous with thaumic glow and alive with a blue tracery of leaves.

Lack shrugged, unperturbed. "There's a few more of us, here and there. And maybe you *could* cut us all down—not that I'd prefer that, of course. Partial to my own throat, you see! Let me make an observation, though. You might not think the Madrigal is *perceptive*, but I can assure you, sir, that she is *persistent*."

Fennus raised the point of his sword, his arm steady as he angled it toward Lack's throat. He paused there for a moment, considering.

Then he sighed, and with a swift motion, sprang toward the left-hand wall, catching it with one booted foot and springing toward the opposite side of the narrow alley, arcing higher and higher with each sideways leap, until he caught an eave with one delicate hand and flipped up onto the roof.

He shook out his cloak in annoyance, tossed back his hood, and sheathed the blade, striding nimbly up the tiles to the peak. He heard a commotion in the streets below, the Madrigal's men circling the building, watching for him to move to an adjoining rooftop or to descend.

There was no easy way for them to pursue him, so Fennus took his time, gazing across the icy cityscape toward the docks and the mast of the ship he'd be catching within the hour.

This was all a minor inconvenience, at best. It really was pitiful. The whole business did nothing to improve his mood, however.

Then he heard a heavy impact and a clatter of tile behind him, followed by a rising, throaty rumble, like an oncoming avalanche.

He whirled to face an enormous, sooty creature, its fur bristling, its fangs huge, green eyes alive with liquid malice.

He had only a final sliver of a second to think, incredulously, *Is that the gods-damned* cat?

Amity leapt.

ACKNOWLEDGMENTS

This book would not have been possible without bringing together a lot of folks, my own "ring of fortune." The version you're currently holding, even more so. In fact, the acknowledgments section needed a lot of expanding given the journey this book has made to reach you in its current form.

Legends & Lattes was originally a self-published title sent into the world with zero expectations, which due to the enthusiasm and efforts of a startling number of people, has now transformed into this new incarnation.

To all those who have made this possible—as Viv would say, "You might forgive too much. But I'm damned glad to have you."

It should go without saying that I'm extraordinarily grateful to my wife and kids for making my life full and for putting up with my nonsense. But I'm going to say it anyway. I love you! Kate, thank you so much for being my wife and partner and support.

I also can't thank Aven Shore-Kind, my NaNoWriMo '21 buddy, enough for convincing me to do this in the first place and for writing alongside me all month. We both finished our NaNos, and it would be entirely accurate to say that this book wouldn't exist without her help, enthusiasm, and encouragement.

I also want to thank Forthright—whose books I've had the pleasure of narrating for years now—who took on the daunting task of editing this one. Her attention to detail in every aspect is unmatched, and I'm so grateful she agreed to keep me from looking like an idiot. Her tireless efforts are why the original version of the book was so polished.

And now I need to add many more thanks to the list, because a whole lot has happened since I pushed the "publish" button on Amazon's KDP site in February of '22.

First, an enormous thanks to Seanan McGuire, who is almost certainly largely responsible for the existence of this edition of the book. She brought *Legends & Lattes* to the attention of a gigantic audience via Twitter when she first saw the cover, and later with her very kind recommendation of the book. I will never be able to thank her enough, and I will never forget it.

Second, to all the booksellers who ordered and hand-sold this print-on-demand, self-published book, I am so humbled. I must mention Kel, and Gideon Ariel, both of whom were huge early champions of my little story. I am in your debt. I can't name all of the booksellers who put this on their shelves, and pointed it out to potential readers, but I wish I could. I remain stunned.

On social media, on TikTok, Twitter, and Instagram, every one of you who championed Viv & friends . . . you have my eternal thanks. I am so grateful for your energy and time and care. The response was overwhelming and kind, and clearly a big part of why you're reading this particular version.

I have received a startling amount of fan art. I am so amazed by every piece of it. I keep a folder of them and just open it to stare at them rather frequently. You will never know how much each one means to me. My heart is full.

A special thanks to Rudee Rossignol of fantasycookery.com for creating a recipe for Thimblets that is unbelievably tasty. Every time we make a batch they disappear almost immediately.

To my now-agent, Stevie Finegan, who reached out to bring up the possibility of making this happen, and who has worked so diligently to make it so—and to the team at Zeno—a huge thank you! I'm so very fortunate to have you! A big round of thanks for my new publishers. The amount of work that has gone into making this happen so quickly, with such a truncated timeline, must be herculean. I want you all to know how much I appreciate it. I hope to thank every one of you in person someday soon.

At Tor UK, my eternal appreciation to Georgia Summers, Bella Pagan, Rebecca Needes, Eleanor Bailey, Jamie-Lee Nardone, Holly Sheldrake, Siân Chilvers, and Lloyd Jones. You have my great gratitude for taking a chance on this book, and for being so welcoming.

At Tor US, my huge thanks to Lindsey Hall, Rachel Bass, Peter Lutjen, Jim Kapp, Michelle Foytek, Rafal Gibek, Jeff LaSala, Heather Saunders, Andrew King, Rachel Taylor, Eileen Lawrence, Sarah Reidy, Aislyn Fredsall, and Angie Rao. You are all so wonderful and generous with your time and care.

Last, but not least, I want to thank all of my original beta readers and advisors, who assisted me hugely and whose comments were so very helpful. All of you made this happen. In no particular order, thank you to Will Wight, Billy Wight, Kim Wood Wight, Rebecca Wight, Sam Wight, Patrick Foster, Chris Dagny, Ibra Bordsen, John Bierce, Rob Billiau, Jennifer Cook, Stephanie Nemeth Parker, Laura Hobbs, Ri Paige, Howard Day, Steve Beaulieu, Ian Welke, Roberto Scarlato, Crownfall, Aletheia Simonson, Suzanne Barbetta, Eugene Libster, Ezben Gerardo, Eric Asher, and Kyle Kirrin.

PAGES TO FILL

A LEGENDS & LATTES STORY

TRAVIS BALDREE

"Mind the blades!" cried Roon.

Viv hurled herself to the side as a pair of dirks whipped toward her. The street was narrow, though, hardly built with an orc in mind. Her shoulder slammed hard into brick, and she couldn't make herself small enough to dodge them both. One purred past harmlessly, while the other sliced a red ribbon across her upper arm. She hissed and clapped a hand over the wound, baring her teeth.

Roon glanced back long enough to confirm that Viv was still breathing, and then the dwarf renewed his pursuit of their quarry. Gods love him, but he was already flagging. He'd never catch up.

As Viv pressed off the wall and stumbled back into a run, she could see the object of their pursuit, a slender elf in full flight, increasing her lead down the curving thoroughfare. Tossing those knives hadn't slowed her up any. In seconds, she'd be obscured by the bend, and losing sight of her would be disastrous. Viv pushed herself to a dead sprint and outpaced Roon after only a few strides.

Gnomes scattered before her thundering approach, and she felt like a giant terrorizing a helpless village. A wild laugh escaped, her breath hitching in her chest.

"Fennus!" bellowed Viv. "We need eyes on her!"

She caught sight of him leaping gracefully across the sloping metal rooftops. He offered no reply—she couldn't imagine him suffering the indignity of raising his voice—but she thought he'd be able to keep track of the fugitive woman.

For the first time since coming to Azimuth, she was grateful her greatsword was too menacing to lug around the city. Without Blackblood weighing her down, Viv began to close the distance.

The elf fled tirelessly, her long braid flying behind her as she tore through the crowd.

An intersection hove into view, and Viv demanded more from her legs. If the woman managed to duck into an alley . . .

Then Taivus flowed into the street like mist pouring from around the corner, his hands up and ringed in golden light. The fifth-finger sigils blazed on both his palms, and the elf's step faltered, her legs scissoring together as though bound. She flew forward in what should have been a skin-shredding dive but recovered into a graceful tumble to her knees, even with her ankles pinned to one another.

Gallina emerged from behind Taivus with a knife in each hand, warily approaching the kneeling woman.

For just a moment, it seemed to Viv that the elf's muscles boiled underneath her clothes. Her whole body flexed, and her skin darkened like a cloud had passed overhead.

Viv reached her first and drew her short-sword. By then, the elf looked just as she had when they'd first tracked her down in the marketplace a few intersections back. She clutched her side as if wounded.

Given who she was, Viv wouldn't put it past her to have a few more dirks tucked up a sleeve, or something a hell of a lot nastier.

"Bodkin?" asked Viv, voice low and steady.

The woman stiffened and glanced over her shoulder at Viv. For a second Viv could have sworn her pupils were horizontal slits, like a goat's.

Fennus dropped from the rooftop and alighted gently, tossing his hair over his shoulder and drawing his slim white rapier in the same motion. The gnomish folk murmured anxiously at the margins of the intersection. It wouldn't be long before wardens appeared, and their crew was all tangled up in something inconvenient.

"You know why we're here," said Viv, patient and reasonable. Better her than Fennus, if they wanted this to go easy. She held her sword angled down, but ready. "My friend Taivus is going to bind your hands, and we'll get you back on your feet. We all run out of road sometime. This is just the end of yours. Doesn't have to be the end of everything, though. The law's fair in Azimuth."

The elf laughed, and her voice was deeper than expected, rich. "You act like you know who I am, but it's clear as rivers you don't."

She pulled her hand away from where she'd been clutching her side and tossed something into the air, then tucked her head and covered it with both arms.

Viv caught the barest glimpse of three tiny silver stones wrapped in lines of green as they reached the apex of their flight and began to descend.

"Shit," said Gallina, flatly.

Taivus was in motion, his hands up again and flickering alight. Fennus drew his cloak across his face and crouched, while Viv lunged forward with her free hand outstretched. If she could just get hold of Bodkin before those things landed . . .

Then the stones struck the street tiles, and a hot flash of light detonated into noxious black smoke.

Viv closed her eyes against it, still falling, fingers reaching.

They slapped bare stone.

Holding her breath and keeping her eyes shut tight, she dropped the short-sword and flailed around, scrambling through the cloud in a crouch, hoping to lay hands on the elf.

She seized an arm.

A squawk, then "It's me!" Gallina grabbed Viv's shoulders.

Viv felt a rush of cold air and opened her eyes to see the smoke winnowing away. Taivus's eyes were closed, his fingers in spidery motion. Fennus stalked out of the shreds of darkness with an expression of cold fury. Viv spun in a quick circle, searching the crowd for any sign of the elf, but her fears were confirmed.

Bodkin was gone.

But in the space she'd once occupied, a small leather satchel lay half-open on the pavers. Viv scooped it up.

"Well," said Roon, puffing up to them and putting his hands on his knees, blowing out his braided mustaches. "'Least we know it was Bodkin.'"

———+———

Viv still couldn't believe that such a precisely organized city could be so disorienting. Azimuth was arranged in concentric circles, with numbered streets expanding from the center like gears of increasing size. It was beautiful, orderly, and Viv couldn't tell one spot from the next most of the time. She would've given anything for a little disrepair or the wobble of an indifferently paved road, just to have some landmarks she could remember.

Viv had spent too much time in one tunnel or barrow or another to suffer from claustrophobia. Still, the smaller scale of the gnomish city made her feel a little short of breath. Most of the structures were multiple stories tall, but more often than not, she found herself able to peer into the second-floor windows.

They'd made a brisk exit from the spot where Bodkin had vanished. No sense waiting for suspicious wardens and suffering a lot of questions. Not that they'd have any trouble tracking a seven-foot orc bleeding all over everything.

The crew followed Gallina back to their rented rooms on the seventh ring road. The little gnome, of course, looked right at home.

While they ascended the staircase, the hosteler eyed them warily, and Viv was grateful her injured arm faced away from him. She kept a hand pressed tight to the wound, doing her best not to bleed on the floor.

The ceilings were uncomfortably low. Although the Spires district had buildings more suited to her height, lodgings had been sparse there, and none had met Fennus's minimum requirements of luxury. Viv hadn't complained at the time but now felt the sting of belated annoyance. Still, she had to admit that the heated floors and flick-lanterns were nice.

She ducked and followed Gallina into the room they shared, and the others piled in after. Viv's greatsword, Blackblood, gleamed on one of the beds beside their heaped packs.

Fennus looked like he was going to start in straight away, but Roon preempted him. "Sit down, an' let me take a look," said the dwarf, patting Viv's leg.

While Roon dug out bandages and some clear alcohol from his bag, Viv slid down to the floor, wincing as her back protested. Honestly, that growing ache was more of a worry than a new laceration.

Fennus couldn't wait any longer. "A less than satisfactory

day's effort, I think we can all agree." His beautifully sculpted face was set. "Neither Taivus nor I will be able to locate her so easily next time. And we certainly can't rely on recognizing her on sight."

Viv grunted as Roon swabbed the deep cut along her triceps and began wrapping it in gauze. "Not so tight," she said.

"Tight's better," he replied.

"If I flex my arm, it's going to pop."

"Maybe don't flex your arm then," he groused. "Think of that?"

Fennus had a way of being absolutely silent that was louder than anything he might have said. Roon sighed—quietly—and they both redirected their attention to the elf.

His unsmiling gaze swept over the room. Gallina sat cross-legged on one of the tiny beds, idly twirling a dagger, while Taivus loomed in the far corner. Finally, Fennus said, "If we intend to collect, there can be no further mistakes."

Gallina snorted. "This is *Bodkin* we're talkin' about. We've all heard the stories. It was never gonna be easy. There's a reason she's a legend—and a dapplegrim into the bargain!" She snatched an artist's rendition of their target from the bedside table and wrinkled her nose at it. The likeness was carefully executed, for what it was worth. "Why'd they even bother? She's never gonna look this way again. She didn't even look like it this time."

"All the more reason for us to be at our best." Fennus flicked his gaze pointedly to Viv's arm.

A tiny spark of anger started to bloom in her, but it was swiftly quenched by a wave of weariness. Swallowing a retort, Viv picked up the leather satchel she'd retrieved and shook it. It clinked softly.

"We're not totally empty-handed." She flipped it open to sort through its contents.

"Could be what those artificers were after, anyway," said Gallina, craning to see.

"Nope," said Viv. She withdrew a few small glass bottles, capped with corks and wax. They shone with liquid in a variety of colors. "No schematics here."

"Looks like paint," supplied Roon.

Viv cracked the wax seal on one and removed the cork, sniffing. "It's paint, all right. So little, though. She's hardly covering barns with it."

"Fabulous," said Fennus. "At least we can enjoy some arts and crafts."

"Still might be a lead. You never know," said Viv. She replaced the cork and held the bottle up to the orange evening light coming through the window.

Fennus looked like he was mustering a rejoinder, but Taivus broke in. "An observation."

They all startled and stared at him. The stone-fey was so gray and silent, it was often easy to forget he was there.

He continued as though he hadn't noticed their reactions. "Radius and Tangent hired us to capture Bodkin and retrieve their stolen property. We might have better success with the latter. Perhaps they'd pay for that alone?"

"Not as much," said Gallina. "But not nothin'. We're a practical bunch." She cocked a thumb at herself, clearly indicating all of gnomedom. "They care more about keepin' her from sellin' it to their rivals than anythin' else."

"Perhaps worth considering, then," said Taivus.

Fennus's mouth thinned. "Find her or find the schematics— one leads to the other. It's moot. And I, for one, don't see any reason to settle for half-measures. Successfully hunting a figure of Bodkin's renown is worth more to us than the bounty alone."

Viv thought about arguing the point, but it wasn't worth the effort. "All right, then we need to be on it tomorrow. The city's big, and I doubt she'll leave it just yet. Why would she need to? She's a dapplegrim. Who knows what face she's using now? Do you think you can still track her down thaumically?" She glanced between Fennus and Taivus.

"Given time," replied Taivus.

"Too much time, but yes," added Fennus. "She'll be on her guard, and she knows our faces now. We can't traipse around the city in plain sight, flashing arcane light wherever we go."

"Well, no reason for the rest of us to sit on our hands," said Gallina.

Fennus arched a brow at her.

"Yep." Viv held up one of the bottles of paint. "We should divide and conquer. Seems some detective work is in order."

And as a side benefit, Viv could enjoy a brief reprieve from Fennus's acid tongue.

—◆—

Viv slept fitfully, stretched out on the floor atop her bedroll, her arm throbbing. Perversely, her wounded side was the only one she wanted to lie on. Lantern light from the street stroked Gallina's profile and the edge of the knife she clutched in one hand as she slept. Her high, squeaking snores normally lulled Viv, but tonight they nettled her instead.

She briefly contemplated settling her mind by sharpening Blackblood but didn't want to wake her companion. Instead, she quietly rose and rummaged through her pack. Withdrawing a notebook, she put her back to the wall under the window, letting the soft light fall across the pages as they opened to the scrap of paper that marked her place. She glanced briefly at what she'd written.

Well-nigh to thaumic line,
the Scalvert's Stone a-fire

On the opposite page, she ran her finger down her notes. Rumors in the highlands north of Cardus. Spoor on a well-trod farm road in the east Territory. Sightings of a creature with a surplus of eyes near the mouth of a played-out iron mine.

Still not enough. Impatience rose in her, the pressing need to act—but she had to be sure. It was the Scalvert Queen or nothing. She'd never convince Fennus to make a second attempt.

And if they succeeded? Well, the future beyond that point yawned white and empty. She'd find something to fill it. Of course she would.

She glanced at her sleeping friend, and her heart pinched with the ache of a truth untold.

Then she crawled back to her bedroll and stared at the ceiling, clutching the notebook to her chest until at last she drifted off.

—◆—

"Luck," said Roon, saluting Viv and Gallina before trotting after Fennus and Taivus. Fennus had insisted on having the dwarf's company, in case muscle was required.

"Eyes open!" Viv called after him, raising a hand.

Fennus didn't acknowledge her, but Taivus matched the gesture.

Gallina took a huge bite of her breakfast. "Hand me one of those bottles," she mumbled around her mouthful.

To free herself up, Viv polished off her own meal—a thick, custardy square of egg and ham the hostel had served warm in the lobby. Her estimation of the place crept up another notch. She wiped her fingers on her trousers and fished one of the paint bottles from the satchel. The line on her arm burned as she stretched to hand it over.

Gallina bounced it off her palm and snatched it out of the air. "I'm thinkin' we head to the Athenaeum."

Viv wrinkled her brow. "A library? I figured we'd ask around a trades district or something. We know it's paint. Why do we need to look it up?"

"Never been to a gnomish Athenaeum have ya?" Gallina grinned up at her.

"Well, no, but—"

"Just trust me."

They headed north. Again, Viv was happy to let Gallina lead, because Azimuth was truly enormous. They passed titanic statues of geometric abstraction, dizzying to follow with the eye. Everywhere, long steam hoses were strung across the streets in tidy bundles and neatly bracketed to the walls. When Viv passed under them, she could hear them hissing. Garlands twined around many of the hoses, and groomed walls of ivy were staggered along the thoroughfares, every vista checkered with emerald. The net effect was overwhelming, at least for Viv.

Even though it was probably useless, she scanned the crowd for signs of Bodkin. Azimuth might have been a gnomish metropolis, but plenty of other folk were well-represented. She saw humans and elves, stone-and sea-fey, dwarves, a hob or two, and even a little crowd of rattkin scurrying past, clad in some sort of religious habits.

Bodkin's reputation as a thief meant they could hardly expect to stumble across her on the street. Given her inborn talent for stealth, it was even less likely. Still, it never hurt to be alert.

Gallina was a game tour guide and kept up a running commentary as they wove through the press. Viv was careful not to tread on anyone and made appropriate nods and murmurs of acknowledgment as her companion pointed out the sights.

Viv saw the Athenaeum long before they reached it, a ring of seven towers, networked with enclosed walkways. The marvelous feat of architecture was embellished with angular promontories and complex linework etched into the facings. It had clearly been built to a scale that most buildings in the city were not. Viv could already tell she wouldn't have to duck to clear any doorways.

"They have *that* many books?" breathed Viv, genuinely awed.

"A fair few," replied Gallina, her eyes twinkling. "Lots more than books though. Like I said, trust me."

They ascended the steps to one of the towers and passed through two sets of big brass doors that hissed open at the touch of a button. Emerging into a cavernous interior hallway, Viv's breath caught at the size of the place. Every wall housed enormous inbuilt shelves, packed with volumes. Narrow walkways ringed the tower at vertical intervals, and a webwork of staircases connected them. Research desks and tables clustered here and there. Tall, dark-tinted windows admitted only muted light, but flick-lanterns cast a steady yellow glow over the whole place.

"How do you even *find* anything in here?" breathed Viv.

Gallina gestured at a set of metal plates on nearby shelves, with labels like ORGANELLE and OVA and OWLERY. Beneath each was a series of black pips in clusters.

"There's a system," she said. "But we're not here for the books."

Viv felt a pang of disappointment. She could spend days in here, given half a chance. Weeks, probably. "You're going to make me ask, aren't you?"

"You want to know somethin', and you want to know it fast, you talk to one of the Scholars of the Seven Aspects," replied Gallina. She shot Viv a sly smile. "You know about the Seven Aspects, yeah?"

Viv gave her a flat look. "You know I don't."

"Want me to explain it?"

"I mean, yes . . . but not right now, I guess."

Gallina withdrew the bottle from a pocket and held it up. "I figure this is Third Aspect, which means third tower. We head there and see what the Third Scholar can tell us. You check the books for what somebody *used* to know. You check with the Scholar for what somebody knows now."

Viv looked around once more and spied a raised platform in the center of the tower with a short staircase curling around it. A line of locals—and a few taller folk—were queued up to speak to a gnome stationed at the center of the platform. She cocked a thumb at him and raised her brows.

"First Scholar," said Gallina, with a nod. "Organisms. Living things. You want to come with me to the third tower, or . . . ?" She trailed off, smiling a little at Viv's expression.

"You wouldn't mind if I looked around here, just for a while?" asked Viv, anxious to do so, but feeling guilty about it. "I mean, if I'd be any help at all, of course I'd want to—"

Gallina laughed, interrupting her. "I know that look. Stay. Knock yourself out. All you gotta do is remind Fennus of how damn smart I am the next time we see him."

"I will extol your genius," said Viv gravely, then flashed a smile.

The gnome was still chuckling as she departed, leaving Viv to her own devices.

—◆—

Alone in what seemed an edifice constructed entirely of books, Viv felt a thrill dance from the tips of her fingers to the back of her neck. She glanced briefly at the slow-moving line of supplicants leading to the First Scholar, then decided she'd rather find her own answers. She didn't know the protocol, and besides, this seemed like the right tower for her subject of interest. That was practically a sign, wasn't it?

A nagging voice told Viv that she was wasting moments she could have devoted to their current task, but she quashed it. Gallina had that well in hand.

Viv made a brief circuit of the floor, noting the alphabetical arrangement of the plates on each stacked tier. There was some sort of subject-based organization in effect as well. The little black pips probably made it clear, but she decided to wing it.

She ascended one of the staircases, feeling absurdly slow tramping up the shallow, gnome-scaled steps. Trailing her fingers along the spines of multicolored volumes, she inhaled the spices of paper and ink.

The first few books she sampled were too broad, treatises on western Territory fauna in general. She needed something more exotic and probably older. She frowned and looked to the higher tiers. Viv had no idea how much time she had before Gallina might return.

At last, she decided she could ask for a *little* direction. Approaching an elderly gnome busily reshelving a series of leather-bound folios, she hunched down and cleared her throat. "Um, excuse me?"

He glanced up and blinked at her over a pair of rimless spectacles. "Can I help you?"

"Yes, I'm, uh, looking for something on . . ." She hesitated, then resolved to be as specific as she could. ". . . on scalverts." Viv felt absurdly childish, like she was asking for a storybook.

He looked her up and down, then pursed his lips. "Histories or practical?"

"Both?"

The gnome nodded and trotted off toward a nearby staircase. Surprised, Viv followed.

He directed her to three different shelves and seven different volumes. She was relieved she'd asked, because even after hours of aimless wandering, she never would have located them on her own.

She thanked him and took the stack to a nearby table. It was too short for her to use properly, and she doubted the chair would hold her weight, so she leaned with one hand on the tabletop and began flipping through them. After a few minutes, she pulled out her notebook and took up her stylus. With growing absorption, Viv filled pages with fresh research.

The sting in her arm became muted, and in her mind's eye, she looked up from her well-trod path toward an indistinct but promising horizon.

—◆—

"There you are!"

The clack of the paint bottle on the table snapped Viv's attention from her reading. She instinctively flipped her notes closed, too fast to be anything but suspicious.

Gallina squinted at Viv's notebook and the hand splayed

protectively atop it. Her smile faltered into momentary speculation, but then flashed back more brilliantly than before.

"Knew you'd keep busy," she said breezily, as though she hadn't noticed.

Viv forced a laugh but didn't think she sounded terribly convincing. "So, what did the Third Scholar have to say? Let me guess, you handed him the bottle, and he told you Bodkin's address and how she likes her eggs?"

The gnome stuck her tongue out at Viv. "Ha. You're very amusin'. No, but I do know exactly what this is. And"—she picked the bottle back up off the table and waggled it—"exactly where it came from."

"I thought we'd all agreed it was paint?"

"Well, sure, but the kind of paint is important. It's an oil paint with metal flakes in it, I guess. Used for real detailed stuff, tiny brushes and so on, something about the mix. Best for very specific kinds of wood. Like you said, nobody's paintin' barns with it."

"Huh. So Bodkin is secretly an artist? All right, maybe that helps us somewhere down the line. How many places in Azimuth sell this then?"

"That's the best part." Gallina's grin widened. "Just one."

━━◆━━

The shop's interior was a startling contrast to the order of the street outside. The smell of linseed oil and turpentine overwhelmed the senses. Densely packed cubbies covered the back wall, stuffed with a riot of hues bottled in glass. Sheets of canvas draped over a few wires strung from rafter to rafter, like laundry on a line. Easels sprawled in a skeletal tangle in one corner, while a set of tables of inconsistent heights overflowed with boxes of paintbrushes in all sizes.

Viv had to lift the dangling canvases with the back of a hand to pass under them.

Behind the counter, a birdlike gnome tied the bristles of a sable brush with thread, then carefully trimmed the ends with a tiny pair of shears, her tongue between her teeth.

She slid the thread off the tip of the brush and examined the result critically, snipping away an errant strand before glancing up at Viv and Gallina.

"Help you, m'dears?" Her voice was as thin as her delicate fingers.

"Sure can!" Gallina set a bottle on the counter, the blue paint gleaming under a low-hanging flick-lantern. "Friend of ours is runnin' a little low on supplies and sent us to see about gettin' a refill."

The woman behind the counter appraised Viv with a frown. She wondered if she shouldn't have waited outside.

To her relief, the shop owner returned her attention to the bottle, picking it up and holding it close. Her tongue appeared between her teeth again. "Hmm. Metal flake. Cobalt forty-seven."

"Sounds right," agreed Gallina brightly. "Big project ahead, I guess. Definitely gonna need more."

"Leyton should know I need time to prepare this," replied the woman, frowning in disapproval. "Of course I don't keep this on hand."

Viv and Gallina exchanged a quick look at the name *Leyton*, and Viv experienced a burst of elation that only one customer bought this particular blend.

Gallina forced a laugh. "You know elves. Got all the time in the world, so they figure the rest of us must, too. 'Specially when they get real focused on somethin'."

"Mmm, yes, the clocks are quite—" The shopkeeper blinked. "*Elves?*"

"Oh, um, *like* an elf, is what I meant to say." Gallina forged swiftly ahead. "Well, anyway, we can leave it here until you can mix another batch. Do you need payment now?" She started fishing in a pocket. Nothing smoothed over a blunder like the promise of money.

"No, that's quite all right." The shopkeeper resettled on her stool, her brow clearing. "I'll need the afternoon, though. Best drop by in the morning."

Sliding a few silvers across the counter top, Gallina insisted, "Just so you know we'll be back for it."

The woman's eyes widened at the coins, and Viv thought Gallina might have offered a *bit* too much, but before any further questions could be asked, they turned and hustled out the door.

—◆—

"So, either Bodkin is walkin' around as Leyton, or she stole that bag of paint from 'em and this is a dead end. Gotta say, my first impression? Bodkin didn't seem the artsy type." Gallina led them under a long—and thankfully high—awning a few hundred paces from the shop and out of the noon sun. She made a sour face. "But I'm not real keen on Fennus bein' right."

Viv shrugged, then winced at the lance of pain in her upper arm. "It's still our best lead. Nothing strange about a hobby. Clockmaking, I guess? Or clock painting, at least. You never know what somebody might get up to in their off-hours."

"Uh-huh." Gallina regarded her shrewdly, leaning against the wall under the shade.

Viv pretended she didn't notice. "Anyway, we've got a name. And how many non-gnomish clockmakers can there be in this city?"

"Best bet is to head to the Spires." Gallina smiled wickedly. "Abso*lutely* gonna find her before Fennus does."

"Maybe it's smarter to wait for the others," Viv mused aloud, worrying at her bandages. "Bodkin gave us the slip last time, and now she's on her guard. Besides, Roon will feel left out."

"Are you gonna make me list all the reasons why we shouldn't wait around?"

"You're telling me there are reasons?" Viv grinned at her.

"I can make some up."

Viv thought about Fennus.

"Nah. Hells with it."

—◄+►—

Crossing the border between Azimuth proper and the district known as the Spires was surreal. The scale of the buildings abruptly changed, and as Viv glanced back over her shoulder, it all seemed a trick done with mirrors. The street wasn't any wider, but seeing doorframes higher than eye-level made her feel like a cramped muscle had suddenly unknotted.

The Spires only occupied three sections of ring-road and relatively little of Azimuth as a whole. Still, due to the curving streets, once you walked a bit and the smaller buildings were out of view, it was easy to imagine you were in any other city in the Territory, albeit one with more gnomes than usual.

Now that they were closing in, the risk they'd be spotted and their target would bolt was much greater. Given the circumstances, there wasn't much they could do about that except hope that fortune favored them. Viv did her best not to draw attention to herself, but she'd seen maybe four orcs during their entire stay in Azimuth. The streets here were much less busy than elsewhere, and it was hard not to stand out like a pig on a poultry farm.

Leyton's name, some polite questions, and a few coppers pointed them in the direction of the right workshop, and Gallina and Viv found themselves in a surprisingly clean alley, at the foot of a set of iron stairs.

"Looks like a clockmaker's sign to me. Kind of out of the way, but this must be the place," murmured Viv. Beyond the railing of a narrow upper porch, a red door was visible, upon which a set of thin metal gears and two clock hands had been artistically mounted.

She waited while a pair of dwarves hauling toolboxes passed them and turned the corner onto the main thoroughfare. Then the alley fell silent and empty, but for the two of them.

"Check nobody's home, then try the door?" asked Viv.

"I mean, she's a thief. It's gonna be locked," replied Gallina.

"Well, when I say 'try,' I mean . . ." Viv made some vague lockpicking motions with both hands.

Gallina snorted. "Wait down here, ya big lump. Try to look small."

The gnome mounted the stairs and peered through a narrow window to the side of the door.

"Nobody there," she called down in a loud whisper. "Not unless they like the dark. Shutters on the other side are all closed." Then she withdrew a tiny wrench and pick and addressed the handle and its mechanism.

Viv was surprised when, a few moments later, Gallina descended, tucking her tools back into a pouch.

"Trouble?"

"Nah, I unlocked it. But look. They're not home. Somebody needs to search the place and wait in case Bodkin comes back. The other should check around the neighborhood and ask a few more questions. I don't wanna judge you based on height or anythin', but if one of us is gonna blend in . . ."

"Yeah, yeah. Duly noted. Be careful, all right? And if you come back to the door, knock twice on the window first. I don't want to bruise you when you come in."

Gallina chuckled and flipped one of her daggers to catch it by the blade between forefinger and thumb. "Tempted to ignore that just to see if you're as fast as you think you are."

They nodded to each other, then Viv ascended the stairs, slipping quietly through the door and locking it behind her.

———+———

The interior of the workshop was dim, and it echoed with Viv's footfalls. The glass housings of flick-lanterns gleamed faintly in what light there was, and as her eyes adjusted, the furnishings of the room took rough shape.

She blew out a slow breath in surprise. There must have been three or four rooms, but the center of this one was completely empty. She almost thought it was vacant, at first, but no. Hulking shapes crowded the corners.

Viv glanced back at the small window beside the door and decided to take a risk. Better that she got a clear picture of her surroundings. She turned the little knob on the base of one of the flick-lanterns until a sharp click sounded. A hiss and pop preceded the blooming of a small blue flame, and she tweaked the knob to bank the light as low as she could manage and still see.

Set into a dividing wall, an archway permitted a dim view into another area with shuttered windows. A long worktable was tucked next to the wall, with a surprisingly small number of tools arranged neatly atop it, a sturdy stool beneath. An ornate, half-assembled clock lay spread out in an orderly arrangement of cogs, gears, and spindles. The facing was finely carved wood, half-painted in some kind of naturalistic motif. Slim brushes and bottles of paint stood ready.

Stacks of shipping crates towered in each corner, and a rug was rolled up and propped on its end against one pile. The walls were bare.

She stepped quietly through the archway into a small kitchen area, again, mostly barren. A few plates were stacked near a basin, and a table and two lonely chairs seemed dwarfed by the room.

Viv spied a bed and dresser through another doorway. A staircase led down to what must have been a front door. She wondered again why the workshop's main entrance was located in the alley but supposed it wasn't exactly a storefront.

She put her hands on her hips and looked around in consternation. "What in the eight hells? This is a master thief's lair?" she murmured.

A nasty suspicion was growing that she and Gallina were going to prove themselves a pair of fools. Still, since she'd already gone to the trouble . . .

Viv didn't like the risk of two points of entry. She hauled one of the chairs down the front stairs and tipped it to rest between the lowest step and the door to prevent it from opening.

Back upstairs, and with no obvious sheets of schematics in evidence, she took a slim wood-chisel from the workbench and popped the lids on a few crates. Several contained little wooden trays filled with clockworks and some completed clocks carefully nestled in piles of shavings.

Viv shook her head. It seemed like more than a hobby, that was for certain. Awfully skilled and detailed mechanical work for a renowned master thief. Although she supposed Bodkin had the finger dexterity for it.

The other crates were packed with folded clothes and cloaks, cutlery and knickknacks.

"Somebody's leaving the city," Viv whispered.

Of course, if this *was* Bodkin's bolt-hole, then she'd hardly have left her prize out to be spied through a window.

Viv swiftly investigated the workbench for any hideaways and riffled through the kitchen, knocking on the cabinet walls and checking the undersides of every surface. She tested the floorboards with one heavy foot for any squeaks or hidden joins.

Eventually, she checked the bedroom, lifting the mattress single-handed and peering into the drawers of the dresser. At last, Viv approached a small vanity. After satisfying herself that it was empty, she rapped on the base, smiling at a telltale click.

Well then. Score one for detective work.

When she popped out the false bottom, a sheaf of fresh, folded parchment slid into her waiting hand.

Viv stood and peeled them open, holding them up to the thin light filtering through the shuttered, street-facing window. Elaborate linework packed each page, sprinkled with measurements, annotations, and more of those cryptic pip arrangements Viv had noted in the Athenaeum.

"And there you are," said Viv, marveling that a few ideas caught on paper could be worth so much. She glanced back over her shoulder, contemplating the rooms behind her. "Now, I'll have to admit that Fennus was right, though. No reason to settle for half-measures."

She returned to the workroom, extinguished the flick-lantern, and dragged the stool into a corner to wait.

—◆—

Viv was impressed. She didn't hear so much as a creak from the stairs outside.

The window wasn't visible from where she sat, but a brief disturbance of the light cast across the empty floor immediately put her on alert.

After a barely audible snick, the door slowly swung open, and evening light spilled across the length of the room. No silhouette.

The door didn't close.

Viv's fingers itched to draw her short-sword from the sheath she'd hung in easy reach from the corner of the table, but she resisted the urge.

Then Bodkin stepped out of an interior shadow and stared directly at Viv.

"Where are the rest of your friends?"

Viv immediately recognized the voice, purring and low. "Might as well get the light so you can see me shrug."

"I see fine in the dark."

"Well, I don't, and I have something to show you before you figure your next move. Humor me so I don't hold it up backward and make an ass of myself."

Bodkin remained motionless for a second before taking a backward step and igniting one of the flick-lanterns. Then she took another sidelong step and smoothly closed the door.

Viv squinted in the sudden glow and tensed in case Bodkin decided to make any further moves. She didn't.

When her eyes adjusted, Viv saw that Bodkin looked mostly

as she had the previous day, which was honestly surprising. She'd have put money on a new guise, given the circumstances. Odd.

Fine elven features, practical clothes, hair in a long pale braid . . . and three of those wicked dirks fanned out in one hand.

Viv held up the schematics, pinched between two fingers. She remained relaxed on the stool with one leg crossed over the other. "You might hit me with all three of those, but I have to tell you, I'll probably keep coming. And I'll be in a really shitty mood."

Bodkin made a disgusted sound, snapped some kind of amulet from around her neck with a jerk, and tossed it to the ground. "Worthless piece of trash. I'm going to *kill* him."

"Oh, whatever that is probably works fine. Didn't track you down with magic. It was the paint." Viv gestured at the bottles on the worktable with the folded parchment. "Unlucky hobby, I guess. So, you're *Leyton*, then?"

For the first time, Bodkin registered something other than icy, impatient fury. Instead, she showed an almost comical expression of shock, and the barest flicker of concern.

The dapplegrim recovered swiftly, however, and Viv recognized the speculative gaze cast between the short-sword, the schematics, and Viv. She'd weighed the odds enough times herself to know the look.

"Anyway, I was a little surprised you hadn't fenced these yet. But I guess it's safer to do that when you're already on your way out of the city." Viv patted the nearest crate.

"You're chatty, and nobody is bleeding yet," said Bodkin. "They want me alive, then?"

"'Left to the party's discretion' is how they put it."

Bodkin nodded.

"So," said Viv. "All things being equal, I'd rather—"

But Bodkin was already moving, and Viv didn't waste her breath on an oath, shoving the schematics down her shirt with her left hand while drawing her short-sword in a whisper of steel on leather.

The dirks whined across the room, but as Viv's blade cleared the sheath she kicked off the stool into a roll, coming up fast to one knee. The dirks thumped into the plaster, jetting plumes of powder.

The elf's flesh flexed and rippled beneath her clothes, and she seemed to expand, even as her skin flushed blue-black, like ink soaking through clean linen. At the same time, her pale braid and irises shot a bloodless white, pupils twisted into slashes, and fingers scrawled into pale claws.

So that's what a dapplegrim looks like, Viv thought. *Chat's over, I guess.* She came the rest of the way to her feet, sketching a quick cross-body slice with her sword to maintain the space between them.

"Don't want to hurt you, but I will. And I think you're out of knives," said Viv grimly, the point of her blade leveled at Bodkin's chin.

"Fuck you."

Viv sighed. Even without the sword and with an injured arm, she had to have five stone over her opponent. In a purely physical contest . . .

With incredible swiftness, Bodkin slapped Viv's blade to the side with the flat of a hand, dodged under her guard, looped an arm behind Viv's elbow, and *threw* her across the room.

Viv's leg clipped the workbench, arresting her motion and cracking her spine across the far edge. Her back lit up in a long line from left to right, and she fell hard onto her shoulders and neck. Tools and paint jumped into the air, bottles shattering across the floor. She tumbled quickly and was on her feet, nauseous and disoriented from the twist to her neck. She'd lost her sword.

Bodkin did not pause her assault, lunging across the room, all patience for witty banter clearly exhausted. Those claws were sharp, scoring several deep gouges along Viv's forearms as she fended off a flurry of slashes.

Viv's mind went cold, submerged in icy waters that only permitted thoughts of survival.

She managed a grip on one of Bodkin's wrists and hauled her in close, then bent, hooked her other arm around the dapplegrim's waist, and heaved up, lifting their feet off the floor. Both of their breaths came hard, panting in one another's ears.

Bodkin managed a few awkward slashes across Viv's back, shredding her shirt, but Viv was already turning and rushing toward an interior wall. She slammed Bodkin into it back-first, obliterating the plaster with the impact as they continued through, snapping a pair of studs in a hail of dust, wood, and gray chunks before tipping over to hit the kitchen floor hard.

Viv's full weight came down on Bodkin and blew the breath out of her. The dapplegrim wheezed raggedly for air and instead got a cloud of atomized plaster. She coughed in short barks, eyes streaming, black skin gray with dust.

Breathing through her nose, Viv managed to get up onto an elbow and then to grab both of Bodkin's wrists. She spat a mouthful of dirt to the side before hoarsely growling, "Don't make me show you how hard an orc's skull is, all right? Already got enough of a headache."

Bodkin managed a few clean breaths, blinking her eyes clear.

Viv could feel the dapplegrim's body tensing beneath her, like a winch cranking tight. *Eight hells, she's not done*, Viv thought wearily.

The dapplegrim bared sharp, pearly teeth.

"There's no way—" Viv stopped short and cocked an ear. Bodkin heard it, too, her eyes flicking to the side.

A clunk from down the front stairs. The chair bracing the door banged against the bottom step as someone tried to push their way in.

"Valeya?" a man's voice called, muffled by the half-cracked door.

Viv blinked down at her quarry and drew her head back. *Valeya? How many damn aliases does she have?*

But a look of genuine fear and panic flashed across Bodkin's face, unmistakable. With an effort she erased it, struggling with renewed fury against Viv's restraining fists.

"Valeya, darling, are you up there? Only, I've got an armload here, and I could use the help!" The door thumped against the chair again, followed by frustrated muttering.

"*Darling?*" whispered Viv. And suddenly several gears slotted into place. "Hey, look at me," she said urgently, voice low. "*That's* Leyton, isn't it?"

Bodkin bucked under her, lips writhing in agonized frustration. This time Viv didn't think the tears squeezing from the corners of her eyes could be blamed on grit.

The fight went out of Bodkin all at once, and she met Viv's gaze. She showed her teeth one last time, then gave a short nod.

Viv was silent for several seconds, staring up and through the dust to the shuttered windows and the light filtering through. Bodkin's heavy breaths pressed in and out against her chest, but they weren't fighting anymore.

She glanced down at the dapplegrim, whose eyes were rapidly searching Viv's face for some inkling of intent.

Then Bodkin whispered one word. "Please."

"You've got one chance here," said Viv, voice still low. "I'm going to let your wrists go, one at a time. Don't screw this up."

Viv slowly uncurled her fingers from the left, then the right, then slid back and up onto her knees, straddling Bodkin.

There was a silent moment where they stared at one another.

"Oh, hells," muttered the voice at the bottom of the stairs, banging the door one last time against the chair. Then the clatter of something dropping in the street and rolling away. "Oh, *hells!*" it repeated. A clamor of tumbling metal, the tinkle of shattering glass, and some sterner curses rang out as Leyton presumably fumbled the rest of his burden.

On any other day, Viv might have winced in sympathy. Now, she felt nothing but relief. His misfortune might have bought them a little more time.

Viv hauled herself off Bodkin's legs and the dapplegrim scrabbled back until she came up against a table leg. Bodkin closed her eyes and took a series of slow breaths in through her nose, while the blue-black skin bled back to pale elven flesh, although heavy bruises now ringed her wrists. Ears shortened and gold bloomed across hair. When her eyes opened again, they were hazel, bloodshot, and their pupils were perfect circles once more.

She kept breathing heavily through her nose, studying Viv, waiting for the orc to make a move.

Viv sighed and fell back onto her ass in the dirt and debris. "He's the clockmaker?"

"Yes."

"You two are . . . ?"

"Yes."

A pause.

"Does he know?" Viv asked, wearily.

Silence.

Bodkin sat with her eyes closed, her mouth working. Viv had a feeling Leyton would be climbing the back stairs any moment now, and the time for deliberating would be at an end. She opened her mouth to speak, but Bodkin beat her to it.

"One last score," she said quietly, in a tone of bleak amusement. "It's a joke. Every job, it's just one last score." She laughed, a broken sound. "And for the first time it *really* was. Leyton gave me a reason to finally *want* out. And I almost made it."

Viv stared down at her own hands, gray and caked with grime. She thought about sleepless nights, furtive research in stolen moments, her notebook, and the blank pages she hadn't figured out how to fill.

After a few seconds, she nodded and hauled herself to her feet, groaning as the wounds and the bruising on her back burned bright, like a brushfire catching a fresh gust.

She patted her chest, where the schematics were tucked away. "I can't let you have these," she said. "And I can't do anything about this." She gestured at the wreckage of the wall and beyond. "But I can leave you to find your way out. You understand?"

Bodkin managed to get to her feet, wincing. The skin around her eyes tightened, but she nodded.

"All right, then. I'd wish you luck, but I'm not really feeling up to it."

Viv turned toward the front stairs, since it sounded like Leyton had given up on the blocked door and was probably circling to the back.

Bodkin brought both fists together with all the force in her body onto the wound on Viv's upper arm. Viv swallowed a shout and fell to the side, reaching for the banister and failing to catch it, hitting the floor hard.

"I can't start at the beginning again," breathed Bodkin, standing over Viv with a knife reversed in one hand. Her skin was still pale, but her irises were black slits again, and her flesh quivered like the surface of water before the boil.

"Then it's gonna be the end," a high, sharp voice broke in.

Gallina stepped into the kitchen, floating dust billowing around her like fog.

"How long have *you* been there?" croaked Viv from the floor.

"Well, it was a real nice moment for a while, and I didn't wanna mess it up." Her gaze hardened as she stared at Bodkin, a brace of knives in each fist. "But I'm happy to mess somethin' up now."

Viv managed to get a hand on the banister and pulled herself up, groaning. "Timing could've been better."

"You turn your back on somebody with a knife, you don't get to make jokes."

"Didn't know she still had one."

"Plus, you were gonna let her go."

Viv stared at Gallina and felt inexpressibly tired. "Still am."

The tension ran out of Bodkin in a rush. She dropped the knife and slid bonelessly to the floor beside it.

"Eight hells, Viv. *No.*" Gallina's exasperation was serious, furious.

"Her husband, lover, whatever . . . he's going to walk through that door any second."

"Don't much care," Gallina replied, gritting her teeth.

"Gallina. If I have to ask it as a favor, I will."

"For *her*?"

Viv held Gallina's gaze. "Not for her. For me."

Footsteps rang on the metal stairs in the rear.

Gallina snarled and snatched Bodkin's abandoned knife from the floor. She didn't spare a look for the dapplegrim. "Well?" The gnome gestured down the stairs with the knife.

They descended quickly. Viv grabbed the chair and tossed it up the steps, where it landed with a bang and a clatter.

Then they were out into the street and away.

———◆———

Limping back to their hostel in tense silence, Viv reflected that she'd leaked an awful lot of blood on the streets of Azimuth in very little time.

There was no hiding her wounds from the hosteler now, and she was grateful to ascend past his disapproving gaze. Odds were good they'd need new lodgings tomorrow, if not sooner.

In the room they shared, Viv withdrew the schematics and tucked them into her satchel. She stripped off her shredded shirt and sat in silence, head bowed, while Gallina unpacked medical supplies with jerky, angry motions.

Still, she was gentle while she dressed Viv's wounds and bound what could be bound. Donning a relatively fresh shirt, Viv couldn't suppress a small moan as the gashes in her back bunched and stretched. The heavy bruise where she'd struck the table edge throbbed in sick waves with every beat of her heart.

"Serves you right," muttered Gallina, speaking for the first time since they'd left the wreckage of Bodkin's home.

"Thank you," said Viv quietly, wringing out a rag over the basin on the side table, then mopping the dust from her face.

When she was done, they stared at each other for a moment, Gallina biting her lower lip fiercely.

And then, in the way of things between old friends, they let the knot of tension untangle and were both glad of it.

"Don't know about you," said Gallina, "but I don't wanna sit around this room and watch you ooze until they come back."

Viv nodded mutely.

Gallina studied her for a second more, then marched to the door and yanked it open. "C'mon. We're gettin' some air."

—◄+►—

Night eased from the shadows in a cool wave. With a pop and a hiss, the streetlamps burst to life all at once. They strolled aimlessly through the streets, although Viv couldn't hide a limp. She was very conscious of the stares she drew, her arms nearly mummified in linen and reeking like a distillery.

Gallina cleared her throat. "So, I'm thinkin' we tell the crew that she got the jump on you, then escaped." She waved generally at Viv's battered condition. "I figure all this backs us up, huh?"

Viv snorted. "Should square with Fennus's estimation of me just fine. I got the shit kicked out of me, and the mark got away? He won't bat an eye."

"He's wrong though," said Gallina quietly.

"Yeah . . . Yeah. But for once, it's useful."

"'Least we got the goods." She grinned suddenly. "And we still found her first."

Viv laughed a little. "We did."

Then she stopped short. Gallina continued onward until she noticed, turning back with a quizzical expression.

"What *is* that?" asked Viv.

"What's what?"

"That . . . smell." It didn't take long to discover the source. Just ahead, yellow light puddled in front of a small establishment

sandwiched between walls of ivy. Tiny tables were scattered
in the glow pouring from two large, glass-paned windows that
fronted the building. The mumble of conversation and the tinkle
and chink of cutlery filtered from inside.

"Oh," said Gallina, wrinkling her nose. "Yeah, I guess that's
sorta new. Coffee. There's a couple places like this now."

The scent wasn't like anything Viv had ever encountered.
She breathed deeply, and it was secret warmth and rich earth
and old wood and toasted nuts and . . . peace.

"Hang on," she murmured. "I'll just be a second."

She drifted in the door, her limp suddenly subdued, forging
deeper into what felt like the comfortable border between sleep
and rested wakefulness.

A long marble counter bisected the small shop. Intricate
gnomish tilework in white and cornflower blue patterned the interior. A massive slate board hung on the back wall, chalked with
a precise list in neat block letters, half the words foreign to Viv.

Two gleaming machines topped the counter, hissing with va-
por, burbling through pipework, gurgling something dark and
steaming into porcelain cups.

Patrons clustered around small tables, deep in soft evening
chatter, sipping hot drinks, stirring with tiny spoons.

As Viv approached the counter, one of the gnomes manning
a machine craned to meet her gaze, brows raising. "What can I
do for you, miss?"

Towering over him, entirely too large for the delicacy of this
place, but nevertheless dreamily comfortable, Viv asked, "Can
I get a coffee?"

"Anything more particular?" He gestured to the board behind him.

"Whatever you think is best."

Viv waited near a window, watching the bustle while remaining absolutely still, as though afraid any sudden movement might crack the world around her. She was peripherally aware of Gallina entering and giving her an appraising look. Her companion must have seen something on her face, and chose to remain silent.

When the gnome behind the counter offered a tiny cup to her, she took it carefully in both huge hands and stepped back, holding it to her face to inhale deeply.

There was nowhere to sit that could accommodate her, but she didn't mind.

Viv closed her eyes, brought the rim to her lips, and tentatively sipped.

The heat of it filled her like heart's blood.

"Oh," she breathed.

In her mind she saw that distant, indistinct horizon.

A landscape began to come into focus, and she wished she'd thought to bring her notebook.

There were blank pages to fill.

ABOUT THE AUTHOR

Travis Baldree is a full-time audiobook narrator who has lent his voice to hundreds of stories. Before that, he spent decades designing and building video games like *Torchlight, Rebel Galaxy,* and *Fate.* Apparently, he has now written one book. He lives in the Pacific Northwest with his very patient family and their small, nervous dog.

CPSIA information can be obtained
at www.ICGtesting.com
Printed in the USA
LVHW041639230123
737765LV00003B/246

NE 02/23

9 781250 886088